A
Ghostwriter
TO DIE FOR

Mysteries by Noreen Wald

The Jake O'Hara Series

GHOSTWRITER ANONYMOUS (#1)

THE LUCK OF THE GHOSTWRITER (#2)

A GHOSTWRITER TO DIE FOR (#3)

REMEMBRANCE OF GHOSTWRITERS PAST (#4)

GHOSTWRITER FOR HIRE (#5)

The Kate Kennedy Series:

DEATH WITH AN OCEAN VIEW (#1)

DEATH OF THE SWAMI SCHWARTZ (#2)

DEATH IS A BARGAIN (#3)

DEATH STORMS THE SHORE (#4)

DEATH RIDES THE SURF (#5)

Praise for Noreen Wald

THE JAKE O'HARA MYSTERIES

"Murders multiply, but Jake proves up to the challenge. She sees through all the subterfuge and chicanery, solving a mind-boggling mystery in a burst of insight. All the characters are charmingly kooky and fun...a good beginning for a new series."

– TheMysteryReader.com

"[Wald] writes with a light touch."

– New York Daily News

"The author keeps the plot airy and the characters outlandish."

– South Florida Sun-Sentinel

THE KATE KENNEDY MYSTERIES

"Sparkles like the South Florida sunshine...Kate Kennedy is a warm and funny heroine."

– Nancy Martin, Author of the Blackbird Sisters Mysteries

"Miss Marple with a modern twist...[Wald] is a very funny lady!"

– Donna Andrews, Author of the Meg Langslow Mysteries

"A stylish and sophisticated Miss Marple, seeking justice in sunny South Florida instead of a rainy English Village, and meeting the most delightfully eccentric suspects in the process."

– Victoria Thompson, Author of the Gaslight Mysteries

"Kate Kennedy's wry wit, genuine kindness, and openness to adventure make her a sleuth to cherish. *Death is a Bargain* is another top-notch entry in a great series."

– Carolyn Hart, Author of the Death on Demand Mysteries

A Ghostwriter TO DIE FOR

A JAKE O'HARA MYSTERY

Noreen Wald

HENERY PRESS

A GHOSTWRITER TO DIE FOR
A Jake O'Hara Mystery
Part of the Henery Press Mystery Collection

Second Edition
Trade paperback edition | March 2016

Henery Press, LLC
www.henerypress.com

ISBN-13: 978-1-943390-73-1

Printed in the United States of America

To Steve, with love

ACKNOWLEDGMENTS

Round up the usual advisors. Thanks to my grandniece, Etta Kavanagh, a Washington, DC editor, and Joyce Sweeney, a Coral Springs, Florida author, for reading and editing the manuscript. William S. Rea, M.D., a psychiatrist practicing in Boca Raton, loves Jake O'Hara. His clever contribution to her banter is much appreciated. My niece, Susan Kavanagh, an editor and writer herself, understood my writing blocks and bursts. I'm grateful to Doris Holland, Diane Dowling Dufour and Gloria Rothstein, dear friends—and long-distance listeners—who spent their time and money on my murders. Thanks to the Henery Press team for putting new life into Jake and Kate. A special thanks to my lead editor, Rachel Jackson. The new covers designed by Kendel Lynn are great. And where would Jake O'Hara and her author be without my agent, Peter Rubie? Finally, a big thank you to my son, Bill, who, during a traffic-filled Christmas Day drive from New York to Washington, suggested the setting for Jake's final conflict.

One

This morning I said to my mother, "I'd ghostwrite for the devil himself." By this afternoon, I'd signed the contract. As our dear friend, Gypsy Rose Liebowitz, Carnegie Hill's favorite psychic and a recent guest speaker at my Ghostwriters Anonymous meeting, said, "Beware of buyers." She, of course, referred to the "authors" who hire us to write their books—and not to the purchasers of those books. Since we ghostwriters are seldom seen—or credited—our readers don't know we exist.

After I'd finished ghostwriting *A Killing in Katmandu*, I realized, once again, I was broke. A habitual state of affairs that, despite over two years in a twelve-step program, I still hadn't managed to change. Some fellow members of Ghostwriters Anonymous have suggested that I continue to spend all my advances—and any meager royalties—because I'm still addicted to anonymity. They may be right.

Certainly, being perpetually poor has prevented me from writing and selling a book with my name on its cover. Once an advance hit my checkbook, it mysteriously took on a life of its own and vanished, sometimes evaporating before it even hit the bank. At least I'd used most of the *Katmandu* money for a down payment on a quaint, charming, and almost affordable cottage on the South Fork of Long Island.

The summer place was an impulse buy—a reward for surviving my last assignment, which had turned out to be murder. Literally. And Mom had needed a change of scenery too. So she'd been easily persuaded.

Towards the end of June, we'd sat with Gypsy Rose, each of us drinking a different designer decaf, in the tearoom/bookstore that occupied her brownstone's entire first floor while we waited for Dr. Brian Weiss to discuss his latest book. The standing-room-only New Age crowd seemed reminiscent of stoned—or maybe only hypnotized—Grateful Dead fans.

I'd plunged right in.

"How about that beach house? I'll finish ghostwriting this bloody manuscript out on Long Island. What do you say, ladies?"

My mother's blue eyes widened. "Wouldn't that be wonderful...but could we really afford it, Jake?"

"Sure," I lied.

Mom grabbed Gypsy Rose's well-manicured hand and asked, "You'll come with us—even if only for a few weeks?"

"Why not?" Gypsy Rose's quick response surprised and pleased me. "Everyone and his psychiatrist are in the Hamptons in August anyway."

Mom giggled, and sounding like the pain-in-the-butt Maura Foley O'Hara I knew and loved, asked, "Now which Hampton shall it be?"

"Well, certainly not South Hampton," I said. "That's old money and we couldn't afford an outhouse there."

"East Hampton is every bit as expensive, but we wouldn't want to summer there. It's all new money." Gypsy Rose wrinkled her nose. "You know, the town is filled with movie stars, directors and designers."

"Gypsy Rose is right, Jake," my mother said. "And West Hampton has the wrong kind of money, so that's out."

"How do you know that?" I raised my voice, swinging several New Agers' frowning faces in our direction.

"Everyone knows that, Jake," Mom answered.

"Yeah? Well, I'd bet my advance—blow the whole bundle—that you read that in a Cholly Knickerbocker column, circa 1960."

Gypsy Rose laughed, shaking her head up and down so vigorously that her wild red curls tumbled into her eyes. "Jake would win that bet, Maura."

We wound up in Sag Harbor, where, in lieu of old money, new money, or the wrong kind of money, the town was filled with writers. Mom, Gypsy Rose, and I spent a blithe, breezy summer, refreshing our bodies and restoring our souls, while strolling Sag Harbor's sandy shore, riding the ferry to Shelter Island, digging up fresh clams for our dinner, coming back to sip cocktails at the American Hotel, and, at my mother and Gypsy Rose's inconsistent insistence, driving to East Hampton to ogle the summer celebrities.

Shelter Island was a sentimental journey for my mother. Its Victorian-era Chequit Hotel had been the scene of my conception, specifically, in a room equipped with a bidet that William Randolph Hearst had bought Marion Davies. While Mom had been long divorced from my father, Jack O'Hara, when he'd died and unknowingly left behind a self-created, grieving grass widow, she'd then chosen to consider him canonized. So I've listened to the saga of my embryo's placement in my mother's womb for years, while wondering if the occasion might have been another Immaculate Conception.

Gypsy Rose and I ordered gin and tonics, then Mom opted for a rum and Coke and asked the Chequit's bartender to show us the room where I'd gotten started. He replied that it was the oddest request he'd had all summer. Stumped, he called over the owner, a charming Frenchman, who wore—as if he knew his guests would expect him to—a jaunty beret. Jean Pierre regretted that Madame Davies's bidet had been sold to an antique dealer, but calling Mom a true romantic, agreed to take us on a pilgrimage to the room where it had once been the star attraction. My mother wept as she showed the bed to Gypsy Rose and me. "Your history began in that four-poster, Jake."

While I wrote on the front porch, my mother continued her quest to find a husband for me. She'd say, "You're thirty-three. Tick tock. Do you think Ben's ready for marriage? Let's ask him out for a few days." Or, "Dennis is in Quogue for the weekend."

Not only were NYPD Homicide Detective Ben Rubin and his father Aaron, a retired District Attorney for Manhattan County, who had a major crush on my mother, frequent weekend visitors, so were many of my fellow ghostwriters. And to Mom's delight, my own childhood crush, Dennis Kim, who owned a nearby oceanfront villa, would, often uninvited, pop over in his cream-colored Rolls Royce convertible.

However, Mom insisted that she and I spend Labor Day alone with Gypsy Rose, who'd agreed to build a bonfire and hold a séance of sorts on the beach. Ever since our visit to the scene of my conception, Mom had been obsessed with chatting with my father in the world beyond. Or, rather, with his spirit guide. The lines of communication to the world beyond are somewhat garbled at best. I guess there's no direct dialing. My mother's guilt about dating Aaron Rubin initiated this channeling. So

Mom would have to ask Gypsy Rose to ask her favorite spirit guide, Zelda Fitzgerald, to ask Dad's guide to ask Dad if he knew Mom was seeing someone else. When last channeled, Dad had reported he was taking dancing lessons from Fred Astaire in that ballroom in the sky. And Gypsy Rose, for no earthly reason, suspected that Dad wouldn't be reincarnated 'til Mom died, so they could come back together. I decided to leave the ladies to their spirits and drove over to Quogue to down a Devil Mountain Ale with Dennis.

Although Gypsy Rose usually has a high show rate at her seances, I found out in the morning that Dad hadn't come through, but Samuel Gompers did make an appearance.

Now, it was October. Taxes and mortgage payments were about to force Mom and me out of the beach house and into the poorhouse, which explains why, when Jennifer Moran called today, acting as Richard Peter's liaison, I'd agreed to see her. *Manhattan* magazine's acerbic book critic, Mr. Peter had been voted the man-most-Americans-love-to-hate in a recent poll conducted by his own magazine. His cruel reviews had destroyed many authors' careers, and his roving eye had destroyed as many marriages. His readers confessed that they were disgusted by his poison pen, but along with most of the literary world's writers, editors, and publishers, they came back every week for more. However, his enemies were legion and loud. One author had reviled Peter in a full-page ad in the *New York Post*. Another had purchased an hour on a network and held a mock trial, in which twelve fellow writers, nursing bruised egos, served as Peter's jury. He was burned in effigy, complete with a better rug than usual.

Jennifer Moran, his latest editorial assistant, sat in the sunshine that filtered through the white shutters of our Carnegie Hill apartment, stirring her third teaspoon of sugar into a tiny

Wedgwood cup filled with Twinings English Breakfast tea. "Richard Peter's in deep doo-doo, Jake," she said. "He needs you, like last Thursday."

"How so?" I asked, as my mother passed the Social Tea cookies.

"Well, here's the script." Jennifer shifted the weight of her chestnut hair from one shoulder to the other using her right hand, then reached for a cookie with her left. "Richard Peter's accepted a high-six-figure advance from Pax Publishing, a murder mystery, but the book's like way overdue and he's still rewriting the synopsis. Keith Morrison's threatening to kill him."

"Just how do you fit into all this, Jennifer?" my mother asked. "Who's Keith Morrison?"

"Morrison's the president of Pax, Mrs. O'Hara. And for some reason, Dick Peter seems to tolerate me. I've lasted two weeks. Longer than my three immediate predecessors combined. Mr. Peter took me to lunch yesterday, got drunk, then spilled out his tale of woe." Smiling, Jennifer turned back to me. "I told him, 'Not to worry. Have I got a discreet, talented, mystery-writing ghostwriter for you.' That's your cue, Jake. Get ready for your grand entrance, prepare for center stage."

Jennifer Moran and I had attended Manhattanville College together, where we'd both been English majors. After graduation, despite an accent more Staten Island than Sutton Place, she'd been an aspiring ingénue. Two years later, realizing that wide eyes, big hair, a tiny waist, and long legs don't always add up to a Broadway star's run-of-the-play contract and tired of walk-ons, she married her high school sweetheart, a boring, brash biker. Jennifer still loved to throw out theatrical lines; however, she'd been earning a living for years as a freelance editor.

I asked, "Do I really want to work for this snake? Am I that desperate?" One look at my mother's face convinced me I must be. Jennifer pulled a contract out of a red leather briefcase that matched not only her ankle-high boots but her thigh-high skirt. My mother shuddered ever so slightly; Jennifer never noticed that her ensemble evoked Mom's disdain.

"Okay, okay. Let's see what he's paying," I said, knowing that if the stakes were high enough, I would sell my services and—as I did with all my employers—a part of my soul to Richard Peter.

At four forty-five, I exited the office of my attorney, Sam Kelley, the dirty deal signed, sealed, and about to be delivered, via Jennifer, to Richard Peter. As always, Sam had managed to annoy and exhaust me, and I scolded myself for about the hundredth time. Some writers change lawyers with every book. Why, after more than a decade, was I still contractually wed to old Sam? He had to be the dumbest bunny in the entire city, perhaps in all of America. Or maybe I was.

Sam almost swallowed his cigar when he saw the advance, and this contract, unlike my last ghostwriting assignment's tricky testament to confidentiality, paid royalties. Of course, that contract had been crafted by the sharpest and foxiest multimedia attorney in New York City and, possibly, the universe—Dennis Kim.

A quarter of a century ago, I'd been eight years old and the scrawny new kid on 92nd Street in Carnegie Hill. Twelve and full of self-importance, Dennis Kim wouldn't let me play street hockey with the big boys, so my first bite into the Big Apple had been on his hand. Jeez. Could that same fine hand have custom-designed my new contract with the literary world's Antichrist?

Two

Autumn in Carnegie Hill still made me smile. On Tuesday morning, as I walked south on Madison Avenue, the city smelled clean, the wind having whisked away the odor of the garbage du jour from all seven of the block's restaurants, the air felt crisp, and the clear sky crowned the buildings like a sapphire tiara. My mother called these balmy late October days Indian Summer and mentioned that a dark plaid, transitional cotton dress would be perfect for this weather. Since I only have two dresses, both black, but neither plaid nor cotton, and I didn't even want to inquire what exactly she'd meant by transitional, I decided to wear a Gap pocket t-shirt, navy linen blazer, and khaki pants. Mom's shrug spoke fashion volumes, indicating that once again I hadn't gotten it quite right.

Manhattan magazine's high-rent location on Sixty-ninth Street between Park and Madison proved perfect. In my Nikes, I could cover the twenty-five blocks in less than the same number of minutes. My leather loafers were in my briefcase, together with a banana and a bagel. Born lazy, I did like to walk for two reasons: plot-hatching and people-watching. This morning, I was on the lookout for women wearing dark cotton dresses; however, in a little over a mile, I hadn't spotted a single one. Wait 'til Mom heard that transitional clothes, along with her long-lamented white gloves, seemed to have totally vanished from the New York City scene.

I switched shoes in the lobby while the uniformed guard announced me. The elegant building had once been a private home; a small bronze plaque next to the wrought-iron front door indicated its designation as a landmark. A century ago, the owners would have graciously greeted their guests in this fourteen-foot-high marble rotunda, leading them up the red velvet steps of the sweeping staircase to the second floor salon. Today, the guard sniffed at me suspiciously as I passed through the electronic archway after sliding my briefcase through the baggage check. Just like a mini midtown airport.

"Mr. Peter is on the fourth floor. The receptionist there will direct you. Elevator's straight away on your right." The guard had an indefinable foreign accent, bad teeth, and a rotten attitude. But the elevator operator was an old charmer. Small, squat, and looking like a street-corner Santa Claus who'd arrived two months early. He greeted me with a warm smile.

"Welcome aboard. I'm Steve." The sounds of Cole Porter's "Anything Goes" filled the elevator. "Anybody ever tell you that you look like Annie Hall? Top floor? You a new critic?"

"Is that where they keep them?"

"Nearer to God," he said.

While assuring Steve I was no critic and, yes, people have mentioned Annie Hall to me, I noticed his uniform matched the guard's, the jacket sporting the magazine's logo, a bright red apple—with *Manhattan* embroidered underneath in leaf green— on the breast pocket. And, like the lobby guard, Santa Steve wore a holster on his hip. Stepping out on the fourth floor, I wondered if the elevator operator had referred to God—as in how most of us perceive the Almighty, or to God—as in how Dick Peter perceives himself.

The receptionist stood at a small Louis XIV desk—no computer in sight—smiled and placed an antique phone, minus push buttons, back on its cradle. *Manhattan's* ubiquitous uniform—Jesus, what would the editorial staffs dress code be?—couldn't hide her shapely figure. "I'm Barbara Ferris. Welcome to *Manhattan.*" Barbara's deep voice oozed warmth as we shook hands. "If you'd follow me, please." Her age could have been anywhere from thirty to forty. I admired her lush dark hair, braided into a plait long enough to swing back and forth over her pistol as we walked. Ripe now, I'd bet that in a few years, when the sand shifted in her hourglass figure, Barbara would battle the bulge big time. Her holster rested on a well-rounded love handle, but the Windsor knot in her tie presented a subtle style statement.

The dentil molding, William Morris wallpaper, and Hopper originals continued on with us as Barbara and I walked through French doors and down a small hall, passing two oak doors on the left. She rapped on the third door.

"Enter." Never had a voice left me less inclined to obey an order.

"Well, good luck now," Barbara said, and retreated at a fast pace.

I placed a sweaty palm on the brass knob and stepped into Richard Peter's realm. Dead ahead were two bay windows and between them, facing the entrance, was a long, cluttered desk. Mahogany, I guessed. Papers and magazines piled on its top obliterated any smidgen of wood, and big boxes of books blocked a glimpse of its legs or sides. Floor-to-ceiling bookcases, crammed with yellowed manuscripts, files, and old and new novels lined the walls. So much stuff—cartons, legal pads, galleys, magazines: *Manhattan, New Yorker, Vanity Fair, Harpers*—covered the rug that I had to forge a path through to greet Dick Peter. He remained hidden behind a stack of manuscripts, but his voice boomed, beckoning me forward. "Come in. Take a seat. And hurry up. I don't have much time for you." Peter sounded like Edward G. Robinson playing Little Caesar. I asked myself could a man surrounded by so many books be all bad.

Jennifer Moran popped out from behind a carton and held out her hand. "Hi, Jake." She cleared some papers off a crushed velvet wing chair the color of old port wine that faced Sixty-ninth Street and Dick Peter's desk. "Please sit down."

I sat. Jennifer wedged an opening between two piles on Peter's desk. His enormous nose, followed by the rest of his ferret-like features, poked through, his head covered with his signature ratty rug. He didn't stand, attempt to shake hands, or even smile. I've worked for some sourpusses in my career as a ghostwriter, but Peter's looked as if it had been pickled in brine. "Ms. O'Hara," he growled.

I couldn't resist. "Mr. Peter, I presume." Jennifer grinned. Dick Peter didn't.

"Let's get you up to snuff." The social niceties appeared to be over. "I've written an outline for a murder mystery." He nodded at Jennifer. "Ms. Moran's read it."

"A plot to die for," she said on cue.

"Yes, isn't it? Well, Ms. O'Hara, you'll just fill in the blanks...dialogue, character development, subplots...the meat and potatoes to go with my soufflé. Do you understand?"

Oh, I understood, all right. "Mr. Peter, as a ghostwriter, turning a soufflé into a full meal is my specialty."

"Good. Now, in my novel, someone's killing all the critics at a glossy magazine. A fictional one, mind you, but an astute reader will glean that the magazine is really *Manhattan*. So you'll need to work here to absorb the atmosphere." Peter tented his fingers and stared at his small hands for a moment. "Yes. You'll work undercover and we'll pass you off as my new assistant. Everyone knows I should have another one. Jennifer will find you a small corner..."

"I usually work at home."

"That's not possible. At least not in the beginning. You need to soak up the scene, and I need to oversee your first few chapters at my convenience."

"But..."

"No buts about it. Review your contract, Ms. O'Hara—Jake—you're a Manhattanite now." Abruptly Dick Peter turned to Jennifer. "Waltz Jake around the floor." He bared tiny teeth in what I supposed passed for a smile. "Introduce her as an editor or a reader, here to help me sift through this garbage." This last was accompanied by a sweeping gesture toward the cartons of books in front of Jennifer. He finally stood up. I'm five-four and about one hundred and eighteen pounds, most of which seems to have settled on my hips. Though he was shorter and slimmer than me, most of Dick Peter's weight had gone to that remarkable nose. Again he tried for a smile, while barking, "Then, Jake O'Hara, you and I will go to work."

I could hardly wait.

Jennifer led me to the employees' lounge, all chintz and charm, and served me a hot cup of tea in a Lenox cup. Somewhat soothed, I asked, "What fresh hell have I contracted for?"

"Did you come to my Dorothy Parker reading at the Algonquin?"

"Yes, Jennifer, and you were awesome, but I'm facing a

minimum sentence of five months here, ghostwriting for this creep."

"Just yes him to death; that's what I do." Jennifer downed her espresso. "Now come meet *Manhattan's* Goddess of Gossip."

I perked up. "Allison Carr?" The "Bites From the Big Apple" editor had taken a page from Walter Winchell and gave great gossip. My mother and Gypsy Rose never missed her column, quoting from it copiously. "Let's go."

Barry DeWitt, the magazine's handsome theater critic, darted out of Allison Carr's office as we arrived. His reviews had ravaged—and closed—countless Broadway and off-Broadway productions—while his words of scorn had decimated playwrights, directors, and actors; however, DeWitt himself was considered a star attraction by New York society hostesses: Heathcliff with Darcy's snob appeal. Now his big frame abruptly barged in front of Jennifer, almost knocking her over. Swinging around, DeWitt looked back in anger at the room he'd just left, his icy voice filling the hallway. "Dick Peter's on his last ego trip, Allison. Don't be a fellow traveler." Then he slammed the door and plowed past us, without as much as an "excuse me." Despite his well-tailored Burberry blazer, shock of black curly hair, and aquamarine eyes, DeWitt appeared to be as rude and miserable as his reviews.

A surprisingly cool and calm Allison Carr jumped up from her seat behind a rattan desk and pumped my hand, treating me like a real live celebrity instead of an incognito ghostwriter. "Don't mind DeWitt; all those melodramas have turned him into a half-baked ham." She spoke with gaiety and gusto. "So, working temp for Dick Peter, are you? Well, a few months in Purgatory beats an eternity in Hell, I always say. But welcome to *Manhattan,* darling girl." Management must have indoctrinated the magazine's entire staff to mouth these words to all newcomers. Allison waved Jennifer and me toward high-back cane chairs. "I like your look. So Annie Hall."

I stared at her in amazement. She had tawny hair and was tall and tight—this woman worked out big time—with long legs, big feet, and a flat stomach. Allison looked no older than I did, yet I knew she'd been writing "Bites From the Big Apple" for almost twenty-five years. But what really caught my attention was her dress. Allison Carr wore a short sleeve Black Watch-plaid cotton sheath, showing off her excellent upper arms. Totally transitional.

"And my mother would absolutely love your style, Ms. Carr. Mom and her best friend are your biggest fans. Your columns have replaced *Photoplay* and Cholly Knickerbocker in their lives. Filled a real void."

"Call me Allison, and do bring your mother and her friend over; we'll all do lunch."

Wow. Mom and Gypsy Rose would be thrilled. And who'd have believed that a woman who wrote so caustically could be so charming?

The door flew open. A big man with bushy black eyebrows and a snow-white crew cut shouted, "I'll have Dick Peter drawn and quartered. I swear I'll—" When he spotted Jennifer and me, he shut up, looking flushed and flustered, then said, "Oh, please forgive me, ladies. I didn't know Miss Carr had visitors."

Allison's smooth-as-Jell-O-pudding response combined just the right amount of amusement and insouciance. "Robert, I think you know Jennifer Moran—she's Dick's editorial assistant. And this is Jake O'Hara, his newest recruit." Allison flashed a rueful smile at me. "Jake, say hello to Robert Stern, *Manhattan*'s managing editor."

Three

If I hadn't been working on my time management skills—almost as appalling as my money management—someone else would have discovered the dead body. If this was my reward for being an early bird, I should have stayed in bed.

On Tuesday night, Mom, Gypsy Rose, and I had dinner at our favorite Italian restaurant. The brisk walk down Madison Avenue always revved up our appetites, while the stroll back uptown burned off a small portion of the pasta and better-than-sex desserts. Well, better than some sex. I scooped up more of the chocolate sauce, spooning it onto the ice cream-filled pastry puff, thinking that the eight blocks home wouldn't be making a dent in these calories and that I'd given my mother a canyon-sized opening for her ongoing diet and exercise lecture. However, Mom not only overindulged herself, but her delight in discussing every detail of my meeting with Allison Carr kept her from harping on my unhealthy lifestyle.

On my third recounting, Gypsy Rose said, "Enough. Now, Jake, tell us why Robert Stern wanted to pull Peter apart. I've met him and he's a really nice guy. Stern that is, not Peter."

"I'm clueless. Everyone at *Manhattan* seems to detest the man. Jennifer says even the elevator operator has a grudge against him. Peter's easy to hate; I felt like killing him myself."

"Do you think you'll be able to work for him, Jake?" my mother asked.

"Well, no one hates him more than his about-to-be-ex-wife." Gypsy Rose adjusted her eyeglasses, halting their slide down her nose and into the sauce.

"I'd forgotten that he's married to Mila Macovich. Do you know her romance novels taught me more about sex than..." My mother's raised brow veered me away from that red flag, and I changed my direction. "How could Mila be married to that Dick?"

"Separated at the moment," Mom said. "And please watch your language, Jake. The *Post* reported that she punched him on his just-lifted jaw at the Miami Book Fair. Must have been quite a row. Anyway, she locked him out of their townhouse when she returned to New York."

"I wonder why. And why didn't he have his nose nipped while he was having his face done? It's as big as the Brooklyn Bridge."

"Cindy Adams says Mila's the top candidate for the Lady Clarice Heartland Romance Writers' Award," my mother said. "The ceremony's next month at the British Embassy."

Gypsy Rose winked at me, then turned to my mother. "Maura, the *Post* ought to give you a loyal readership award."

"Do you know why they were fighting, Mom?"

"Who, darling?"

"Come on, Mom. Mila Macovich and Dick Peter. Why did she bop him at the Book Fair?"

"I only know what I read on page six." Mom reached over and snatched one of Gypsy Rose's puffs. "Mila wasn't talking, but her punch sent Dick flying to the hospital for a few new stitches to replace the ones that she'd ripped open. Then again, Mila's a big, beautiful, bold woman; she refers to herself as a yogurt-eating Russian peasant. Of course, her family's been here since 1917, but..." Thankfully, just then the waitress brought us the check, interrupting Mom's history lesson.

During our faster-pace-than-usual jaunt from the restaurant to our house on 92nd Street, I had Mila on my mind. I'd cut my adult lit teeth biting into Mila Macovich's romances. The first throbbing member I'd ever encountered had been on page thirty-six of *The Virgin and the Vagrant*, her biggest blockbuster. A Macovich romance still occasionally popped up as a miniseries. But somehow all those aching loins performed better in the pages of a book than on a television screen. The adaptations of her novels were worse than those of Judith Krantz.

She'd married Peter, following his messy, rumor-riddled divorce from exotic dancer Glory Flagg. New York's literary community had been aghast; however, compared to Mila's flamboyant past, she'd kept a low profile ever since. Why had two such gorgeous women married a gnome like Dick? Maybe his member was as huge as...

All my ruminating remained unresolved as I fell asleep.

Then I walked into the office this morning at eight-fifteen, only to find old Dick facedown on his desk. He'd been stabbed in the back—a killer with a sense of irony?—with a Delft dagger. His rug had shifted to the right; his nose protruded to the left. I screamed, "Jesus, Mary, and Joseph!" When no one answered, I dialed 911. Standing pat, still using my phone and touching nothing, I called all three of Ben Rubin's numbers, leaving frantic messages, as I tried to decide if I'd rather wait alone or fetch the guard—who seemed to work from dawn to dusk—from the lobby. The elevator operator hadn't been at his station when I arrived and, apparently, hadn't gotten here yet—or he'd have heard me scream. I glanced at my watch. 8:18. Maybe I should go...

"Oh my God! What happened? Who killed Dick Peter? Jake?" Jennifer stood in the doorway, staring at me, a tremor in her voice and horror in her eyes.

"Well, you can be damn sure I didn't, Jennifer. The police should be here any minute."

My cellphone rang. One of the things I love about Ben Rubin is that he doesn't ask a lot of foolish questions. "I'm on my way."

"Thank God. And Ben, hurry."

Jennifer had heard my end of the conversation, but far from being reassured, she appeared to be in shock. I cleared off a chair, facing away from the corpse, and led her to it.

"Sit down, I'm going to..."

"Don't leave me alone with him. He's dead. I'm afraid of dead people; I want to go home. Take me with you. Now." All color had drained from Jennifer's face and she closed her eyes, while her white knuckles clutched the arms of the chair the way mine did at the dentist.

"We can't go anywhere, Jen. Dick's been murdered; the police will..."

"Jake, listen to me." She sounded sick. "I can't talk to the police."

"And why would that be?" a burly policeman asked from the doorway. Steve, the elevator operator, stood two paces behind him, holding the door open, probably in acknowledgment that the officer's uniform outranked his. Jennifer threw up. All over the Persian carpet, all over a pile of books and all over her shoes. As a second cop, an attractive woman about my age, entered, the first one looked over at me, pointed to Jennifer and said, 'Take her to the ladies' room; Officer Conway will wait there with you until she gets cleaned up. Who called 911?"

"I did." My voice cracked. Damn him. I couldn't be more nervous if I'd done it. And it showed.

"And you are?"

"Jake O'Hara. I work for Mr. Peter—er, that is, I would have been..."

"I'm Officer Franco." He looked grim. "We'll talk when you get back." Then he turned away from me, heading for Dick Peter's body. Jennifer slumped in her chair, weeping softly. Officer Conway and I each grabbed one of Jennifer's arms, gingerly attempting to lift her up, while sidestepping to avoid the mess.

In slow motion, we half-carried, half-dragged Jennifer down the hall and into the john. Conway propped her up against the sink and I scraped the gook off her shoes, washed her face and combed her hair. Not only wouldn't Jennifer respond, but she seemed to have left the zip code. I couldn't reach her.

By the time the three of us returned to the scene of the crime, we found the room filled with busy people. Someone had strung yellow tape around the door and across the hallway on either side of it. An Abbott and Costello lookalike team from the coroner's office were spreading plastic on the carpet, covering up Jennifer's breakfast, while a third man laid open a body bag. A fingerprint expert, an older woman, severely impeded by the clutter, dusted Dick's bookcases. In one corner, I spotted the medical examiner, holding his little black bag, talking to Ben Rubin.

Ben waved at me, just as Officer Franco, appearing no less grim than when I'd last seen him, stopped me. He flipped his notebook to a clean page. "Okay, Ms. O'Hara, please take it from the top." I threw a help-me-I'm-desperate look at Ben, who grinned, gave me a thumbs-up, and continued to chat with the M.E. If I didn't know better, I'd swear Ben was getting some perverse pleasure from my impending inquisition by Officer Franco.

We stood near the wing chairs where Jennifer and I had sat only yesterday...when Dick Peter had been very much alive and bitching.

"Officer Franco, Jennifer needs medical assistance." I somehow managed to sound both impertinent and intimidated.

"I'll ask the doc to take a look at her after he's done with the stiff. But first, why don't you tell me what happened, Ms. O'Hara?"

"Now see here..." I began just as my phone rang. Damn. Only Ben—who'd given it to me—and my mother had the number. And Mom had strict instructions to only use it in an emergency. God, had something happened to her or Gypsy Rose? "Excuse me, I have to take this call." Franco stared at me as if I were certifiable. Then he glowered. I pushed the "accept" button.

"Jake, are you all right, darling?"

"Sure, Mom." I hoped that was accurate. "Why?"

'Turn on the news. They just broke into *Ramirez Now*. Dick Peter is dead! Did you know?"

The question was, how did they know? My money was on Santa Steve, who seemed to be among the missing at this moment.

"I'm with the police now in Dick's office." I favored Franco with a smile as Officer Conway led Jennifer out of the room. I whispered to Conway, "Where are you going?"

Conway replied, "To the lounge. Jennifer can rest there."

My mother said, "Is Ben there?"

"Yes. Mom, I've got to go."

'Tell Ben to hurry up and put it on, Jake. Glory Flagg is on. She's been telling all of America that throughout their six-year marriage, she and Peter were part of a sadomasochistic ménage à trois! With another man. The audience is going crazy. And just as Wendy Wu came on with the news bulletin announcing his death, Glory was screaming that Dick's suing her for twenty million dollars—because she's going public with a tell-all book!"

I dropped the phone on Officer Franco's foot and yelled, "Ben!"

Four

Every eye in the room—well, except for Dick's—was glued on Glory Flagg, resplendent in a red, white, and blue star-spangled jumpsuit. The Abbott and Costello team had unearthed a television set from under a crumpled raincoat. Enthralled, we all listened along with host Eduardo Ramirez as the glorious Glory bashed Dick Peter—her verbal assault punctuated by her brash Brooklyn vowels and missing consonants.

"Dickie and I were the odd couple, ya know. Him a graduate of Harvard, wit seven letters after his name, me a Lafayette High School dropout—I quit in my junior year to woik as a stripper. Kinda the college of bumps and grinds..." Glory was saying in response to Ramirez's last question—how did she feel about Peter now.

"And the sex was sensational," she continued, "once you got past the kinky stuff. Being polyamorous can be a joyful journey for those ready to explore alternate erotica. I'm quoting from the deceased here."

"Polyamorous? Would you explain that term for our audience?" Eduardo Ramirez asked, an eager grin crossing his made-for-television face.

"Yeah. Ya know, when a goil gets to boff more than one guy at a time. Or vice versa. But Dick's favorite sexual sandwich has always been two guys with a masochistic miss spread like mayo in the middle. So I can't understand why he was all bent outta shape about my upcoming book..."

"Glory, regarding Dick Peter's demise, how do you think that will impact you?" Ramirez's ad-lib sentence structure certainly lacked his writer's style. The camera moved in for a close-up of Glory; tricolor makeup encircled her eyes.

"Eduardo, my guess is that his twenty-million-dollar lawsuit against me and Harvest House will be as dead as Dick is." Glory flashed her fabulous smile. Either her dentist had managed to bleach her teeth far whiter then mine or maybe contrasted against her scarlet lipstick, her teeth just looked brighter. No wonder Mom still used Revlon's Fire and Ice.

Officer Franco, who'd reluctantly joined our queue around the television set, said, "This broad just gave Senor Ramirez and most of America her motive for murder."

Ramirez asked Flagg, "Had Dick Peter been ill?"

Glory giggled. "Eduardo, you're an old acquaintance of Dick's." Ramirez nodded sagely, as she rattled on, "Ya know, spiritually, he's the sickest soul around—and wouldn't ya jest love to cover his Final Judgment on Court TV?—but physically that little sucker was the healthiest specimen I ever slept with. I ran into Mila, she let Dick back into the house over the weekend, and she said he's still full of piss and vinegar. Um, that is, he was as of last night. I wonder what did do him in." The network broke away from the show for a Volkswagen Beetle commercial.

Ben said, "Whoever called with the news of Peter's death obviously neglected to mention murder."

"And maybe on purpose," I said, revising my rush to judgment of Steve the elevator operator as the caller, unless he also turned out to be the murderer. If Jennifer ever pulled herself together, I'd have to ask her why Steve held a grudge against Dick. For now, I went on with my theory. "Say the killer called in, knowing that Glory had been scheduled as this morning's guest on *Ramirez Now*—he might not have wanted to reveal that Peter had been murdered, hoping that Glory would hang herself verbally. Which, as if I need to remind you, is exactly what happened."

Ben said, "Any one of the critics and editors with offices on his floor who passed by here this morning could have placed that call."

"Yeah, but, Ben..."

Back on the air, Ramirez interrupted both my assessment of the murderer's state of mind and Glory's medical evaluation of the dead Dick. "I've just been informed that Allison Carr of *Manhattan* magazine and a frequent contributor is on the line." The television screen split three ways: a headshot of Eduardo to the left, a glowing Glory in the middle, and to the right, a network file photo of Allison Carr, with *Manhattan*'s "Bites From the Big Apple" editor and the magazine's famous logo underneath. Suddenly Carr's photo filled the entire screen and we heard her cheery voice.

"I arrived at work a little while ago, just ahead of the police. Things are buzzing in Dick Peter's office. A homicide detective from the Nineteenth Precinct is in there...So is the coroner. I overheard a heavyset uniformed policeman say that Dick's been stabbed in the back. My condolences, Glory. I know how you must mourn your dear departed Dick."

Ramirez in the studio and I in the victim's office gulped in unison. I said to Ben, "Well, there you go. I guess Gypsy Rose is not the only psychic I know. And just how much do you think they contributed to Carr for this phone-in reportage?"

For once Eduardo Ramirez seemed speechless. But not our girl Glory. "Allison, the reason everyone reads your column is because of your compassion. I'm sure you'll miss old Dick as much as I will." Glory Flagg gave Allison's picture the finger, and we went to another commercial break.

"Welcome to the age of instant information," the medical examiner said.

The lady fingerprint expert sighed wearily. "Gentlemen, there's some instant information I could use right now." She looked from the doctor to the detective. "When is Dick Peter's ETA into the body bag? I've got to dust his desk." Ben Rubin clicked off the TV, telling Officer Franco, "Go get that woman off the phone. Tell her that her next interview will be with me and meanwhile to keep her mouth shut." Then he turned to me. "Do you know where that Carr woman's office is?" I nodded. 'Take Franco there now." The rest of the crime scene staff went back to work.

Allison, all smiles, hung up the phone when Franco and I walked in.

"Hi, Jake. Did you happen to catch me on TV? I just got through talking to Eduardo Ramirez and Glory Flagg." And she was still smiling after Officer Franco read her the riot act. "Oh, great, I'll look forward to chatting with Detective Rubin." Did this lady ever lose her cool?

There was precious little I could tell Officer Franco. From the time I'd discovered Dick's body 'til Jennifer's appearance, less than five minutes had elapsed. Franco, whose patrol car had been cruising Sixty-ninth Street, made the scene only moments later. We talked in the hall. "No, I didn't touch a thing. Yes, I'll be available for more questions." My answers seemed to satisfy him and he dropped me off at the employees' lounge, where Officer Conway was having less success with Jennifer.

Since Jen remained semi-collapsed and Officer Conway had gathered neither evidence nor information, I spent the next few minutes essentially repeating what I'd told Franco.

"Then you have no idea why Jennifer's in such a state?"

"Only that she told me she was afraid of dead people." We spoke as if Jennifer weren't there. I didn't think she really was— at least not listening or caring. She was beginning to spook me.

Michael Moran, dressed in motorcycle mod, pushed the door open. Like Dick Peter, Michael was a small, slim man, but much more wholesome-looking. Huck Finn in a biker's helmet. I've always questioned what it could be that Jennifer found appealing about him; I'd tried to like him for years. Eventually, I just stopped trying.

"What's wrong? Jennifer, are you okay?" Jen, her head hanging on her chest, her mouth slack and her fingers twitching, said nothing. Michael shouted at me, "Jake, what the hell's going on here? I got a call from the police," he sneered in Officer Conway's direction, "saying Jennifer had some kind of a spell. I demand to know what happened to her!"

Conway spoke up. "It would seem murder made her sick." That shut him up.

While the officer advised Michael that the police weren't through questioning Mrs. Moran and that they shouldn't plan on leaving town, Barbara Ferris, the uniformed receptionist, joined us.

"Hi, Jake. Detective Rubin sent me to help get Jennifer down to the lobby." I wondered where she'd been all morning.

Michael managed to get Jennifer on her feet. As I handed Barbara her shoulder bag, they each grabbed one of Jen's arms, half carrying her out of the room. I hoped Michael didn't plan on driving Jennifer home on his motorcycle.

Sally Conway and I walked back to Peter's office. I wanted

to have a word with Ben, if he'd ever stop talking to the medical examiner...and ignoring me.

Maybe this was payback time. Ben and I had met when he'd interviewed me—as a possible suspect—in a previous murder case. And even though I'm certain that he'd decided on my innocence as quickly as I'd checked out his Antonio Banderas looks, Mom, Gypsy Rose, and I had driven him crazy. Probably still did.

Currently, we were—to use my mother's term—courting; we sometimes double-dated with my mother and Ben's father. "Weird," Modesty M., a wordy gothic novelist and my fellow member of Ghostwriters Anonymous, had said. And for once, Modesty, an odd duck herself, had been totally accurate. However...My phone rang.

Mom. I'd cut her off. "Hi." I put my hand over the phone and said to Officer Conway, "Excuse me. Why don't you go on ahead?" Conway nodded and left me alone in the hall, dwarfed by a huge print of Maxfield Parrish's painting of a group of American Indians staring off into the distance at what looked like skyscrapers.

"Listen, Mom, everything's okay, I'm..."

"Sorry to disappoint you, Jake, but this is not your mother." The sexy voice, chuckling as he spoke, belonged to Dennis Kim.

"How did you get my number?"

"You gave it to me the day you were almost killed. Remember? I've kept it next to my heart ever since."

"Right." Jesus, I was getting forgetful. "Look, Dennis, I'm in the middle of a murder here. What do you want? This phone is not to be used promiscuously."

"What kind of a guy do you think I am? Would I make promiscuous phone calls? This is a matter of life and death."

"Yes? I'm listening."

And curious, but I'd never give him that satisfaction.

"I represent Pax Publishing, Jake. Dick's murder presents a major problem for them."

"Did you draft my contract with Peter? Dennis Kim is written all over it."

"Yes, but only to protect Keith Morrison and Pax's interests, not Peter's. My first loyalty is to my client." Wherever this conversation was going, it was good to know that up front. Dennis continued, "With their best interests in mind, I told them how you'd turned *A Killing in Katmandu* into what looks like a blockbuster—after the author's death. And that you'd worked that miracle from a twenty-page outline."

"With no royalties in my pocket, thanks to your crafty contract."

"My point exactly. Your employer was my client. But this time you have a share in all the royalties and that holds true even though Dick's dead."

"You mean...?"

"Yes. Keith Morrison would like to talk to you about completing the manuscript, under the same financial agreement. Maybe a tad more. If you're interested, I'll set up a meeting. Only you'd have to write fast, Jake. Dick should have been finished with this book long before he died. Keith said he'd discuss a bonus if you can deliver a manuscript in less than three months."

"God only knows I can use the money. Hey, thanks, Dennis."

"There's something else, Jake."

"Oh?"

"Robert Stern would like to meet with you and me in his office. I'm pulling into a diplomat's parking place in front of the Russian Embassy around the corner on Madison as we speak."

In all the years I've known Dennis, he's never parked legally. "Stern's office is on the fifth floor. Go on up, I'll meet you there. Take the marble stairs in the center hall. The elevator doesn't go to the top floor." Why was I not surprised?

Barbara Ferris rose from her desk across from the elevator. "Jennifer should be home by now, Jake. Mr. Stern had his limo waiting to drive her and Michael."

"That's great. I'm on my way up the stairs to see Mr. Stern."

"Yes. I've been given clearance for you." She handed me a big badge in the shape of an apple. "Pin this on your jacket; it gives you access to the top floor."

Jeez. Security couldn't have been any tighter at the Manhattan Project than it was at *Manhattan* magazine.

Robert Stern fussed over me as his secretary served tea. "Your first two days with us have proved distressing, my dear. I do apologize. That unpleasantness in Allison's office yesterday and then discovering Dick's body today. You're probably asking yourself what tomorrow will bring." The question had occurred to me. Mr. Stern plopped a piece of lemon in his tea. "Our meeting will be brief. Then I want you to go home and get some rest." He came across as avuncular and sincere.

"Jake. Robert. What a pleasure to see two of my favorite people enjoying a chat." Dennis charged across the threshold like a stunning Korean martial arts master wearing a Brooks Brothers suit. And, as it has done for over a quarter of a century, his presence pumped up my heart rate.

The tea sandwiches were better than the Plaza's or the Palace's. Surprisingly, I was hungry. I reached for two more. Robert Stern said, "Dick's sudden departure for the world beyond leaves us rather muddled here at *Manhattan*. I intend to put our best investigative reporters on the case. This crime will not only be covered, it will be solved. I shall make that promise to our readers. But my immediate need is a temporary replacement for Dick. Someone to do the reviews for the next two or three months. I understand Jennifer is ill. And while she's a fine editor, her writing lacks bite. Dennis tells me you have plenty of bite."

I grinned at Dennis as memories of our childhood fight in Carnegie Hill flooded my mind; however, I hoped he hadn't violated my ghostwriter's anonymity while raving about my writing skills to Robert Stern.

"Jake, I need a witty, pithy critic, and I need her now." Mr. Stern's washed-out blue eyes smiled at me.

"You've just hired one." I smiled back.

Which is how I wound up in my own office—a room with a view—and a title: associate editor. Before settling in, I called my mother, invited Dennis for drinks at the Polo Lounge, and dashed back to Dick's office to have that chat with Ben.

Five

Dennis Kim waved to Joe Klein. Then he raised his glass in a salute to me, saying, "Stop thanking me. I'm always at your service. If you want me, all you have to do is whistle. You do know how to whistle, don't you, Jake?"

I laughed and took a sip of my extra dry martini. He'd accepted my cocktails and conversation offer, then asked if we could change the venue to the Royalton on 44th Street, which was far too trendy for my taste, but what the hell. Because of Dennis Kim's intervention, I was going to remain gainfully employed...whether he wanted to hear about it or not. The lounge, almost empty at four o'clock in the afternoon, seemed soothing, despite the stark Euro-Mod decor—or maybe it was the gin that soothed.

I changed the subject. "If the police round up the usual suspects, half of Manhattan would be in custody. It's the people who didn't want Dick dead who'll make the short list."

Dennis nodded. "Just the authors alone would fill volumes. Maybe the Writers Guild chipped in and hired a hit man."

"Did you know him well, Dennis?"

"Not really. Only through Stern and Keith Morrison—hey, don't forget, I've set up a meeting with Morrison in the morning. Anyway, dealing with Dick was like dancing with the devil. Not a nice guy."

"I found that out, and I dreaded the idea of working with him. This is an awful thing to say, but his death and your connections have placed me in a dream job. Ghostwriting for the dead is so much more fun than working with a real, live pain."

"Jake," he said, and his gold-flecked eyes looked amused, "I didn't bump him off to make your career path easier."

"But you did resurrect the ghostwriting assignment from hell and turn it into a heavenly opportunity."

"That's what I do for a living. If you'd ever get rid of Sam Kelley and have me represent you, all your ghostwriting would be glorious."

I ate the first of my three gin-soaked olives and steered the conversation back to the murder. "What's Robert Stern's story? In Allison's office yesterday, he sounded as if he might murder Dick any minute."

"Yeah. Robert would certainly be high on that long list of suspects. About seven or eight years ago, when Dick Peter was still married to Glory Flagg, he had an affair with Stern's wife."

"How did Stern find out?"

"When Dick dumped Catherine, she had a nervous breakdown. Robert had to put her away. Then she hanged herself. The suicide note told the whole sordid story."

"Jesus. How come Stern didn't fire Peter on the spot?"

"Oh, he tried. *Manhattan's* board of directors voted him down. Dick's scurrilous style sold millions of copies."

"That must have been hell for Stern. What was his wife like?"

"Catherine Stern exuded class. Came from old money, a real

lady...Miss Porter's, Vassar, riding to the hounds at their estate in Virginia...yet she had an earthy charm. I liked her. And Stern adored her. They'd been married thirty years."

"She must have been considerably older than Dick at the time of the affair."

"Almost twenty years. She was a beautiful woman with the figure of a schoolgirl. What could she have seen in Dick? I never understood it. And Robert never got over it."

It almost sounded as if Dennis had harbored a yen for Catherine himself. I chewed on the second olive.

"But I had the impression that whatever had Robert's knickers in a twist yesterday had been a recent development. And why would Stern confide in a gossip columnist, for God's sake?"

"Let's just say that Allison Carr comforted the grieving widower for years. And while she spreads rumor and innuendo for fun and profit, she's never mentioned the Robert-Catherine-Dick triangle. Not in the magazine. Not on TV."

"When I told Allison that Mom and Gypsy Rose thought she was the greatest thing since acid skin peels, she invited us all for lunch. She seems totally charming and unflappable. Is that for real?"

"Wendy says Allison's so cool that she could have sunk the Titanic quicker than the iceberg."

Wendy Wu was not only a top news anchor but Dennis Kim's ex-wife. She'd annoyed me even before she married Dennis. "What's that supposed to mean?" I snapped.

"I guess it might mean watch your back."

"That's not very funny, Dennis."

He didn't answer me but instead motioned to the waiter for another round. "I have some other news for you, Jake." I glared at him. "According to my source at the *New York Times*, *A*

Killing in Katmandu will make the bestseller list this Sunday. Number four. Congratulations."

"Great. However, thanks to your confidentiality clause in that ghostwriter/client contract, no one but you, me, Mom, and Sam Kelley will ever know I wrote a bestseller. No royalties. No recognition. A ghostwriter doesn't have a chance in the fame game. The dead 'author'—who never wrote any of her own books—will get the credit. And her estate will get the money. What I get is the shaft." I speared the last olive, almost stabbing the waiter as he whisked away my empty glass and replaced it with a fresh martini.

Dennis ignored both my comments and my attitude. "So can I take you to dinner tonight, to celebrate?"

"Why don't you have Gypsy Rose channel your former client's sorry spirit? That is, if she can be reached in the bowels of Hell. Maybe the devil will give her a weekend pass so you can take her to dinner." I swallowed half the martini in one gulp.

Was I angry with Dennis over that old contract and the fact that he'd become a big-shot entertainment attorney while I remained an unaccredited ghostwriter? Or was I angry because Dennis Kim's presence still made me feel like one of Mila Macovich's waiting-to-be-ravaged virgins?

I went home to take a two-martini nap. My mother woke me in time for *Jeopardy!* She served dinner on a tray—turkey sandwiches with crusts trimmed, a pot of decaf tea, Jell-O, and Social Tea cookies—Maura O'Hara's panacea for all life's ills, including discovering a corpse before breakfast.

We both knew the Final Jeopardy question: Who are Amy, Beth, Jo and Meg? The answer had been: the first names of the four March sisters in *Little Women.* Literature was one of our best categories. Before Alex shook hands with the winner, Mom switched off the TV. "Jake, I need to talk to you."

My mother was dressed for bed, saturated in Vaseline Intensive Care Lotion from head to toe and swathed in an old, long-sleeve cotton t-shirt, sweatpants, and white socks. Her face and hands, the only visible parts of her body, glowed.

"Isn't it a little early to be all greased up and ready to slip between the sheets?"

"I'm getting up at five. Gypsy Rose and I are going to a sunrise ceremony in Central Park."

"Who's getting married at dawn?"

"Not a wedding, Jake. Some witches from Westchester are holding their fall coven. Gypsy Rose is considering having one or two of them speak at the bookstore's Halloween Happening—so we're going to Strawberry Fields to audition them."

Gypsy Rose's New Age bookstore drew large crowds from all the boroughs and out of town as well. Conservatives, compared to some of the crazies in that movement, but sometimes both Gypsy Rose and her audience were over the edge. I try to reserve judgment regarding the world beyond and the spirits residing there whom Gypsy Rose calls friends. Occasionally, she and they have awed me. It's the live, seemingly certifiable fruitcakes who scare me.

"Well, be careful trotting through Central Park in the dark," I told my mother, using a stern voice.

She smiled. "Don't worry, dear. Too-Tall Tom is coming with us. He used to date one of the warlocks. And he's hired a hansom cab to drive us there."

"Wow. Those suburban witches will be totally impressed." But I felt better. Too-Tall Tom was not only far more sensible than Mom and Gypsy Rose; he also belonged to my Ghostwriters Anonymous group and was my closest confidant.

"Anyway, what I wanted to tell you," Mom said, as she stacked the remnants of our gourmet dinner on the tray, "is that Mila Macovich came into the store today." I trailed after her carrying the empty teacups.

"No kidding."

"She wanted an out-of-print Edgar Cayce book. Mila's past-life-regression therapist told her how Gypsy Rose had dated Edgar in her previous incarnation—and that her bookstore had the largest Cayce collection in the city."

"Mila's therapist knows Gypsy Rose?"

"Not from this lifetime. But it seems this therapist—his name is Bruce Wexler—had been a woman the last time around and he...uh, that is, she, was Gypsy Rose's chief competition for Edgar's affection."

Conversations like this tended to close my open mind.

"But it's why Mila wanted to read up on the world beyond that's of interest here, Jake."

'Tell me."

"Well, Mila told us that she had to contact Dick Peter. And how her therapist believed that Cayce's books could be a start. But when I told Mila—and God, she's stunning—about Gypsy Rose's successful séances, she said she'd be interested in attending one. We decided the spiritual climate would be perfect on All Soul's Day. If you're interested, I think we might have room for one more ghost."

"You're an angel."

My mother's hug smeared me with Vaseline.

Six

I dreamed of Delft daggers, their blades brightly covered in red blood and green bile. The loud ring of my bedside phone jarred me awake. Edgy, my hand trembled as I reached for the receiver.

"Jake, I'm sorry to wake you, but..."

"That's okay, Ben. What time is it?"

"Six forty. I'm operating on zombie time...got to bed at two. I'm at headquarters now, but wanted to see how you were doing before I head down to the morgue."

I really did like this man. And felt guilty that I'd allowed Dennis Kim to tickle my toes, yet again, yesterday afternoon. I guess I could just chalk that up to a bad mix of murder and martinis.

"Confronting corpses has become a regular part of my career path. I'm doing fine." Like he'd believe that. "How about you?"

"Good." He sounded harried. "Just be careful at work, Jake. Don't play Nancy Drew. Watch out for Allison Carr; all her charisma could just be a cover-up. Don't trust that woman, and tell her nothing."

"Do you think she…"

"I asked her to keep her opinions to herself, but there she was last night on MSNBC, then later being interviewed by Larry King. Glory Flagg was on too. Spewing venom. What a pair they are."

"Ben, for God's sake, Allison's a gossip columnist. For her, talk is money." Why was I defending her? I didn't even know her, but she'd turned me into an instant fan. "Hey, she's not really a suspect, is she?"

"The possible suspects in Dick Peter's murder outnumber Scarlett O'Hara's suitors."

I laughed. "This O'Hara would enjoy a visit from a certain suitor. Any chance of that happening tonight?"

"I'll ring you later. Right now I have a date with a corpse."

"Stiff competition."

"Ouch. It's too early for your bad jokes, Jake. Save them for tonight."

As I left the house to meet Modesty for breakfast at Sarabeth's, the temperature had dropped into the low fifties and the wind whipped scraps of paper high off the ground, blowing my blunt cut and too-long bangs into a bad hair day and leaving any trace of Indian summer as only a warm memory. I'd put on a camel blazer, a beige cotton turtleneck, khakis, and caramel-color socks, matching my new Bandolino tasseled loafers, but I still felt chilly.

Modesty sat at a table overlooking Madison. She was dressed in her favorite outfit: a black wool monk's robe, belted with amber rosary beads that, unintentionally I'm sure, matched her short, fluffy hair. The cool weather had forced her to leave her St. Francis sandals at home—so black lace-up granny boots completed her ensemble. Petite, pale, and green-eyed, Modesty might have been considered perky, even pretty; however, she worked too hard at being just plain weird. Clothes from the crypt have long been her fashion statement. And her personality matched her style. Years of ghosting for wannabe romance novelists—mostly women—had turned Modesty into a card-carrying misogynist. She tolerated me and Jane D., another member of our Ghostwriters Anonymous group, because we were the only two people in the world who'd read and critique her work-in-progress, a Gothic horror—now heading for two thousand pages.

Difficult as dandruff on a daily basis, she always came through in a crunch, and I considered her a friend. God only knows what she considered me. We ordered two cappuccinos and decided to share a fresh-baked muffin, an order of cinnamon toast, and Dick Peter gossip.

"Did you catch Glory Flagg with Larry King?"

"Damn, Modesty, I must be the only person in America who missed it."

"Glory certainly spoke ill of the dead. And that gossip monger Allison Carr wasn't a fan of Dick's either. I can't believe that you discovered the body. Your new assignment as his *editor* has certainly proved to be exciting. What was he like?"

I knew Modesty suspected that I'd been hired as more than an editor for Dick, but as members of Ghostwriters Anonymous we never revealed—even to each other—the names of the authors who employed us as ghostwriters.

"Grim. As big a horror as reputed. Remember, I only met him the day before his murder."

"Well, I met Glory Flagg at that Holistic Happening I went

to with Too-Tall Tom in NoHo last weekend," Modesty said between bites of blueberry muffin. "The three of us sat together at the 'How to Control Your Chakras' lecture. It was all about managing your body's inner energy and healing yourself both spiritually..."

"We'll work on my chakras later." I wasn't even sure what or where they were, but figured I could contain my curiosity. "Tell me about Glory."

Modesty smiled—such a rare occurrence that I'd forgotten what well-shaped, pretty teeth she had—and said, "Now, Jake, what would you expect a woman, formerly known as Gladys Fuchs of Flatbush, who's reinvented herself into Glory Flagg, a nationally acclaimed stripper, to be like?"

I laughed. "Does she always wear red, white, and blue like she did on the *Ramirez Now* show?"

"Yeah. Glory honored our chakras class with an exhibition of her patriotic dance. Started out wrapped in the Stars and Stripes—with Sousa's eponymous march as her music—wound up in a spangled G-string. And she has a Statute of Liberty routine where the torch-twirl is hot stuff."

"You're joking."

Modesty reproached me. "You know I never joke."

"Right. Sorry." I wiped cinnamon flakes from my chin. "So did you get a chance to chat with her?"

"Glory doesn't chat, Jake. She addresses her audience loud and clear, like Adelaide in *Guys and Dolls*. And in the same accent."

"Did she discuss Dick?"

"Her favorite topic. Glory held her hate for him in high esteem. Claims Dick's deviancy had closed down her second chakra. She hoped this healing session would reopen the floodgate of her passion."

"So Glory told the whole crowd that Dick ruined her sex drive?"

"You got it."

"Listen, Modesty, do you think you know her well enough to arrange an introduction?"

"I would hope that after your last foray into detective work you're not planning a sequel. Let Ben Rubin, whom the City of New York overpays, do his job."

"I just want to talk to her about..."

"Actually, you should ask Too-Tall Tom to give her a call. He became quite cozy with our girl Glory. They bonded. Seems his second chakra had gone into neutral too after he'd broken up with that tacky John Wilson. That's why we were there, you know."

I didn't know, and I felt a pang of jealousy that my best friend, Too-Tall Tom, had shared his dysfunctional chakra problem with Modesty instead of me. I said, "Well, he's off this morning on some witch-hunt with Mom and Gypsy Rose. So will you phone Glory?"

"It's your funeral, but I'll arrange a meeting. Maybe for today after work."

"You're a doll." I smiled at her.

Modesty shuddered, then in a stern voice, advised me, "Watch your mouth."

Seven

Once again, the guardian of the lobby greeted me with a curt nod and gestured toward the electronic bag check conveyer. I flipped out the pass card that Barbara had given me yesterday, flashed a smile, and extended my hand. "My temporary ID; I'm a Manhattanite now. Jake O'Hara. How are you doing this morning?"

His cold gray eyes met mine. "Hans Foote." I blinked, stifling a giggle. He reached for the card, ignoring my hand. After a few seconds of intense scrutiny, Hans pointed to the subway-like turnstile to the left of the visitors' electronic walkthrough. "Slide it into the opening, logo up. If your card is inserted the wrong way an alarm will go off here and at the police station. You must do it correctly. There is no margin for error." I heeded his instructions. Not mechanically adept, I've had major trouble with hotel room doors, ATMs and, when visiting Washington, riding the Metro. When using a programmed card, I assume that it's smarter than I am.

A NYPD patrolman standing by the elevator door also checked my ID, but he returned my smile. Santa Steve appeared somber. "Good morning, Miss. A sad chapter for *Manhattan,* isn't it? And what a way to start your career here, finding a body. So depressing. But I wish you well with your new assignment. Replacing Mr. Peter, aren't you?" The melodic strains of "Dancing in the Dark" almost drowned him out. He opened the gate; we'd arrived at the fourth floor.

"Dick's irreplaceable," I answered him over my shoulder as I exited the elevator.

Barbara followed me down the long hall, hauling a dolly filled with manuscripts and files. My office, pristine when I'd left yesterday, was now piled high with cartons from Dick Peter's accumulated clutter. "The police released this stuff a little while ago, after Mr. Stern called the mayor and told him we had a magazine to publish. He's a big campaign contributor, you know." I wondered how Barbara was privy to that bit of information and why she would share it with me. She dumped a pile of files on my desk and continued, "Of course, the cops still have all the appointment books and correspondence and the like, but Jennifer should be able to answer some of your questions."

"Have you spoken to Jennifer? I called her this morning but reached her voicemail."

"She's having a series of GI tests and X-rays taken; says she'll be here this afternoon. Miss O'Hara, I told Jennifer that you were the new book editor. She seemed somewhat surprised." I'll bet.

"That's just a temporary move...and I'm only an associate editor." God, I hoped Jennifer hadn't expected the job. "And, Barbara, call me Jake."

Alone, I sat and stared at the mountains of work strewn across my desk and all of the chairs. Should I sort it out now? Or wait 'til I returned from my meeting with Keith Morrison? In my greed and glee about working alone, had I dealt myself a losing hand of solitaire? How the hell could I...

"Jake?" Allison Carr's cheery voice caught my attention. She stood in the open doorway, glowing. "Are you okay, my dear?" Her warmth spread like sunshine, brightening the room.

"A bit overwhelmed, but fine otherwise. Please come in, Allison." I shoved a bunch of books onto the oak floor, clearing a club chair for her.

She sat, crossing one well-toned leg over the other, then smoothed her navy gabardine skirt. "I wanted to tell you how well I think you've handled a ghastly situation. If there's anything I can do to ease your transition from Dick's drudge to having his job as *Manhattan's* book editor, just let me know." Allison waved a hand over the mess and grimaced. "Mr. Peter never was Mr. Clean. Ask either of his wives."

"Did you know Mila Macovich?"

"Not as well as I knew old Glory. Mila is something of a misanthrope, my dear. She never made the social scene, which is, of course, my bread and butter."

"Did you meet Glory while she was married to Dick?"

"The naked truth is Glory Flagg and I are old acquaintances. I've known her for decades. We were in the same class in Lafayette High School in Brooklyn."

I felt my mouth drop. Allison's velvet vowels rolled right on, "Oh, yes. Gladys Fuchs and Annie Carriano. One entered burlesque, the other Barnard. Gladdie had sex appeal, I had a scholarship."

"But..."

"If you're wondering why I sound like Grace Kelly, it's because I worked almost full-time at Bloomingdale's while I went to college so I could hire her voice coach. My Brooklynese diction proved to be more of a challenge than Grace's Philadelphia twang. The old boy suffered a fatal stroke the week after I'd mastered mid-Atlantic vowels. However, he died happy, having heard me turn 'owfill' and 'coughfee' into 'awful' and 'coffee.'"

"That's totally awesome." Allison's true confession had further endeared her to me. "Are you...er, that is, do most people know about your background? It's a great story."

"Certainly. Gladdie's never let me forget that I was a homely giant of a nerd while she was the Brooklyn Bombshell. I once did a column on our past and present collision course. She then threatened me with a hit man."

I laughed. "Such drama."

"Don't laugh, Jake. She was dead serious." Allison stood, adjusted her blazer, and mustered a smile. "Enough about vain Glory, I'm here to issue two invitations. Please ask your mother and Gypsy Rose Liebowitz if they can join me for lunch tomorrow. At noon."

Wow. Allison was a fast promise keeper. "I'll just bet they can."

"Good. And naturally you're included as well, my dear. Give me a buzz later to confirm. Then mark your calendar for ten a.m. Monday. Dick's invitation-only funeral will be at St. Thomas Church on Fifth Avenue. Mr. Stern is working with the merry widow to make this a special occasion. A *Manhattan* requiem to remember. He asked me to be sure and ask you personally. You'll sit in my pew."

"Thanks. I'll be there."

Allison's long stride had her across the room in seconds. She turned at the door and said, "Oh, Jake, do you think you could ask Gypsy Rose if I might attend Mila's séance?" Quid pro quo? Damn.

I stalled. "How do you know about that?"

"My dear, you of all people should be well aware that a journalist never reveals her sources. We Manhattanites would die first."

Did she know I was a ghostwriter? "Allison, I don't..."

"Just see what you can do. You can share the results of your inquiry with me when you call to confirm our luncheon. Thank you in advance." She swept out the door, gently closing it behind her, before I could reply.

What the hell was the matter with me? Obviously Ben had Allison Carr pegged, while I'd behaved like a fawning fan club of one. The phone rang. Dennis, calling from his car, to tell me that he was double-parked on the northeast corner of 68th and Madison, and could I move my fanny?

Pax Publications had its main offices on the second floor of the Chrysler Building, the grand dame of art deco skyscrapers, but Keith Morrison reigned at the top, in the tower suite on the sixty-ninth floor. His secretary, Margaret Bourke, a slim, youngish woman sporting a sleek, dark 1920s bob, toured us through the publishing house's library before whisking us up to Morrison's domain. I'd once dated an Ivy League bookworm. This library rivaled Princeton's. And the Jacobean desk placed in the center appeared as large as the university's football field. Comfortable sofas and overstuffed armchairs were scattered strategically around the desk. The smell of new books was intoxicating; the walls were lined with classics as well. I wanted to move in, send out for food to the deli across Lexington Avenue, and never leave. Books were a real turn-on for me, often delivering what their covers so tantalizingly promised, and, on many occasions, providing more fun than sex.

Ms. Bourke let Dennis and me savor the ambiance for a few minutes, then led us to one of the building's magnificent deco elevators. We stepped back in time into something not unlike a set design from an old black and white Fred Astaire-Ginger Rogers musical. The ascent proved as thrilling as Coney Island's Cyclone, *swoosh*, and we were expressed to the top floor.

The rooms located in the scalloped steeple of the Chrysler Building were dramatically narrow. Here, with sky-high ceilings and windows to the floor, the views blew you away. Scary too. The city loomed large, from the Bronx to the Bowery. What a great spot for a suicide jump; I'd have to work that into Dick's, or some future, plot. Morrison, greeting us at the elevator, surprised me, looking more like Norman Mailer than Michael Korda, dressed in blue jeans and a Gap t-shirt. He grabbed both of my hands in his and, almost as if he were praying, said, "Pax vobiscum." I couldn't wait 'til we got to the filthy lucre discussion.

In his sanctum, we sank into art deco leather chairs, the color of Gallo Burgundy, facing Morrison with New York City at our feet. I couldn't tear my eyes away from that awesome sight. We were so close to the window that the view made me dizzy as it dazzled me. Dennis was all business, fiddling with what looked like a contract. Morrison's monologue droned on. "Dick is—I mean, was—something of an enigma. That *Our Gal Sunday* syndrome."

"Who?" What was the man talking about?

"You know, Ms. O'Hara, the one from a poor mining town who pulled herself out of the coal dust and grew up to marry an English earl."

"When did that happen?"

Morrison smiled, swung his chair around, stared out the window in the direction of the Empire State Building, for at least a New York minute, then swiveled back to look at me. "In another world, young lady. And in a far, far better place. Radioland. Around sixty years ago. *Our Gal Sunday* was a soap opera. One of the best."

"Oh," I said, wondering where he was going with this. "Anyway, I've envisioned Dick Peter's dreary childhood, growing up as he did in a small mining town, to be much the same as I've always pictured Sunday's." He sighed. "Even today, when faced with life's little sorrows, I ask myself: How would Sunday handle this one?"

Dennis squirmed, shifting his right leg to a new resting place, crossing it over his left knee. He caught my eye and winked. "Keith, we wanted to firm up Jake's contract..."

Keith straightened up and seemed to shake off Sunday's storyline, returning from radio days to the world of publishing. I watched the process with amazement. The remembrance of soaps now past, Morrison seized control of the conversation. "Well, let's see what the little lady is worth. Does Ms. O'Hara have a price in mind, Dennis, or shall we open the bidding?"

I bit my tongue but pictured the publisher with a Delft dagger in his back. Dennis kept quiet too. Morrison continued, "Dick's untimely demise does put Pax in something of a quandary." Dennis nodded. I wondered why I'd bothered to come to this meeting. Morrison peered over a crystal paperweight at Dennis. "Frankly, because of our Dick's caliber and his being a later grad from my alma mater, the editorial board waived Pax's standard requirements of so many pages by a given date, and advanced him considerable monies...rather too freely, I'm afraid."

Suddenly, he swung his chair around to face me. I figured it must be my turn to nod. "Pax prides itself on hiring only the best. We had every confidence, Ms. O'Hara, that you could ghostwrite our Dick's book when he was alive and contributing, but now that he's dead..." Morrison spread his hands delicately, "we realize..."

I looked him in the eye. "That you should have taken your Dick in hand instead of waiving him so freely."

Next to me, Dennis choked. The publisher arched his eyebrows. Then he slid his chair back, walked around the desk and extended his hand to me. "Ms. O'Hara, that is exactly the mordant mirth our own dear Dick would have shown. You are our ghost Dick. Please consent to stay on and finish the book for us."

"I would be delighted..."

Dennis stopped choking. "For another twenty percent..."

"For another twenty percent," I finished.

Eight

Jennifer was a no-show. A message from Michael on my voicemail assured me she'd be in tomorrow morning, but for today the doctor had prescribed a sedative and a good night's sleep. Sounded good to me. Instead, I started to create order out of the chaos in my office. Now that Dennis had negotiated two great-paying but demanding jobs for me, I knew I'd better get to work. As I sorted and prioritized, I wondered if Jennifer could be pregnant. And felt a twinge of envy. As my mother frequently reminded me, "Christ was dead at thirty-three, and you aren't even engaged."

Or maybe Jennifer's tummy trouble was seriously connected to Dick's murder. Did she know something? Suspect someone? And why had she said she couldn't speak to the police? That odd remark had almost gotten lost in her gut-wrenching performance. Jeez, I should be ashamed of myself, but murder made me suspicious. Even of Jennifer.

I stuffed the new book by Harry Brett, whose adventure sagas conjured memories of Hemingway, into my briefcase, deciding that *Bordello in Borneo* would be my first book review as associate editor. I'd planned on reading it anyway. I'd start tonight. Then I called and ordered a pizza.

When we'd left the Chrysler Building, hordes of men were spilling out of Grand Central onto Lexington Avenue. The Pledged-For-Lifers, a quasi-religious all-male movement of reborn husbands, would be holding its annual convention in Madison Square Garden starting this afternoon. Gridlock. East, west, north. and south. Both Park and Madison Avenues had been jammed with Range Rovers and Jeeps sporting Montana and Texas license plates; Manhattan had never seen so many minivans. It took us over an hour to drive from 43rd and Lex to 69th and Park. Dennis hadn't even suggested lunch, and it looked like this would be a long, lonely afternoon.

The phone rang as I finished the fifth slice. "She'll see you," Modesty growled. "But only because I told her you were working for Dick."

"You're terrif...er...I mean, thanks."

"Yeah. No question, Glory's after something, and I'd guess she thinks you can help her get it."

"Whatever it takes. Where?"

"Where all the hookers hang...the bar at the Pierre."

"I never heard that."

"Well, you just check it out when you meet Glory there tomorrow at six. She's taping a *Dateline* segment, so she can't make it this evening." Modesty hung up. Cool. Even though I had no tangible game plan, just loads of questions—like why had Harvest House, a highly respected publisher, wanted to be associated with Glory's book?—I was dying to meet her.

By four o'clock, I'd gone through three of the files that Morrison had given me—only twenty-three more to go. And some ABCs might be lurking, misplaced in the XYZs. But Peter had these notes in far better order than his *Manhattan* files. I opened the "D" folder, and Barry DeWitt's dossier jumped out at me. Dick Peter hadn't even tried to turn the theater critic into a fictional character, except for a notation in the margin: Call him Ben Arnold. Barry's behavior and lifestyle—according to Dick— made Don Juan look like a slacker. In addition to claiming that he'd slept with both Glory and Mila, this information indicated that Barry went both ways. One of his male lovers had been the late rock star, Mercury Rising. Peter's vile verbs and acid adjectives both shocked and amused me. Ghostwriting in his voice wouldn't be easy. But his murder mystery had real potential, and since the characters all appeared to be based on people Dick knew, might his notes somehow lead to his killer? Jeez. Could DeWitt be the missing link in the Peter-Flagg ménage à trois? How about Stern or Morrison? Picturing prim Robert Stern rolling around as part of a threesome, naked except for his trademark bowtie, with Glory in a star-spangled G-string and Dick wearing only his ratty rug, I laughed aloud. Polyamorous sex suddenly seemed more hilarious than hot. Imagining Keith Morrison, the old windbag, cavorting in bed with Flagg and Peter, proved even more difficult. He'd need a radio, retro-programmed to *Our Gal Sunday,* to make the scene. However, powerful men in their fifties and sixties have been known to choose some mighty strange playmates. Anything's possible, I suppose. Still giggling, I returned to the "D" file.

"Girlie, can you handle a flash?" Startled, I glanced at the door. I hadn't heard it open. A long, lean man, bald and at least seventy, stood there looking around the room. "You all alone? Laughing like a hyena in heat? You must be a regular Woody Allen, entertaining yourself like that."

"Er—I was reading something funny." Embarrassed and annoyed at being addressed as "Girlie," I gestured vaguely toward the files.

"So, can you use a flash camera?"

I hesitated. He hopped from one foot to the other in a movement resembling an Irish jig, and peered over his glasses at me. "Well, I once photographed a friend's wedding. The pictures were pretty good...Why? Just who are you, anyway?"

He bowed. Deep. Sweeping. Courtly. Like Ivanhoe or Rhett Butler. Yet I felt the gesture to be somehow mocking, not of me, but rather himself. "Forgive my bad manners. Please permit me to introduce myself, Jake O'Hara. I'm Christian Holmes, *Manhattan*'s religion editor. Though it's Christian in name only; I've been a practicing atheist for over fifty years."

"How do you know who I am?"

"Miss O'Hara, don't be modest. You're the woman who discovered Dick."

We both laughed. And, for a moment, his lined, basset-hound face lost its haunted expression. "I'm really desperate, Girlie. The other reporters and feature writers have snatched every staff photographer; they're all running around New York, trying to grab a quote and a picture of the sundry suspects in Dick's murder in time for the whodunit pieces that'll run in our next issue. Apparently, you're the only one here. Even Stern's left his ivory tower and is personally interviewing the widow, Mila Macovich, for his editorial. Barbara Ferris steered me to your door."

I hadn't realized everyone was out on assignment. "What angle are you covering, Mr. Holmes?"

"Nothing to do with Dick. And the name's Christian. I'm doing a profile on Isaac Walton, the Pledged-For-Lifer's spiritual leader. I need a cameraman...um, cameraperson. Will you please shoot the good reverend for me?"

"Now how could I turn down an invitation like that?"

"Well, come on, Girlie, shake a leg. We don't want to miss

the opening prayer-a-thon. We'll grab a camera on our way out."

"Listen, I'll call you Christian and you'll call me Jake or the deal's off. Okay?"

"You got it, Girlie."

Juggling the camera, my briefcase, and cellphone while hustling to keep up with Christian, I was attempting to place a call to my mother when I literally ran smack into Ben in *Manhattan*'s lobby. The yellow tape had remained wrapped around Dick Peter's office door, with a flurry of police activity in evidence as Christian and I passed by; however, there had been no sign of Ben. "Hey, Ben, I'm trying to reach Mom to see if she heard from you."

Christian, a few feet in front of me, stopped and glared at me for causing this delay in his mission. "Girlie, we'll miss the opening sermon."

"Christian Holmes, meet Ben Rubin; he's the homicide detective in charge of the Peter investigation." The religion editor grunted, but he did shake hands with Ben.

"Nice to meet you, Mr. Holmes. I never miss your column." Could that be true? I'd never read a one. Ben smiled. "I especially enjoyed that recent piece on the Big Bang and the Baptists. I'll be dropping by tomorrow to ask you a few questions...about the article...and about Dick Peter's death."

"Why would you want to talk to me? I wasn't even in the office yesterday. I spent the day at the New York Public Library, researching the history of the Pledged-For-Lifers and Reverend Walton." Christian sounded snide. But he certainly hadn't been at the library before eight a.m.

"Just covering the bases. As a writer, I know you under-stand." God, Ben had to be the most charming cop in New York. As well as the smartest. He'd finished in the top ten percent at Columbia Law School, even made Law Review, but preferred chasing down killers to prosecuting or—God forbid—defending them.

"Christian, I need to ask Ben something. Walk on ahead, I'll..."

"Your legs are too short, Girlie. You'd never catch up to me. I'll wait outside, but make it snappy." Christian marched out the door, and I pulled Ben away from Hans Foote's earshot.

"Well, are we on for tonight?"

"We are. But it won't be a romantic evening, Jake."

I winked at him. "Don't be so sure about that, Detective."

"My father, Gypsy Rose, you, and I are dining with your mother. Dad made a brisket; Gypsy Rose is doing dessert."

"That only leaves the salad for Mom to screw up. But why, Ben? I'd hoped we'd have some..."

"Girlie." Christian barged back in. "Come on!"

"Dinner at eight," Ben said, and motioned for Hans to pass him through the gate.

I felt guilty not telling Ben about the possible motherlode of clues that I'd tapped in Dick's notes for his book. Then I decided—oh, what the hell—I'd deal with that tonight.

We took the Lexington Avenue subway downtown. The city was a zoo; you wouldn't get a cab if you bartered your firstborn. Christian and I clung to a pole shared by another half dozen hands amidst throngs of standing-room-only passengers. It made for instant intimacy.

"Have you been at *Manhattan* long?"

"Since the beginning, Girlie. Before you were a gleam in your father's eye."

I wondered if Christian's writing style was as chock full of clichés as his speech. "So I guess you must know where all the skeletons are hidden." Clichés must be contagious.

"What's on your mind?"

There you go, Jake, a direct question. Should I tell him what I was after? Well, I did want to know, didn't I? "Okay, Robert Stern, for starters." I'd been wondering if what Dennis told me was common knowledge. "In Allison Carr's office on the day before Dick's murder, Stern practically threatened to kill him. In front of three witnesses. A longstanding feud?"

"No mystery there, Girlie. Everyone at *Manhattan* knows how much Stern hated him. Dick Peter screwed Robert Stern's wife. Then told anyone who'd listen. He liked bragging about bedding anyone above his social position, which in Dick's case could have included a streetwalker. Then he dumped her. Catherine Stern later killed herself and Stern, the cuckold, still had to face that ugly, strutting little rooster every day of his life. Peter had both an ironclad contract and the bitchiest book column in the country. The board loved Dick. They all kissed his sorry ass. One or two of them, literally."

A young women standing next to Christian and clinging to our pole burst into laughter. An older, conservatively dressed woman, seated beneath us, glanced up in disgust. A fully covered—complete with face veil—woman gave up her seat to distance herself from us. Fortunately, we would be getting off at Grand Central—the next stop—to take the shuttle to Times Square and then board the train down to Penn Station.

Nine

Madison Square Garden was as fully packed as any Rangers playoff game or Ringling Brothers Circus opening day. Every race and national origin seemed to be well represented. What was missing were women. I may have been the only female in a field of fervent, flag-waving husbands. The Omaha Symphony Orchestra played "America the Beautiful" as the Pledged-For-Lifers sang along. On the stage, its backdrop swathed in red, white, and blue—Glory Flagg would have been right at home here—the Reverend Isaac Walton's head was bowed, but his baritone boomed out: "From sea to shining sea." Amidst deafening applause and loud cheering, he stepped up to the white marble podium. Walton's preaching clothes—crisp, white linen jeans and matching collarless shirt—blended right in. As he held up a thick gold cross, the crowd went crazy. "Jesus! Jesus! Jesus!" Their chants rocked the rafters.

Stunned and a little scared, I turned to Christian. "Holy crap."

"My sentiments exactly." He opened his notebook. "Aim that camera, Girlie, you don't want to miss him waving that cross."

The vast audience grew quiet. The sea of male faces and I all focused on Reverend Isaac Walton. Small and wiry, he was not a good-looking man and, somehow, he seemed vaguely familiar; but then he'd been plastered all over the papers and had appeared on more television shows than even Glory had graced over the last few days. His deep voice, filling the arena, was confident, charismatic, and cajoling. And his message resonated like country music; "Please, Mister, Please, Don't Play B 17" came to mind. I realized that somewhere offstage a guitar player softly strummed that song. This conference was well choreographed. The reverend spoke of broken hearts, broken homes, and children broken in spirit, split asunder by divorce. The men's commitment would mend, repair, and prevent such breakage. Lots of "Amens" from his assembled brother Pledged-For-Lifers accompanied him. He closed with, "You are Christ's shepherds. You will lead your family—your own small flock—to heaven."

If men were shepherds, were women sheep? Isaac Walton had better get another line. "Come on." Christian grabbed my elbow, ruining my last shot. "We want to beat *Newsday* and *Time* backstage. Walton's press agent's an old drinking buddy of mine. He's arranged a fifteen-minute exclusive. You can reload when we get there."

Christian Holmes knew the myriad nooks and crannies of backstage Madison Square Garden better than I knew Carnegie Hill. Again, I found myself struggling to keep pace with the septuagenarian; maybe I would rethink Mom's exercise program suggestion. My power walks weren't doing it. We arrived at a dressing room sporting a huge star before either Walton or any of our media competition. I reloaded while Christian rapped on the door.

"That was quick," a female voice shouted from behind the

closed door. "You must have beaten your own record for rabblerousing."

Christian looked as puzzled as I felt. When the door finally opened, a pretty, plump, blatantly middle-aged woman stood in front of us. She wore a frilly pink and white check apron and held a rolling pin in her left hand. Almost by reflex, I snapped a close-up. As the flash went off, she lashed out at the camera with the rolling pin and screamed, "Damnation! Who are you?"

I didn't need to turn around to know that Isaac Walton had arrived. His baritone soothed, "Young lady, don't you worry, I've got it." And sure enough, just inches from a crash landing, the reverend's firm hand caught my camera. Then he addressed the lady in waiting. "Now, Mother, don't you fret. These good folks are from *Manhattan* magazine. Did I forget to tell you that Jack set up an interview?" Andy reassuring Aunt Bea. Only this lady had to be Isaac's age, not a generation older...and, despite the arcane appellation, no doubt his wife. Could Reverend Walton be a certified chauvinist?

A few minutes later, the four of us sat in a dressing room as well furnished as a Plaza suite. A clothes rack holding starched white linen shirts and crisply creased jeans stood in the center. Our chairs circled a large oak table.

Sally Lou Walton had dropped her rolling pin on the chintz-covered couch and apologized profusely in an accent I could barely decipher. Country fer sure. But where were them thar hills located?

"Any friends of Jack Willis are more than welcome to visit in our home away from home. Now can I serve you all a bottle of pop or cup of tea?"

"No thank you, Mrs. Walton." Christian favored her with a big smile. "That's mighty kind of you, but we promised Jack we'd only take up fifteen minutes of your time." What an absolute hoot...Christian suddenly sounded more country than Loretta Lynn.

"Yes. Jack promised me that you and *Manhattan* magazine would give the Pledged-For-Lifers a fair shake. He swore you weren't some big-shot New York writer who'd make our movement look like a pile of manure. I always have believed that *Manhattan* is a road map to Hell, but I didn't want to pass up this chance to reach the scarred souls of its sorry readership. So I hope you plan to honor Jack's word, Mr. Holmes." The Reverend Walton leaned forward and aimed his steely gray eyes straight into Christian's tired baby blues.

"I treat all spiritual causes and their leaders with the respect they deserve," Christian, the atheist, responded, sincerity oozing from him like the manure Isaac wanted to avoid. I'd bet my latest twenty percent that Walton's press agent—Jack What's His Name—had neglected to inform the reverend that his old pal, *Manhattan*'s religion editor, didn't believe in God.

However, Walton seemed delighted with Holmes, accepting his answer as gospel. "Then let's get started; you have twelve minutes 'til the mayor arrives."

As Walton talked and Christian took copious notes, I snapped candid shots of him, Sally Lou, and the room, figuring I could photograph the faithful on our way out. "Watch those profiles, Miss O'Hara. I prefer full face. No need to draw attention to my nose." Isaac Walton issued his request lightly, but I treated it like the order I suspected it was. He returned to what was obviously his favorite topic. "Family values have been flushed down the toilet; I blame television. And sex..."

"Sex?" Christian asked, echoing my thought process. "Without sex, we'd have no families to value, would we?"

Ignoring Christian's question, Walton plunged forward. "Feminism, situation comedies, gays, divorce, and the internet are instruments of the devil. Too many Americans have succumbed to Satan's temptations. The Pledged-For-Lifers movement is God's antidote to these pervasive evils. I am but the Lord's messenger. His scribe, if you would." While Christian was scribing as fast as he could, I zoomed in for a close-up of the rapture on Sally Lou's pudgy face.

"How do you respond to critics who call your group an odd mixture of old-time religion, New Age touchy-feely spirituality, and EST? Or those who claim you hook the husbands by preaching manly virtues reinforcing their roles as heads of their families? Or that you reel in the absent wives by sending home God-fearing, committed partners who also change diapers?" Christian asked. "After all, CNN did a special on a local chapter in Butte where the men lay supine on the floor, begging God's forgiveness for trespassing against their wives."

"We were infiltrated by media spies. And, of course, shown in the worst possible light. What's wrong with religion, spirituality, and confession? And absolution is good for the soul. Didn't Christ build His church on those very principles? Like the good Lord, I'm used to attacks on my faith. The media is run by godless commies." Isaac Walton turned florid with fury. Not a pretty picture. He recovered quickly. "The men who are Pledged-For-Lifers will save the world, and our Christian belief in the sanctity of marriage will open the gates of heaven. You may quote me, Mr. Holmes."

"Alleluia!" Sally Lou cried. I busied myself with the camera.

On our way out the door, Isaac Walton pulled a Columbo. "There's just one more thing..."

"Yes?" Christian asked.

"A rather ugly secret. I never discuss my past, but under the circumstances, and with you working for *Manhattan*...Well, the truth will come out now anyway, so I might as well give you the exclusive. I've already had a call from the police." For the first time, Walton held my total attention. What was going down here?

Christian closed his notebook. And waited. A good ploy, I thought. People speak more freely when a reporter isn't jotting down their every word.

"The thing is...er, well, that dreadful, evil man who wrote for your magazine...the one who was murdered..." Isaac Walton floundered. Sally Lou nodded encouragingly. I raised my camera. Christian stood pat. The reverend gulped, then spit it out. "I'm Dick Peter's only living relative. He's my first cousin."

"Holy crap," I said, repeating my first impression of the preacher's persona, speaking for first time since entering the dressing room and staring at the face I found so familiar. "Sorry about that, Reverend Walton."

But Isaac, now on a roll, plowed on. "We were long estranged. For over thirty years...ever since he absconded with our mutual grandmother's insurance money, and went off to study literature at Yale, leaving me to dig my way out of a West Virginia coal mine."

Jesus. The Dick Peter/*Our Gal Sunday* connection! I should have paid more attention to Morrison's musings. Keith Morrison had attended Yale, but many years before Dick Peter was a student there. He'd also been a current friend of Dick's, despite being much older. Did Morrison know cousin Isaac? And could the cousins have held a reunion before Dick's death? But how...?

A discreet tap on the door signaled the mayor's arrival. Our interview was over.

Ten

"I knew there was something fishy about that Isaac Walton," my mother said, scooping a potato onto my plate. "Ben, please pass the gravy to Jake. Take another slice of the pot roast. And Aaron's carrots have such character."

Gypsy Rose Liebowitz waltzed around the round table, pouring all takers another glass of wine.

"His style's an interesting mix of Elmer Gantry's carnival barker zeal, Deepak Chopra's spiritual spice, and St. Francis of Assisi's love of children and small creatures. The problem—as I see it—is that Walton's sermons are for the birds and he's full of...their droppings. White or red, Aaron?"

"Did you call Walton, Ben?" I asked. "He said he'd spoken to the police."

"Yes. Early this afternoon. I found his name in Peter's address book; that intrigued me—the critic and the clergyman—but I had no idea they were non-kissing kin until I talked to him. You and Christian Holmes seem to have gotten far more information out of him than I did." Ben checked his watch. "Joe Cassidy's at the Garden now taking the reverend's statement."

"Well, it was Christian who asked the questions; I just took the pictures. We do know that Isaac arrived in New York before the murder; he was all over the local news, but could he also have made an appearance at Dick's office?"

"How would a visitor penetrate that fortress after hours?" Aaron asked.

"Good question, Aaron. Ever since I'd received my pass card, I've been wondering about that myself."

Ben swallowed his forkful of Mom's salad—iceberg lettuce topped with her homemade Russian dressing, an equal mix of Hellman's mayonnaise and Hunt's ketchup—before answering. "Well, the medical examiner places Peter's time of death somewhere between ten p.m. and two a.m. The guard, Hans Foote, went home at six. After that the security's all electronic."

"You're putting us on. His name isn't really Hans Foote, is it?" Gypsy Rose shook her head full of red curls.

"It's his name all right, and he behaves like a reincarnated storm trooper," I said.

"Yes. He would," Gypsy Rose said. "So many of them choose to go back into some sort of police work. They love wearing uniforms through all their lifetimes."

Ben reached for the bottle of Mouton Cadet.

"You were saying, Ben?"

I didn't want the pragmatic policeman and Carnegie Hill's favorite channeler to get into a philosophical discussion that would throw this conversation onto another plane.

"Well, I think either Peter went down to the lobby and handed the killer his electronic pass, or possibly, the killer was someone on the magazine's staff who'd stayed late for a rendezvous."

"A rendezvous with death...that's a great title, Jake," my mother said.

"I'll see if I can write a book around it, Mom. There's a third possibility, isn't there? The killer could be a staff member who went home at his—or her—regular time, but returned later and used his card to get back in."

"No. The tracking system would have picked that up."

"So, it was an insider," my mother said.

"Or an outsider Dick had trusted enough to escort up to his office after hours. Great salad, Maura," Ben said.

"When did Hans get to work yesterday morning?" I asked.

"He said he'd arrived at eight, just in time to process you through. You were the first one to arrive at work that morning and you didn't have your employee card yet."

"Hans works long hours. What, eight to six?" Aaron sounded like the D.A. he once was.

"Right, Dad. And he loves being the lobby police. Said he wouldn't trust anyone to cover part of his watch."

"Hans is totally creepy, makes me nervous. And Barbara Ferris told me that he had good reason to hate Dick Peter."

Gypsy Rose laughed. "Only one of a million motives for killing Dick...but I can assure you that SS attitude will always be with Hans Foote."

"I'll check it out," Ben said.

"Okay, who would Dick willingly have handed his card to? His long-lost cousin?" I asked. "Revenge would be a casebook motive."

"But, darling, do you really think Reverend Isaac Walton is capable of murder?" my mother asked.

"Mom, I believe anyone can be capable of murder."

"Oh, Jake, I only pray you're wrong; otherwise, how very sad for all of us." Mom took another sip of white wine.

"There's another thing..." Ben buttered one of Gypsy Rose's home-baked rolls with a vengeance. "You'll read all about it in the morning paper or see it on tonight's late news, so I can tell you now."

"What?" Gypsy Rose and I demanded.

"The coroner says there was semen in Peter's boxer shorts."

"Did he make it with his murderer or did he have more than one caller that night?" I asked.

"I do wish you could find a more tasteful way to describe intercourse, Jake," my mother said.

"Maybe I should try to summon Peter's spirit guide from the world beyond before All Soul's Day, Jake. Who better to help us?" Gypsy Rose offered.

While I was giving serious consideration to both Mom and Gypsy Rose's suggestions, Peter's book-notes files flashed through my head. There was something...

"Dick Peter might have been entertaining Mila Macovich—she is his wife, after all. Or maybe Glory Flagg," my mother said as she started to clear the dishes.

"Let me do that, Mom. You made the salad."

"And set a beautiful table. Thank you, Maura. I'll help with the dishes." Aaron stacked as he spoke.

"Glory Flagg hated Dick. I don't think she'd...er, have sexual relations with him in his office," I said.

"Well, it wouldn't be the first time," Gypsy Rose said. "They used to have matinees there all through their marriage. Sometimes with a rumored mystery guest."

"Who? And where did you hear this?" I sat back down. Let Aaron help with the cleanup. He wanted to score brownie points with Mom. This could be his golden opportunity.

"From Robert Stern. I spoke to him this morning," Gypsy Rose said. "We're both on the Met's board, you know. Nice man..." She sounded defensive. "Anyway, he said that most of the staff thought the other member of their sexual trio had to be

Barry DeWitt. This was in the sexy seventies. *Manhattan*'s good old days before AIDS, armed guards, and electronic cards. Glory liked to torment Peter, flirted with DeWitt at every opportunity, but Robert says it could have been anyone. Male or female."

"I guess Glory and Dick ran an equal opportunity ménage à trois," I said.

Over the rim of his goblet, Ben stared at Gypsy Rose. "I'd be interested in your opinion of Robert Stern. You've known him for a long time, haven't you?"

"Well, yes, but..." Gypsy Rose fiddled with the flower arrangement. It occurred to me that she must have known about the affair Dick Peter had with Stern's wife; however, she'd never mentioned it, or Catherine's subsequent suicide. I had no doubt the same thought had just occurred to Ben.

"Do you think he could be our killer?" Ben asked.

"Oh God, Ben, I don't want to think so. You know about Robert's wife, don't you? And how he hated Dick...blamed him..."

"Yes, I do."

Gypsy Rose bent her head and, suddenly, looked her age. She sighed. "And the Delft. Do you know about the Delft?"

"What about it?" I asked.

Ben answered me. "Robert Stern has one of the largest collections of Delft in the country. And now he claims he's misplaced one of his daggers."

Eleven

The pianist's magic fingers spread across the keyboard as I hummed along. Quietly. *Casablanca* was Mom's and my favorite flick—even though a few years ago it was rated number two in the One Hundred Best Ever Movies list. Who quotes from *Citizen Kane* on a daily basis, for God's sake? In the immortal dialogue spoken by Claude Rains—"I'm shocked! Shocked!"—at those results. There's no one in the city who can play "As Time Goes By" like Bobby Short, but this was close.

When Ben had suggested that we skip dessert and catch the last set at the Carlyle, I jumped out of my seat so fast, I almost knocked Gypsy Rose, still pushing the wine round the table, on her fanny. A little romantic nightcap might help me get murder off my mind.

The song reached the line "...the fundamental things apply" and I nibbled on Ben's ear. As intended, that move caught his attention, but it also reminded me of my first, brash childhood encounter with Dennis in front of his father's fruit stand. I turned my attention back to humming along with the smooth rendition.

By the opening bars of "Someone to Watch Over Me," Ben and I were on our second round and again mired in murder.

"Do you really believe Robert Stern could be the killer, Ben? He seems like such a decent sort, giving me this job and all...and Gypsy Rose thinks he's a saint."

"You said yourself that he threatened to kill Peter the afternoon before he was murdered. And Stern doesn't deny that he had a motive, even admits the dagger used as the murder weapon might be his—there were no prints—but there's no way he can be sure. Claims he only discovered it was missing after the fact...and that there must be thousands of those Delft daggers in Manhattan."

"Thousands. Really? Where does Stern say he was the night of the murder?"

"Home alone. The butler's night off. Says he came straight to his townhouse from *Manhattan* around nine, ate in the kitchen, worked in his den 'til midnight, then went to bed. And that he neither made nor received any calls."

"But there's no way of knowing if any of the magazine's staff stayed later than ten, is there? You don't need a pass card to get out of *Manhattan,* only to get in."

Ben sipped his Remy Martin. Brandy snifters are so cool, and brandy enthusiasts always make such a production out of imbibing their after-dinner drinks. If only I could stomach the stuff, I'm convinced I too would enjoy cuddling the big, fat glass in my hands to keep it warm, savoring the smell, and twirling the amber liquid round and round for most of the evening.

Instead, I'd finished my second pedestrian wine spritzer and was ready for bed.

"Allison Carr seems to have been the last one to leave that night," Ben said. "Says she went home at nine thirty, and never noticed if Peter was still in his office...with or without company."

"Oh damn. Allison asked Mom, Gypsy Rose, and me to have lunch tomorrow, but the invitation smacked of a bribe. I have to call her and..." I checked my watch.

Almost eleven fifteen. "Guess I'll have to wait 'til morning to cancel."

"What did she want in exchange?"

I hesitated, knowing how Ben felt about Gypsy Rose's dallying with the dead, then figured what the hell. "I don't know how she got wind of it, but Allison wants to crash a channeling. Mom told me that Mila Macovich asked Gypsy Rose to contact Dick Peter. Apparently Mila has some unfinished business with her dead husband."

"So that's the All Soul's Day séance Gypsy Rose referred to at dinner. I wondered what the hell she was talking about but was afraid to ask. Is Mila a friend of Gypsy Rose's too?"

"Well, actually, it seems Mila's therapist recommended her." I abridged the information that the therapist and Gypsy Rose had been romantic rivals for Edgar Cayce's affections in their most recent mutual past lives.

Ben's response surprised me. "I'd like to crash that séance too...and, Jake, by all means, arrange for Allison Carr to attend."

During the cab ride home, my mind wrestled with not one, but two, moral dilemmas, thus missing out on the full measure of enjoyment I should have been deriving from Ben's seriously skilled kissing.

Would Ben's requesting Allison's presence at the channeling make her bribe-induced invitation to a fancy lunch ethically acceptable? It sure as hell would make Mom and Gypsy Rose happy. Why look a gossip monger's gift in the mouth? Better to fill ours with pate de foie gras.

And why hadn't I told Ben what I'd discovered in Peter's "D" file? Barry DeWitt might very well be the third member of

Glory and Dick's ménage à trois. If so, he could be our number one suspect. Something still ragged at me about those notes. Yikes. Carr, of course. I'd gone through the "C" files. There'd been no mention of the lady. Why?

Certainly, Dick Peter would have planned on using a character based on Allison. Could she somehow have stolen her data from the "C" file? When? How long did Keith Morrison have Dick's notes in his possession?

Then again, maybe Allison might still show up under her character's fictional name, in a file further down the alphabet. I had to turn Peter's notes over to Ben, but selfishly, I wanted to go through them first. Lord, would I be guilty of obstructing justice?

A sudden wave of pleasure as Ben's tongue tickled my teeth pulled me out of the files and into the now. We behaved like two horny teenagers for the rest of the ride up Madison Avenue.

My mother had waited up. She wore her cotton jammies, a pound of grease and a pained expression. "Jake, I need your advice."

An absolute first. "What's wrong, Mom?"

I'd swear that she blushed, though it was a tough call, viewed through all that slime covering her neck, cheeks, and forehead. "Well, I...er, that is, I..." She sat, then hopped back up and rearranged the pillows on our sofa.

"Mom, please, tell me. It's twelve thirty in the morning."

"I just wonder what your father would say about it."

"He'd say let your daughter get some sleep. Just what are we talking about here?"

"Aaron's invited me for a drive this Saturday. Upstate to see how the leaves have changed color."

"Well, that's great. Remember how Dad used to take us every fall when I was a kid? Go, you'll love it."

"Oh, Jake." She sounded close to tears. "You don't understand. He suggested that we stay overnight in Saratoga. In a bed and breakfast."

There you go. My mother was going to get laid before I did.

"I can tell by your face that you're shocked by the thought of my..."

Shocked? More like jealous. "No, Mom. I think it's a great idea. Like we say in Ghostwriters Anonymous...don't project, take it one day at a time. How long has it been since you...well...had some fun?" Now, there was no doubt. My mother blushed.

"So, you think it's okay?"

I giggled. "It's great. You want to borrow a condom?" She threw a pillow at me.

By one o'clock, I was in bed and ready for sleep, having made some ethical decisions regarding my sundry moral dilemmas. Mom had jumped at the chance to dine with Allison at a fancy French restaurant. She and Gypsy Rose would be spending Friday afternoon doing second interviews with those witches and warlocks who'd made the first cut for the Halloween coven—or whatever the devil they were hosting at the bookstore—next week. However, they had no plans for lunch, and Mom had no compunction, even with the quid pro quo caveat, accepting at once for both of them. "You know that Gypsy Rose would love to have another believer, especially one willing to spring for such a nice lunch, at her séance. And maybe Allison Carr will plug our bookstore in her next 'Bites From the Big Apple' column." I decided to wait a while before mentioning to Mom that Ben, definitely not a believer, would be there too.

Then I got to thinking...a ghostwriter needs to know her

employer's characters, especially if he's dead. Not to mention my compulsive curiosity disorder. And after all, Peter's book was fiction, and the entire contents of his file could be figments of his imagination. Maybe that was why there'd been no mention of Allison in the "C" file. My second decision was to get up early and to copy Dick's files as soon as I arrived at work. When that task was completed, I'd call Ben and offer them into evidence, as if it had just dawned on me to do so. Then I'd go see Allison Carr and tell her we were on for lunch. Ethics with ease. Or, maybe, easy ethics? I rolled over.

Twelve

Feeling perkier than I ought to after only five and a half hours' sleep, I walked briskly by Mr. Kim's fruit stand well before sunrise. The city that never sleeps seemed to be snoring...at least on Madison Avenue. Two joggers, three or four cars, a few alley cats. Spooky. Suddenly, the door to Mr. Kim's store popped open, startling me. "Hi, Jake, what are you doing out so early?" Dennis. What was he doing here at dawn? "I was on my way home and decided to give Dad a lift to work." He certainly didn't look like a man who'd been up all night. His Brooks Brothers suit appeared freshly pressed and his white shirt couldn't have been crispier or cleaner. Where had he been? Why did I care?

The lights went on inside the store and Mr. Kim stuck his head out. "Hi, Jake. Wait a second." He joined Dennis and me on the sidewalk in less than that. 'Take this banana with you. And don't walk downtown in the dark. Dennis will drive you to work. Right, Dennis?"

Mr. Kim, a late-blooming poet who composed in the style of Rupert Brooke, was a charter member of my mother's regular last-Friday-of-the-month cocktail party for the lesser literary lights of Carnegie Hill and a dear friend to Mom and me. I didn't want to seem ungrateful, but the last thing I needed this morning was a ride in Dennis Kim's Rolls Royce.

"Well, I could use the exercise..."

Mr. Kim waved the banana at me. "Nonsense. Dennis, get the car."

Knowing better than to argue with his father, Dennis headed across 92nd Street in the direction of the Wales Hotel, where his car was illegally parked in front of the lobby door. I followed him.

As always, the rich aroma of the cream leather seats and their comfortable fit which almost embraced me soothed my body but troubled my soul. Dennis Kim's extravagant consumerism could turn an overextended credit-card capitalist like me into a communist.

"Sitting up all night with a sick client, Dennis?" I shoved the banana in my briefcase.

"You're almost on the money. You may have noticed that Keith Morrison is a little strange."

"I'd say that a guy who makes this century's judgment calls based on the moral values of a 1940s soap opera heroine would qualify as being more than a little strange. How does Morrison manage to run a huge operation like Pax?"

"Actually, very well. His obsession with Sunday hasn't interfered with his sound publishing decisions. Pax has more bestselling authors than any other house in Manhattan. I will admit their list is a bit top heavy, tilting toward '40s trivia."

"I'll bet."

"Part of his success comes from his hands-on approach. You know, Keith plans on personally editing Dick Peter's...er, your manuscript."

"Yuck."

"You'll enjoy working with him, Jake. All his authors think he's cool. And you might even learn something."

"So what was Morrison's problem last night?" Had Dennis really held the publisher's hand 'til six thirty in the morning? Now if his client had been Glory Flagg or Mila Macovich, I'd have no trouble believing he'd spent the night counseling her...or whatever. And, for all I knew, either one—or both—of those women could be his client.

"Suffering from some soul-searching," Dennis said. "Says he's reached the age where he's asking himself: Is this all there is?"

"Running a multimillion-dollar publishing empire would be enough for most people. What does Morrison want?"

Dennis swung onto 69th Street. We must have set a new record for a morning drive down Fifth Avenue. Early birds catch every light. Double parked, he turned his golden eyes toward me and smiled. "What Keith wants is purpose and passion in his personal life. Client confidentiality prevents me from giving more details. But isn't that what we all want?" Dennis placed his hand on my cheek. "Don't you harbor that desire, Jake?" The charge that surged from face to feet left me faint but furious. "Well?" he asked.

"I have plenty of purpose and passion in my life," I said, struggling to unbuckle my seatbelt. Dennis Kim's loud laughter followed me as I exited the car and entered *Manhattan*.

I planned on putting all that purpose and passion into copying Dick's files as quickly—and privately—as possible. It turned out I wasn't the only early arrival. Grumpy Hans Foote stood at his post in the lobby. Maybe since the murder he'd decided to work round the clock. Then I ran into *Manhattan*'s editor-in-chief in the photocopy room, where he was almost straddling the machine. "Hi, Mr. Stern. Can I finish those for you? I've a pile of my own stuff to copy," I said, as if he could miss my bulging briefcase hanging heavy from my shoulder and my arms filled with files.

"That's okay, Jake. I'm finished." Like a startled buck, he lurched, then grabbed his copy and original, clutched them to his heart and bolted from the room. Now wouldn't I like to know what he was holding so close to his vest?

I'd reached the "X" file when Jennifer Moran popped in. "Oh, Jake, here you are. I thought we were the first to arrive...but then I heard a noise." Her husband, Michael, dressed in his usual biker's black, stood behind her, scowling.

"If you're sure you're feeling okay, Jennifer, I'll head on downtown. I don't want to miss the opening." Michael managed to sound solicitous.

"I'm fine, Michael." Jennifer, wearing a brown suit the exact color of her chestnut curls, kissed her husband on his unshaven cheek. I remembered Dennis Kim's hand caressing mine. "You've got to stop pampering me. Isn't that right, Jake?"

How did I get to be the arbitrator of the Moran family's health concerns? If Jennifer had recovered, I certainly could use her help. I knew that she would be a damn good editorial assistant if she wasn't throwing up or passing out. I answered with a question, one of my mother's favorite ploys. "Are you ready to come back to work?"

"Able-bodied and reporting for duty. Let me finish copying that stuff for you."

Figuring Jen would find out most of what was in the files as the manuscript progressed—maybe she already knew from working with Peter—and there were only three files left to copy, I picked up a pile of folders and said, "Bring the rest when you finish."

Michael and I started down the elegant little hall papered in one of Mom's favorite William Morris prints. "Keep an eye on her, Jake."

"Listen, Michael, did Jennifer discuss anything...well, odd about Dick's murder with you? She reacted so..."

"No. But this was her first up-close-and-personal corpse. She wouldn't even go to my Uncle Henry's wake. Jen's always had a morbid fear of violence. So any murder would have set her off. I think seeing Dick's body has affected her soul as well as her stomach. Now she'll never go to another slice-and-dice flick with me, and my cousin Gaston just been cast in a totally gruesome one." He adjusted his helmet. "Hey, I've got to make a pit stop in the men's room. Take care of my little girl."

How could Jennifer have married this moron?

DeWitt came out of the john, jamming something in his pocket, as Michael opened the door.

He spotted me and smiled. I had to admit he was stunning. "Welcome to *Manhattan*, Miss O'Hara." Barry oozed cordiality. Was this the same crude man I'd watched in action on Tuesday afternoon? "I'm sure you'll find it challenging. I must dash. On deadline, you know. But do stop by my office later." His voice and body language were poised, but his marine blue eyes, darting left to right, were filled with terror or anger. Maybe both. "I'll be glad to advise you on Dick Peter's approach to book reviewing; then you can do the exact opposite." He laughed, then was gone before I could reply. There was a lot of that going on around *Manhattan*. I watched him walk toward the elevator and continued on to my office in the front of the building, wondering why all these employees were on dawn patrol.

I'd barely opened the "F" folder when Barbara Ferris, her lipstick matching her red-apple logo and her uniform parade-ready, called from the doorway, "Jennifer asked me to drop off these files. Where do you want me to put them?"

Oh, wonderful. How could I have been so stupid, trusting Jennifer with Dick's files? Maybe she made copies for the entire staff. "Thanks, Barbara." I tried to keep my tone pleasant as I cleared a space on the top of my desk. "Where's Jennifer?"

"Getting you some tea and scones. Christian stopped at that wonderful bakery on Lexington and they're still warm. He's brought in some homemade strawberry jam too." Homemade by whom? Christian didn't strike me as the domestic type. Was there a Mrs. Holmes?

Barbara placed the files in front of me. "Every time I walk past Mr. Peter's office and see that yellow tape, I get chills all over." She crossed her arms and hugged her shoulders. "Do you think the murderer could be one of us? A Manhattanite?"

"What do you think?"

"Well, everyone hated him, you know. But I can't picture any of my coworkers sneaking around stabbing each other. It's all too horrible. I can't sleep. That's why I came to work so early."

Yeah. And the rest of the staff seemed to have shared her insomnia. *Manhattan* was as crowded as Grand Central Station this morning, and at this ungodly hour. I checked my watch—not yet eight a.m. "That's too bad, Barbara, but I'm sure..."

"You don't know the half of it. I've been having nightmares ever since Mr. Peter died. Always the same one. I'm trapped in that messy office of his, and all the books turn into daggers. They take on a life of their own, then all of them stab me at once. I wake up sweating." Barbara rubbed her wrist across her lips, staring at the bright red streak the gesture left on the back of her hand. "Goddamn it. Excuse my language, Jake." She grabbed a tissue from the box on my desk and rubbed at the stain.

Jennifer bounced in, carrying a tray filled with goodies. "Hi, Jake. I thought we'd work better on a full stomach." Her timing sucked. After a little dream interpretation discussion, I'd planned on asking Barbara about Santa Steve's grudge against Dick Peter.

"You must be feeling better, Jennifer," Barbara said, blowing her nose with another of my tissues. "Well, I'm out of here. Now it really is time to start work."

I admired the white ceramic pot tied with a red and white check ribbon as I spread the strawberry jam on my scone and lectured Jennifer on the importance of a ghostwriter's confidentiality. "No one, I repeat, no one must discover that I'm the author of Dick Peter's book. Only Dennis Kim, Keith Morrison, you, and I can share this secret. Never let another living soul see Dick's files. Do you understand?"

"Of course, I do. What was I thinking? It won't happen again, I promise. And I'm sure Barbara didn't look at the files...she'd have no idea what they contained. But more than four people know you're ghostwriting this manuscript, Jake. Your mother's one of them, but family's different, right?"

"Oh, God. Don't tell me you've told Michael."

"Only that you're completing Dick's project...not that you're writing the whole thing." Jennifer's color drained, and I was afraid I'd made her sick again. Why was I being so hard on her? In publishing, as in politics, leaks happen. And after all, she didn't have to follow the twelve steps of Ghostwriters Anonymous. The program's principles had saved my butt more than once. Thank God tomorrow was Saturday; I could dump all this trash at our regular weekly meeting. Too-Tall Tom and Jane D. always offered sound suggestions for restoring my serenity. This had been the week from hell, but my fellow recovering anonymity addicts would help me cope.

"Okay, Jennifer. We can't change the past, but we can put it behind us. Let's take it a day a time. And, thank you for the scone. It's wonderful." I could see that Jennifer was puzzled—but pleased—by my attitude adjustment.

I was finishing my second cup of tea when Jennifer, who'd gone over to the window to raise the blinds, shouted, "Look at this! I can't believe it. And poor Michael was so afraid he'd be late."

"What's going on down there?" I crossed the room to join Jennifer in her intense scrutiny of 69th Street. "Why, that's Christian Holmes, isn't it?" I watched as my older colleague hustled another man into a cab, then climbed in beside him. "Who's that guy he shoved into the taxi?"

"Isaac Walton, you know, the Pledged-For-Lifers' spiritual leader." Jennifer sounded starstruck. "Michael's gone to the Save Your Marriage & Save Your Soul session as we speak. So what in the name of heaven is the reverend doing here?"

Good question. But whatever Christian Holmes and Isaac Walton had been talking about at *Manhattan* this morning had proved intriguing enough to keep thousands of husbands waiting at Madison Square Garden.

Over a third cup of tea, Jennifer poured her heart out. For months, she'd suspected another woman—a strange scent on Michael's briefs, too many wrong numbers on calls that he'd answered after he dashed to grab the phone first, boys-only biker overnights, and no sex, claiming he'd pulled his back. "All the tawdry, typical telltale signs, Jake. Michael never was an original thinker. Then he joined a local cell of Pledged-For-Lifers. Never misses a meeting. He knows I've always been a God-fearing Christian. Now he's one too." She beamed. "He's become a much better husband. Helps with the housework, even asks me to balance the checkbook. Only thing is..."

I leaned forward. "Yes?" This fascinated me. A dark character, filled with eternal lust but promising a lifetime of fidelity, was in full development mode, to be tucked away in a corner of my mind for future use.

"Michael's so caught up in spirituality, you know, he can't be—well—carnal. At least, not yet. We both hope his attending this conference will change that."

"Has Michael met Isaac Walton?"

"Oh, yes. He had the next-door neighbor babysit me last night, though I'd assured him that I felt better, and he went to the opening prayer service. Michael is his cell's delegate. All the delegates enjoyed a private preconference social with Reverend Walton. Michael says he's awe-inspiring."

This case's connections bordered on incest. I switched the topic, hoping to catch Jennifer while she remained off-guard and chatty.

"You said something odd on Tuesday..."

"No doubt. Dick's death just about killed me. I've never seen a body before. I don't do funerals."

"Michael mentioned that. But this was something you said...just before you collapsed...that you couldn't talk to the police. Why? What did you mean?"

Jennifer flushed. "Did I really? I don't remember saying anything like that. Must have been because I felt too sick to speak."

I shrugged, sure she was lying. "It wasn't said in that context, it seemed to me..."

"Jake, if I don't remember saying it, how could I know what I meant? Please excuse me, I have to go to the little girls' room."

As she left, I checked on the time, wondering when I'd stopped liking Jennifer. Almost eight thirty-five. Allison should be here. Everyone else seemed to be. I'd go tell her she was on for both lunch and the séance. That ought to make her morning.

Spotting Ben in the hall as I passed Dick's yellow-taped

office, I said, "Hey, I've copied Peter's files for you. Notes for the book. They might shed some light on his death."

"When and where did you find them, Jake?"

"You can pick them up when I get back from Allison's office. I'll even stop by for you...won't be but a minute or two." I kept on going.

The door to Allison's office was closed. I knocked, then went in. She lay on the Persian carpet, legs and arms akimbo, her stylish blue skirt and matching blouse soaked in blood and the Delft-handled dagger stuck in her chest, seemingly color coordinated.

Thirteen

"You've got to stop going to work so early!" my mother screamed into the phone. After discovering two bodies before nine a.m.—my first week on the job—I tended to agree with her. Then she sobbed, "Please quit, darling, and come home now. You know it's dangerous and I'm so frightened." This advice came too late. During my frantic dash down the hall to find Ben, in a flash of clarity, I'd promised myself I'd find this killer before he—or she—stabbed someone else...maybe me. And to do that I had to remain part of the *Manhattan* scene.

I could only promise Mom I'd be careful, reminding her that our favorite homicide detective would be here to watch over me. Then I hung up.

As soon as I'd told Ben about the second murder, the death knell swept through the office like a hurricane. Barbara Ferris had witnessed my hysteria as I led Ben to Allison's body and followed us. When Ben opened the door, Barbara let out one massive, manic moan, then took off like the town crier. For sure, some *Manhattan* staffer had Ramirez on the line right now. The coroner, fingerprint, and DNA experts, along with Ben's partner, were on their way. Two cops, who'd been patrolling Madison in a police car, arrived a few minutes ago, and I'd ducked out, tap dancing around the barrage of questions from my coworkers, fleeing to my phone. I hadn't wanted my mother, an avid cable fan, to hear about Allison Carr's murder on television. There'd been no sign of Jennifer. Could she still be in the ladies' room? Maybe I should have joined her. I felt a lot like throwing up myself.

Instead, to calm my jangling nerves, I decided to peruse the files. Who knew what clues might lurk inside? The residue of our scones and tea stood front and center on my desk. I cleaned up, stacking the plates and cups back on the tray, then placed it on the chair that Jennifer had vacated. Next, I arranged my copies in alphabetical order. "M" seemed to be missing. While making the copies had I somehow skipped a file? I quickly flipped through all the folders. Then, starting from "A," I went through them again, searching more thoroughly. The original "M" file had vanished too. Who? When? Where? Why was easy. "M" might be the answer. Assuming Dick Peter hadn't already changed real names to reflect his fictional characters' names, several of the suspects in this case were "M's." Keith Morrison, Jennifer Moran, Michael Moran, and Mila Macovich. The last two were double "M's," for God's sake. If only I'd had a chance to glance through that file before...and why hadn't I turned all of them over to Ben? They could contain real evidence. I was probably an accessory after the fact. He'd want my head. And I couldn't say I'd blame him.

I jumped when the phone rang, then knocked two of the files on the floor as I reached to answer it.

"Jake, are you okay?"

"No, Dennis, I really don't think I am." My voice cracked.

"I'll come and pick you up. Since your luncheon engagement with Allison Carr has been permanently canceled, perhaps you'd like to join me at the restaurant?"

"It's nine thirty in the morning."

"So we'll drive through Central Park first. You need a change of scenery."

"How did you find out about Allison?"

"Call me the Asian-American Gypsy Rose Liebowitz."

"I smell a plot. Did my mother put you up to this?"

Dennis sighed but didn't even try to evade the question. "Yes. Maura's worried sick. Why don't you just come home?"

"Jesus, Dennis, I've discovered my second murder victim in less than a week. The police will want to go over a few things with me. And I do have two tough assignments to finish, as you well know."

"Nothing else keeping you there?"

"God, isn't that enough?" Unbidden tears rolled rapidly down my cheeks. I hoped Dennis couldn't figure out that I was weepy. I swallowed hard. "Look, I appreciate your concern. Please tell Mom I'm fine." I placed the phone back on its cradle, put my head down on the desk, and wailed.

Jennifer returned a few minutes after my tears had run their course.

"Where have you been?"

"I'm sorry, Jake. I needed some fresh air, so I walked over to Central Park."

"Before or after Allison's murder?"

"As I stepped into the elevator, Steve told me that you were the one who'd found Allison stabbed to death." Did I, once again, imagine an ever-so-slightly accusatory tone in Jennifer's voice? "God. What happened?"

"It sounds as if you know as much as I do. Just be glad you didn't walk in on Allison too."

"I wouldn't be standing here if I had. I couldn't survive another death scene. Jake, you look awful. Can I get you anything?"

As much as I craved another hot cup of tea, I didn't want to risk her disappearing again. I opened my briefcase "No thanks. Let's get to work while we can. I'm sure Ben will have some questions for both of us later. But first, do you have any idea what happened to the 'M' file?"

"I only copied the 'XYZ' files."

"That's not what I asked you." My attitude adjustment seemed to have vanished along with the folder.

"What's wrong, Jake? Why are you treating me like a suspect? I only want to help here."

"Sorry, Jen. Maybe I'm the one having trouble surviving these dead bodies. Look, I'm going to run these files down to Ben." I opened my briefcase and pulled out my homework. "Why don't you edit my review of Harry Brett's new book?"

Though I'd indicated that I had no notion of what they contained—or I'd have delivered them to him at once—when Ben found out I'd held onto Dick's folders for almost twenty-four hours, and that the both the "M" file and its copy had gone missing, his rage ran rampant. "You're a mystery writer, for Christ's sake. Haven't you ever heard of obstruction of justice?" Then, before I could protest that Keith Morrison had held onto them even longer than me, he'd stormed out of Allison's office, leaving his partner behind to take my statement. Since the coroner still hovered over Allison's body, Joe Cassidy had conducted my interview in the hall. With two of its offices now designated as crime scenes, and the police investigators sleuthing out of the coffee room, privacy had become a premium at *Manhattan* magazine.

I spent the rest of the day polishing my column, reading the

"F" file, looking for a lead on Glory Flagg, and thinking about Allison's murder. The latter took up most of my time. That blood had appeared fresh—I'd bet she hadn't been dead for more than an hour, probably less—when I found her. Round up the usual hordes of suspects. Robert Stern, both the Morans, Barry DeWitt, Christian Holmes, Barbara Ferris, and Hans Foote were all early arrivals this morning. Not to mention our mystery guest, the Reverend Walton. Did one of them have more than *Manhattan* on their mind?

Jennifer fended the phone calls. I gave her strict orders—I'd only talk to my mother, Ben, or Christian Holmes. Mom called eleven times. Ben neither called nor stopped by to see me. And, when I—dying from curiosity about Christian's early morning meeting with Walton—buzzed his office, his voicemail informed me that he'd be out of the office all day.

In between phoning her daughter, Mom, together with Gypsy Rose, had met with the coven's callbacks and selected the witches and warlocks for their upcoming Halloween Happening. This diversion, together with her indecision as to whether or not to go ahead with her regular last-Friday-of-the-month-lesser-literary-lights cocktail party, seemed to reduce her anxiety about my safety. I urged Mom not to cancel the party; we could all use a few hours of fun. During our last conversation, she'd finally agreed, and I reminded her that I'd be home late.

Then on my way out, Joe Cassidy stopped me in the lobby, full of disturbing questions and obviously not happy with my answers. Finally, I escaped from *Manhattan* to keep my date with Glory Flagg.

The setting sun still shimmered through Central Park's autumn leaves, softening the city's rough edges. The horses and the hansom cabs they were harnessed to—so often sad and scruffy in the cruel daylight—had turned into an Impressionist painter's tribute to the elegance of the Edwardian era, making me wish the automobile had never been invented. And the fountain in front of the Plaza glistened with glamour. This was Hollywood's New York, where Doris Day rebuffed then romanced Rock Hudson, and where Barbara Streisand ran into Robert Redford after all those years in *The Way We Were*. The New York I loved. It sure beat the melancholia, murder, and madness prevailing at work.

Glad to be out of *Manhattan*, I savored Fifth Avenue's passing parade. As dusk approached Sixtieth Street, the city's chic crowd favored Klein and Karan, with an occasional Versace exuding an international flair, contrasting sharply with the tourists' jeans, sweatshirts, and Nikes. My own outfit, chocolate brown twill pants and a caramel-colored wool blazer, bridged the fashion gap; however, as I stepped into the Pierre's tiny bar, I noticed most of the people sipping cocktails there were dressed in banker gray or basic black. And for the life of me, I couldn't spot a hooker among them. Could Modesty actually have been teasing me?

Fourteen

Glory's grand entrance—fifteen minutes late—certainly brightened up the cocktail lounge. Her red catsuit, slinking like second skin around the thinnest thighs I've ever seen, was tucked into boots covered in stars and stripes. What she wore as a scarf looked like the real thing. Wasn't it against the law to drape the American flag around your neck? Weirdest of all, her hair was red, white, and blue spiked stripes. Food coloring, I hoped, for her sake. All eyes followed her from the door to my table.

"Jake O'Hara? Ya know, Modesty told me you looked like Annie Hall if she'd been played by Meg Ryan." That had to the nicest thing Modesty had ever said about me. Probably about anyone.

"Thanks for meeting me, Ms. Flagg." I gave her a big smile.

"Sure, sweetie. And the name is Glory. We might be mutually helpful to each other, if ya catch my drift. And ain't it a shame about Allison Carr? I hated that broad, but like, I'm real sorry she was offed. We tawked on *Ramirez Now* on Tuesday morning, right after Dick's moider, ya know."

The waiter appeared at Glory's side. "What would Madame like to drink?"

"A Scarlett O'Hara. That's in honor of you, Jake." She turned back to the waiter. "And make it light on the grenadine."

I ordered another martini, and when the waiter left, said, "I watched the show."

"Good. Then ya do know what a total piece of woik Allison was. May she rest in peace, of course."

I decided to go for the gold. "Allison told me that you and she were childhood classmates. Since you two go back so far together, there must be..."

"Sweetie. Fuchs and Carriano died twenty-five years ago. Their pasts were buried with them. Glory Flagg and Allison Carr wouldn't even have recognized them two broads. But I'm more interested in Dick's book. I hear you're his editor—right—I betcha you're writing the whole damn enchilada. That no-talent bastard sometimes even used ghostwriters to write his columns. Didja know that, Jake?"

"No. I didn't." God, could that be true?

"Trust me. Dick earned his reputation. And in all areas of his life. Now, what I want to know is this: Where are his notes? They could hurt a lotta people, ya know. Might even get someone else moidered."

Was that a veiled threat? "Why do you believe there are notes?"

Glory laughed. "Sweetie, I lived with the son of a bitch for years. The notes were always with us. Dick's secret formula for someone else to do his writing. Get it?"

"Well, the files for the book are now in police custody."

"But not before ya read them, right?"

Bartering information might give me a lead. I shrugged, then said, "I glanced through the folders."

"I'll bet that a bright young lady like you made copies. Ain't that what ya did, Jake?"

"What do you expect to find in Dick's notes?" I clutched my briefcase, wondering if Glory guessed I had those copies with me and that I planned to finish reading them tonight.

"The identity of the killer. That's what's in them files. But the cops might not figure it out. So, if you do have copies, let me take a look at them. Ya know, woiking together, we could crack this case, Jake."

I was tempted to say I work alone. But instead, I only smiled.

"Think it over. We'd be like Nick and Nora Charles." Glory giggled. "In the meanwhile, to show my heart is in the right place and all, what can I do for ya? I gotta say, ya look like your fourth chakra's giving ya some big-time trouble. Modesty and I could help out there."

Afraid to even inquire as to the location of my fourth chakra, I said, "Well, there are a few things that have been puzzling me..."

Glory Flagg waved at the waiter. "Another round."

"Not for me." I indicated my almost-full martini.

After the waiter served Glory her second Scarlett O'Hara, I got down to business. Glory had been married to Dick for over two decades; she must know all the skeletons he'd slept with—in or out of the closet. "So Glory, I understand that even the elevator operator had a grudge against Dick."

"Goes back years. Dick loved to play dress-up. Our trios were like damn costume parties. Every freaking night was Halloween." At the next table a women in a chic cocktail hat dropped her drink in her lap. Her escort ignored her predicament; he seemed mesmerized by Glory. I held my finger in front of my lips, silently signaling Glory that she had an audience. She spun around to confront her eavesdroppers. "Whatsa matter with you two? Didn't your mothers ever tell ya not to listen in on other people's conversations?" When she picked up her story, her voice had lowered dramatically. "One Christmas Eve, Steve played Santa at *Manhattan*'s annual party. We all got wasted. Including Santa. Dick invited poor old Steve to join us for a nightcap in his office. Let's jest say, that year, Santa's Christmas memories really sucked. It's all in my book. Of course, I changed Steve's name. So don't tell anyone."

I gulped down the rest of my martini. "And your publisher is Harvest House?"

"Yeah. This ain't their usual stuff. But the editorial board smells a bestseller."

Talk about tawdry. But Glory was a detective's dream. I wondered if Ben had unearthed all this dirt. Well, if he ever spoke to me again, I'd share it. Meanwhile, I'd keep digging. "And Hans Foote, what's his story? I wouldn't want him for an enemy."

"Hans hated Dick. Maybe even more than the rest of the world did."

"Why?"

"Easy. Dick told him to keep his day job. Ya know, Hans wrote this book, then gave it to Dick to read. That Nazi wannabe thought Dick would recommend an agent. Fat chance. Dick ripped Hans a new rear end. That's figuratively, not literally. I learned all them literary terms from Dick. I used to think a metaphor was something from outer space."

"Hans resented Dick because he massacred his manuscript? That was Peter's M.O. Doesn't sound like much of a motive to me."

"The story ain't over. Dick took Hans's plot to one of his in-favor-at-the-moment, pseudo-intellectual hacks. When the book came out, it was a huge success. Ya know, ya probably read it: *Right in Step.*"

"How did Dick get away with that? I'm surprised Hans didn't kill him."

Glory winked. "Maybe he did. Better late than never. Anyhoo, Hans wrote in longhand on legal pads. Dick never returned the manuscript. The only copy. It would have been that Nazi nut's word against Dick's reputation and bucks. Hans knew he'd never win in a legal battle. But who knows? He may have wielded his revenge with a Delft dagger."

The Delft reminded me of Stern. "Glory, how well do you know Robert Stern?"

"Well enough to know he has a lot of them blue and white plates hanging in his house."

"Do you..."

"Jake, I'm outta here. This was jest the overture. Act One begins when we read Dick's notes together. Thanks for the drinks." Glory stood and stretched. Her catsuit moved with her, showing off that great body. Then she raised the flag around her neck. A man at the bar saluted.

Fifteen

The party was in full bloom when I arrived home at six thirty. Strategically placed russet and yellow mums filled Mom's best vases, and on the faux Regency console in the dining room, a well-stocked bar was doing a brisk business. Dennis had been enlisted as bartender. The buffet held a wide variety of elegant finger food, a gourmet oxymoron that only Gypsy Rose could have prepared. Too-Tall Tom passed a tray of fruit, cheese, and biscuits, held high over most guests' heads, but he graciously stooped to serve. Lights were dimmed, candles glowed, and Mom had achieved a roaring blaze in our temperamental Edwardian-era fireplace that often as not backed up, triggering the smoke alarm.

I loved our co-op's high ceilings, arched moldings, and chair rails. And this evening, Mom and Gypsy Rose had succeeded in creating an atmosphere so warm—and filled with so many good friends—that it did far more to soothe my jangled nerves than the two martinis had.

Mom, deep in conversation with a tall, beautiful woman

whom I'd never met but immediately recognized, spotted me and dashed across the room. "Jake, darling, thank God you're home. Come, I want to introduce you to Mila Macovich."

"How did a megawatt like Mila wind up here among the lesser-literary-lights?" Sometimes my mother amazed me.

"Oh, she showed up at Gypsy Rose's this afternoon, just after we'd finished the final casting for the Halloween Happening. Naturally I invited her to join our little group." I guess Mila, like most people, had a hard time responding negatively to Maura O'Hara's positive attitude. Glancing around the room, I observed how mother's "little group" now included about twenty budding poets, screenwriters, and novelists. Their ages ranged from eighteen to eighty.

Modesty glowered at me from her perch on the ladder-back chair in front of the fireplace. I gave her an I'll-be-over-as-soon-as-I-can wave, then trotted after my mother to meet Mila, the woman who'd replaced Glory as Dick's wife.

Mila in person turned out to be every bit as magnificent as the photograph on her most recent book jacket. That doesn't happen often. Her eyes shone with vitality and joie de vivre, while her posture exuded robust health, honed by long hours of discipline. I wondered if she'd worked out with Allison.

"Your mother's been raving about you, Jake. I'm delighted to meet you. Dick's death has left me devastated. And now poor Allison's been murdered. It's all too grim." Mila extended a slim, pale hand. "Your mother's party couldn't have come at a better time. I deserved a break from making funeral arrangements, shopping for widow's weeds, and meeting with my late husband's financial advisors. They're even worse—if possible—than the morticians."

"I've always agreed with Jessica Mitford," my mother said. "Just have me cremated, Jake, and scatter the ashes over

Central Park. You know, near the reservoir, where Jackie Kennedy used to walk."

Mila grimaced. "My Russian ancestors would turn over in their graves if I were cremated. I have chosen a coffin and a crypt for my departed Dick that will last forever. We all will need our bodies when we rise again for the final judgment, no? I certainly wouldn't want Dick to miss that day."

A picture of Peter as Count Dracula, sleeping his days away through an eternity of nightlife, flashed across my mind. I blinked, trying to erase the image.

"Please accept my condolences, Mila. I'll be at the funeral and at the séance too, if that's all right with you."

My mother said, "That's why Mila dropped by the bookstore this afternoon. The séance is off. Mila's going to work on her nightmares with dream therapy instead."

I stared into Mila's olive green eyes.

"Nightmares? I thought you wanted to contact your dead husband."

"Actually, I want his scurrilous spirit to stop bothering me. He haunts my dreams every night, driving me crazy just like he used to do all day long before he died." Mila pushed her long hair away from her face. "Enough is enough. My therapist has sent me to an expert in dream interpretation. We decided that channeling that slime from the bowels of Hell wouldn't get him the hell out of my bedroom. Gypsy Rose understands." I was glad someone did. "But I will be at the Halloween Happening at the bookstore. Will you be there?" Mila seemed to have gotten over her rage rather quickly.

"Wouldn't miss it."

As I pondered the meaning of Mila's marvelous meandering, I spotted Christian Holmes at the buffet. "Mom, when did Christian get here?"

"He came to see you just as the first guests were arriving, and I asked him to join us."

Modesty's frantic waving caught my mother's eye. Mine too. Then Christian beckoned me. I excused myself, but Mila—as I kept praying she wouldn't go there—was in the middle of explaining how Dick had invaded last night's dream and never even noticed that I was moving on.

My mother widened her eyes at me. I wasn't sure if she thought me rude for walking away or if she wanted to join me.

Christian looked weary. "Jake, I'm sorry I didn't get back to you. I didn't want to let Walton out of my sight."

"What's up?"

"Isaac called me at home late last night. Said Homicide put the fear of God in him. He thought he was about to be arrested for Dick's murder."

I could hear my heart thump. "Why? What did he tell the police?"

"That he'd been in Dick's office the night he was killed."

"No way."

"Yep. Isaac says he went over to end their quarter-of-a-century-old feud. Sally Lou had pushed him, believing that as a man of God, Isaac should forgive his only living relative. However, the reverend swears he was out of there by nine thirty and when he left, Dick was alive and kicking."

"Why would Walton tell you?"

"He'd thought we'd been fair with him during our interview and he wanted to have his side of the story in *Manhattan* magazine. Isaac knows this looks bad; he left his fingerprints all over Dick's office. The only reason Walton hasn't been arrested is that the office is filled with yet-to-be-identified prints."

"What happened today at the Garden?"

"If I didn't know better, I'd never have guessed the preacher had a problem. Slick as Satan. And he had those guys crawling on the floor and loving it."

"Come on. Crawling?"

"You're too young to remember EST. Those participants groveled, wallowing in their woes while rolling around on the floor, trying to face up to their faults—or some such garbage. Anyway, the Pledged-For-Lifers made EST look like a day at Disney World."

"God Almighty."

"If I believed in God, I'd say he had nothing to do with it."

"Jake, I need to talk to you!" Modesty's bellow sounded belligerent.

Christian chuckled. "Go ahead, Jake. I want to have a word with your mother's friend."

"Which one?" I asked, distracted by Modesty's pacing in front of the fireplace.

"Gypsy Rose Liebowitz." Christian beamed. "Now there's a woman."

On information overload, I went to see what the hell Modesty wanted.

Dennis trailed behind me. "Want a drink? I've just made a fresh batch of martinis."

"No thanks—but I'd love a glass of ice water and some Tylenol. Could you...?"

"Your wish is my whatever." Dennis left. My head was now pounding harder than my heart. I hoped he'd hurry up.

"Okay, Modesty, what's so damn important? You've been dogging me since I walked in the door."

"And how are you this evening, Jake O'Hara?"

'Totally whipped, if you really want to know."

"Yeah? Well, wait 'til you hear this—you'll wake up." Curiosity has its own adrenaline.

"I've heard more than I wanted to today, but maybe my mind hasn't maxed out yet." I sighed. "What, Modesty, what?"

My mother, now chatting with Aaron Rubin and Mr. Kim in the dining room, smiled at me as Dennis returned with the water and Tylenol. "Is this a private conversation, ladies, or may I join you?"

"No," Modesty snapped.

Dennis winked at me and walked over to join my mother's circle. I swallowed, gulped the water, and said, "Shoot."

"Barry DeWitt threatened to kill Allison Carr in the Algonquin lobby late last night."

"How do you know? Were you there?" God, if I'd only given the "D" file to Ben sooner.

"No, I was in the bookstore." I waited; there had to be a segue here somewhere. "I just came from there, researching in the poison section," Modesty said. "Barry DeWitt was next to me with his nose in *Cause of Death*. I was almost in his lap; you know how crowded it can get. Anyway, this woman came and stood next to him and said, 'So you stabbed the bitch.' DeWitt said, 'Are you crazy?' And this woman said, 'I sat a potted palm away from you in the Algonquin last night. I heard you tell Allison if she didn't lay off, you'd kill her. And I've just passed that tidbit along to Detective Ben Rubin. Maybe *Manhattan* can have a field day when they fry you.'"

"Jesus. What did DeWitt say?"

"Nothing. He glanced over at me. My chin must have fallen to my fourth chakra. Then he grabbed the woman by the elbow and led her toward the cozy section."

"Modesty, this is important. What did she look like?"

"Forty or so. Too much makeup. Incipient hippo hips. Oh—and she wore a uniform with some sort of red logo."

"Barbara Ferris."

If I didn't feel so lousy, I'd drink Dennis Kim's entire pitcher of martinis.

"Who?"

"The receptionist at *Manhattan*."

"Is that uniform standard issue for all their employees, or are editors allowed to wear civvies? You really should quit that job before someone stabs you in the back."

Mr. Kim put his arm around my shoulder and said, "Why don't you sit down, Jake? I've fixed you a plate of food. The pastry is great. And you're pale as a ghost."

I grinned, grateful for both his humor and his concern. "Good idea, Mr. Kim." I followed him to the couch and collapsed into its chintz cushions, balancing the water glass in one hand and a full plate in the other while Mr. Kim went to fetch my mother.

Gypsy Rose sank down next to me. "Please listen to me, Jake. You're a magnet for murder. Maura and I are worried sick." She plopped my plate on the coffee table and held my hand. "Can't you work at home for a while, honey?"

"We'll see, but I'll be careful." I mouthed the same empty promise I'd made Mom, while averting her scrutiny as tears welled up. Mr. Kim, Gypsy Rose, Mom, Dennis, and even in her own strange way, Modesty were all worried about me. I gave Gypsy Rose a big—if forced—smile. "Thanks."

She patted my hand. "Eat something." I reached for a tiny turkey sandwich, checking out Mr. Kim's selection of sweets. "You're not the only one I'm worried about, Jake. Mila's canceled her channeling session. Strange. I'm sure Dick's been trying to contact her and I know she's frightened. Dream therapy, indeed. Takes too long. It will be a waste of her time and her money." So much for Mila's believing that Gypsy Rose had understood. "Dick's evil spirit could cause Mila serious psychic damage if we don't arrange for Zelda to have a chat with his guide. Not to mention all the information that only her dead husband can provide for us. Maybe we'll just hold the séance without her and find out what Dick Peter's up to in the world beyond."

"But..."

"We'll do it, Jake. Mark your calendar. Nine p.m. All Soul's day. And invite the ghostwriters; the spirits love a good crowd."

I changed the subject. "Did you have a chance to talk to Christian Holmes? He seemed to be most intrigued with you."

Under her perfectly applied makeup, Gypsy Rose appeared to blush. "What do you know about him, Jake? Besides the fact that he's an atheist. I never miss his religion columns and I'd never have guessed that he's not a theist. Christian says he'd like to do a piece on my psychic ability. It could be wonderful publicity for the bookstore's events—and for the entire New Age movement. Do you think I should consent to be interviewed? Or will he turn my gift into an object of ridicule?"

"I think he's one of the few good guys in this whole sordid case. But, hey, I only met him yesterday. Let's wait and see how this goes down."

"This isn't my first time around the block with him, Jake. Your mother and I knew him during the French Revolution."

I tasted the napoleon.

While loading the dishwasher, between urging my resignation from the magazine, warning me not to play Nancy Drew again, and fretting that I could be the next murder victim, my mother got into a little girl talk. "I'm not going upstate with Aaron to see the autumn leaves."

"Not because you're worrying about me, I hope?"

My mother fussed with the Wedgwood server, trying to stack it behind a full load of plates. "Not really." She placed the server in the sink. "I'd better wash this by hand."

"You're a lousy liar, Mom."

"Well, it's true that I don't want to leave you alone—it's also true that I'm just not ready for an overnighter."

If not now, when? But who was I to offer advice on anyone's love life, least of all my mother's? Maybe on some level, I was glad she wouldn't be going away. Ben hadn't called. I worried that he never would. And I couldn't face the prospect of going through those bloody files tonight. Not even if Dick's notes would prove conclusively who done it.

Exhausted, I fell into bed but couldn't sleep. I counted suspects instead of sheep.

Sixteen

Serial Sue led the Serenity Prayer as I entered the second-floor meeting room of the Jan Hus church on 71st Street. The Ghostwriters group shared the quarters with several other twelve-step programs, including Alcoholics Anonymous, Narcotics Anonymous, and Sex Addicts Anonymous. But at eleven o'clock every Saturday morning, the room's occupants were all ghostwriters, and its atmosphere was filled with our unique brand of frustrated anonymity.

Sue's long-term ghostwriting for numerous "authors" of young adult novels—their series sometimes spanning thirty years and as many books—had left her bitter. Trite tripe takes its toll; however, she'd been making real progress in her recovery. This morning there was a lilt in Serial Sue's voice as she followed our opening prayer with the introduction of today's speaker.

"I'm delighted to present a dear friend and fellow member of Ghostwriters Anonymous, a man who has helped me work the steps and accept my own anonymity. When I joined this program almost a year ago, I'd finally reached my bottom and had to confront my lifetime addiction to anonymity. I'd suffered far longer than all of you. After all, I've been a ghostwriter for over sixty years." Some new members gasped. "And next month, I'll be eighty-two years old." This admission provided Sue with her usual round of applause. "And, despite writing twenty-six different series, I've never had my name on a cover." Nods of empathy were accompanied by murmurs of sympathy. Serial Sue really knew how to work our crowd. Next to me, Modesty groaned loudly.

Sue peered over her Ben Franklins, gave Modesty a look combining disdain with sorrow, and rattled right on. "The books you've all read as children, the Honey Bunch Series, the Beverly Grays, the Cheryl Cranes, I was one of a committee of writers who produced these books as a joint effort, but under one nom de plume. While her fans awaited Clair Blank's newest Beverly Gray mystery, what they never knew was that there was no Clair, only a horde of anonymous hacks writing as Clair. Most of our committee are dead." Serial Sue lowered her voice. "Several suicides...prevalent among us ghostwriters, you know."

I'd swear Sue made some of this stuff up as she went along. Maybe she wasn't really that far into her recovery after all.

Modesty whispered to me, "That old broad's on the pity pot. Who'd remain an anonymous hack for sixty years? It's depressing for the membership to have to listen to..."

"Shush," I said, although I tended to agree with her.

Serial Sue continued, "So, here's my friend, Too-Tall Tom, to share his experience, strength, and hope with us."

I perked up. Too-Tall Tom would be leading our discussion and he was always funny and upbeat. We'd been friends for years, long before there was a Ghostwriters Anonymous group. He ghostwritten how-to handyman books while practicing his talent for interior design working for big bucks as a carpenter, turning Manhattan box-shaped apartments into art deco or

Edwardian gems. No conversation was taboo between us. We'd shared everything, from love lives gone awry, to dreams of having our names on the cover and our pictures on the back of the jacket of our future bestsellers, to being miffed—at times— with our mutually overprotective mothers. I loved Too-Tall Tom and totally trusted him.

Once again, this morning's topic was my nemesis, the third step: Make a decision to turn our will and our lives over to the care of God as we understood Him. Too-Tall Tom said, "I have no problem calling my Higher Power God. Where I have trouble is turning my will over to Him. I still want to be me...and in total control." I certainly identified with that.

At the coffee break, Jane D., a self-help ghostwriter and another old pal, hugged me hard. "Jake, you've gone and gotten yourself mixed up in murder again. Why did you ever agree to edit for a man like that dreadful Dick Peter?"

"For the same reason most of us have remained addicted to our anonymity, Jane. I needed the money."

"I didn't mean to sound cross." Sometimes Jane sounded as old as Serial Sue. "But we're all so worried about you. Is there anything I can do to help? This is a 'we' program, you know. You're not alone." Concern crunched her fine features into a full-face frown. Her eyes, almost the exact same shade of toasty brown as her hair, held mine, forcing me to admit that all my simmering fears had come to a full boil.

"Maybe we can talk about that after the meeting. I could use some advice."

Serial Sue called the ghostwriters back to order.

Formula Fannie, a police procedural ghostwriter who could probably outscore Barry Scheck on a DNA test, took the floor. "I agree with Too-Tall Tom. When my love affair was dying a slow death, my addiction turned me into a control freak. My latest lover, as some of you know, is the Brooklyn M.E. In the beginning, I only dated him for selfish motives. Who could be a better beau? Think of the time and money saved on research. During pillow talk, I had my arms around my own forensics expert. Then I fell in love and discovered he was much more interested in cold, dead bodies than in my hot, live one." I heard a moan from the fellowship. Formula Fannie was famous for choosing the wrong man. A stickler for detail, she simply spent too much time in the morgue. As Modesty reminded me so often, "Some of us are sicker than others."

Too-Tall Tom comforted Formula Fannie by reading the third step prayer. The words, tumbling out in his warm baritone, comforted me too. Yet, when he called on me to share my feelings on the step, I passed. I had a lot of trouble working the steps, and I resented putting anyone in charge of my life, even God.

Maybe that's why I remained addicted to anonymity, found excuses not to write my own book, and my life was murder.

By twelve thirty, Modesty, Jane, Too-Tall Tom, and I were ordering salads and iced tea at Sarabeth's Kitchen. I'd decided to use the tools of our program and ask the ghostwriters for help. The first step told us: We are powerless over our anonymity. And I knew the road to recovery came via the fellowship, not a solo trip. Maybe that would be the road to the killer as well.

"Listen, you guys, I need your help."

Jane adjusted her Hermès scarf—self-help ghostwriting pays better than murder—and looked pleased. Too-Tall Tom smiled, reached across the table, and patted my hand. Modesty, dressed today in a new Franciscan habit, twirled her rosary bead belt and asked, "Solving the *Manhattan* murders?"

"Yes. There are too many suspects for me to sort through alone and I'm afraid..."

"There might be more murders," Jane finished my sentence. She really ought to watch that character defect, I thought, then scolded myself for taking her inventory.

"That's possible—"

"What do you want us to do, Jake?" Too-Tall Tom asked.

I guess interrupting each other is just what good friends do, especially if they're New Yorkers.

"The way I see it, though half of New York City hated Dick, the police should have a baker's dozen of actual suspects. And most of them would have had the opportunity to kill Allison as well. I figure she was murdered because she knew who'd killed Dick...or had uncovered some evidence that could prove whodunit."

"Who are these people?" Jane asked.

Modesty said, "I can give you a banner suspect: Glory Flagg."

"And why is she a frontrunner?" Jane asked.

"Don't you watch TV or read the headlines?" Modesty asked Jane. "Glory's telling all of Manhattan why she's better off with Dick dead. And aside from the ménage à trois..."

"I had the impression Ms. Flagg rather enjoyed the threesomes." Too-Tall Tom grinned.

"No doubt," I said. "But she hated Dick and a twenty-million-dollar lawsuit is a strong motive for murder. What's more, she and Allison Carr had hated each other for decades; they'd been childhood combatants on the battlefields of Brooklyn."

The food arrived. I spread strawberry jam on my biscuit and took a bite, glancing out the window at the Madison Avenue passersby. Saturday morning in Carnegie Hill was like Saturday morning anywhere in the USA. Its residents, dressed in jeans and sweats, were running errands...except here, picking up your clothes at the dry cleaner could cost a day's wages and Mr. Kim's melon prices seemed to rival those in Japan.

Jane said, "Look, I've been attending a shrinks' convention in Chicago for the last few days. Fill me in on the players, will you, Jake?"

"Well, in addition to Glory, there's the current wife, Mila Macovich."

"I just love her books," Jane said.

"You would." Modesty waved a forkful of romaine in Jane's direction.

Even though I shared Jane's feelings about Mila's books, I didn't say so, not wanting to distract the ghostwriters with a literary discussion. "Mila says Dick's haunting her dreams. She scheduled a séance with Gypsy Rose, then canceled. Gypsy Rose still wants to contact Dick's spirit guide, so she's going ahead with it. You're all invited. Nine p.m. Tuesday. All Soul's Day."

"Isn't Dick being buried Monday?" Too-Tall Tom asked. "Then the Halloween Happening?"

"In lieu of a wake," I said.

"It's going to be a busy week for you, Jake," Modesty said. "But you can count me in for the séance. Gypsy Rose runs the best spook show in town."

"She's a channel to the spirits in the world beyond, Modesty," Jane scolded. "I'll certainly be there."

Too-Tall Tom looked glum. "Look, I have a date." We all stared him down. "Okay, okay. I'll cancel it."

"Good," Modesty said. "Jake, quickly give us a rundown on the other suspects and tell us what we can do to help you. I have a chapter to edit this afternoon."

"How many pages?" Jane asked. With Modesty's Gothic

novel rumored to be over twenty-one hundred pages, we all wondered how she found time to be a gainfully employed ghostwriter.

"We are not here to discuss my book," Modesty growled. "Go ahead, Jake."

I moved on, "At *Manhattan* magazine, there are three armed, uniformed employees—the place is run like a detention center—and they all have potential. Dick Peter stole Hans Foote's—he's the guard in the lobby—manuscript and it became a bestseller. Then Steve, the fat, jolly elevator operator, played Santa at a Christmas party, got wasted, and wound up in a holiday masochistic ménage à trois with Dick and Glory. According to Glory, it was really ugly and Steve never got over it. Barbara Ferris—the receptionist—hasn't a clear motive and would be on the bottom of anyone's list. Yet, she had opportunities to commit both murders, appears to know something, is quick to accuse, and appears overly protective of Robert Stern, *Manhattan*'s editor and a prime suspect. She's another one suffering from nightmares."

"What's Stern's motive?" Jane asked.

"His wife had an affair with Dick and it drove her to suicide. Furthermore, he was at work the morning of Allison's murder, claims he was home alone on the night of Dick's death, but he could have been at *Manhattan*. And, most damning, a Delft dagger's gone missing from his collection."

"But wasn't a second Delft dagger used on Allison?" Too-Tall Tom asked.

"Right," I said. "But how do we know how many daggers Stern had in his collection? More than one could be missing."

"Or someone could be using Delft daggers to throw suspicion on Stern," Modesty suggested.

"What about the theater critic, Barry DeWitt?" Too-Tall

Tom asked. "I've heard that he and Peter hated each other."

"He's so handsome," Jane said. "I can't believe he's a killer."

"Cretin..." Modesty began, venom in her voice.

"Tell everyone what you overheard, Modesty," I said.

We were on coffee and dessert by time Modesty finished her recounting of Barbara's accusation against DeWitt. Too-Tall Tom had pulled out a yellow pad and started taking notes. Not a bad idea.

"Jennifer Moran told me that Pax's publisher, Keith Morrison, had been ready to kill Peter because he was so late with his manuscript," Modesty said. "Anything to that?"

"Morrison's one weird happening," I said. "He did hang on to Dick's files when he should have turned them over to the police...not to mention me. And Dennis had to hold his hand the other night...'til dawn. I wouldn't count Morrison out, but could Dick's being late for his delivery date really be a motive for his murder?"

"If it were, we'd all be dead," Modesty said.

"It would have been at my last publishing house." Too-Tall Tom sighed.

I noticed Modesty looking at her watch and hurriedly explained the rejected-relative Walton angle, certain that he was Homicide's hottest prospect. And why not? He'd been, by his own admission, in Dick Peter's office on the night his cousin had been stabbed. All the ghostwriters knew and liked Jennifer, so I went easy over my concerns regarding her possible involvement; however, everyone was shocked to hear that Michael Moran had become a Pledged-For-Lifer, and that he and his new best friend, Reverend Walton, had both turned up at *Manhattan* on the morning of Allison's murder. Feeling as if I were betraying my new friend, I added Christian Holmes to the list. He'd been there, keeping company with Isaac Walton, the morning of

Allison's murder, and earlier he'd given Ben that goofy—indeed, useless—public library alibi.

"Okay," Modesty said, counting on her fingers. "The guard, the elevator operator and the receptionist. That's three. Add the two wives, that's five. DeWitt and Stern...that's seven. Reverend Walton, Michael Moran, and Jennifer—though we all know she couldn't be guilty—for starters, she's too dumb—that's ten. This Keith Morrison guy, that's eleven. Christian Holmes is twelve. You said a baker's dozen. Who's number thirteen? I have to get our game plan and go home."

"Jennifer Moran's a good person, Jake." Jane sounded distressed.

I reverted to program talk. "Hey, I'm only sharing my feelings here."

Modesty stood. "Okay, two questions. Why aren't we leaving this mess to the cops—as incompetent as they may be? Second, if we are going to solve these murders, who's the thirteenth suspect, for God's sake? I need to know. I'm leaving. Now!"

I swallowed hard. "Me. Ben's been avoiding me, and as his partner, Joe Cassidy, pointed out, I was not only on the scene for the murders, I discovered the bodies. And I had a motive. Two, in fact. I wound up with both of Dick's high-paying assignments."

Seventeen

The ghostwriters, strongly motivated by our mutual anger—how could any homicide detective, even one as dumb as Cassidy, believe I might be a possible whodunit?—agreed our biggest chore would be to pare down that juror-long list of suspects. If we divided the list four ways, each of us would have three potential killers to spook. For our first assignments, we decided to check out all those flimsy alibis. Then we staked our killer-candidate claims. The only major area of disagreement was who got whom. Everyone wanted Glory Flagg.

But Modesty, who'd changed her afternoon plans from editing to sleuthing, declared that Glory belonged to her, citing chakras as their common ground and refusing to budge. No one else could win when Modesty balked, so we gave her Glory. She also insisted on Jennifer Moran, determined to clear her—though none of us considered her a true suspect. "Listen, she's suffered enough being chained to that biker. And we all know that Jen couldn't plot a *Reader's Digest* excerpt, never mind two murders." Then Modesty snorted, almost an embarrassed grunt. "I'd better add a guy to my list—maybe that nutty publisher, Keith Morrison—or else you'll believe I've either lost my mind or compromised my position on detesting dumb broads by rushing to defend these twitty women." I'd swear I spotted a faint, rosy blush spread across her pale cheek.

"No way," Too-Tall Tom assured her.

"None of us would ever believe that of you, Modesty," Jane said.

I giggled.

"Watch it," Modesty said. "I could be home editing. Do you want my help on this or not?"

Too-Tall Tom opted for Barry DeWitt. If the "D" file's information about Barry's bisexuality proved correct and he'd ever made the Tribeca scene, Too-Tall Tom's many friends would provide both accurate information and lots of great gossip. "Give me Christian Holmes too. My friends all read his column. Think he's a hoot. Wait 'til I tell them that the religion editor they love to hate is really an atheist. That'll inspire them more than the Holy Ghost." He poured yet another coffee. We were all over-caffeinated. "Oh, and put Michael Moran down for me. I've always wanted to check out the straight biker scene. Hey, maybe I can go to a Pledged-For-Lifer's meeting. Do you ladies think I could pass for a born-again heterosexual husband?"

While Jane thought it over, Modesty and I voted a re-sounding "No."

Jane took on the uniforms: Santa Steve, Hans Foote, and Barbara Ferris. When she heard that Hans acted like a Nazi she told Too-Tall and me—at double-feature length—how she just loved old black and white World War movies. "I have to confess that I find all those uniforms, especially the air force bomber jackets and those white silk scarves, very sexy." Fortunately, Modesty had gone to the john and missed Jane sharing her secret lust.

That left me with Mila Macovich, Robert Stern, and Isaac Walton. The two men were the police's prime suspects. Stern because of his story about the conveniently missing dagger from his Delft collection—the means. Add Dick's death-inducing affair with Stern's wife—the motive. Walton because he'd lied about, then admitted to, being in Dick's den of iniquity on the night of his murder—the opportunity. Then there was the reverend's lifelong resentment and jealousy of his cousin—the motive. However, I wouldn't consider murder to be beyond the realm of that beautiful Russian, Mila, either.

In fact, most of the twelve had strong motives and most of them could have purchased or stolen two Delft daggers, maybe from Robert Stern's collection, if he hadn't used them himself. But how "comfortable" had Stern's relationship with Allison been? While we would investigate each of the twelve's past history with Dick Peter and Allison Carr, opportunity appeared to be as a large a consideration as motive or means. We agreed that the key to solving these murders could well be the suspects' ironclad or Teflon alibis. Where exactly had all these people been during those two tiny *Manhattan* windows of opportunity for murder?

After deciding to have dinner at eight at Grazie to exchange our progress reports, we adjoined at two thirty, all of us revved up to go find a killer.

I stopped at the co-op to check my phone messages and email. Nada. My mother was working this afternoon at the bookstore. New Agers were kept hopping as Halloween approached. Feeling a little guilty—Mom had stayed home this weekend to be with me—I left a note saying not to expect me for dinner and suggesting she hang out with Gypsy Rose. Then I brushed the cinnamon from my teeth, looked up Robert Stern's home address, put on my sneakers, and went out to play Clue.

*   *   *

Mr. Kim's outdoor stands were loaded with mums and pumpkins. Row after row of gold flowers and orange fruit, quickly turning into greenbacks. His business as brisk as the weather. I waved as he filled a young mother's big basket with two truly ugly jack-o'-lanterns. But her preschool-age twin sons were beaming, fighting over who would get the more garishly painted pumpkin.

"Jake," Mr. Kim shouted. "I've saved some of my biggest and best pumpkins for Gypsy Rose's Halloween Happening. Please tell your mother she can pick them up, or if she'd prefer, I'll bring them with me on Monday night. The carver's a true artist, don't you think?" He pointed to the hideous hollowed-out horrors lined up in front of me. "And we're so lucky, he's created a theme for the evening. I swear, Jake, this Adrian's a magician; he's turned each of the pumpkins into one of the seven dwarfs." Next Mr. Kim would be telling me that Dennis was planning on coming to the party as Snow White.

Robert Stern turned out to be a neighbor, living only a block north and an avenue west, but beaucoup bucks and social strata away from my co-op's front door. I walked to 93rd Street, crossed Madison Avenue, heading west, admiring one of the best maintained and prettiest blocks in New York City. Stern's five-story townhouse was located on the north side of the street, steps off Fifth Avenue. I stood awed in front of the limestone mansion, its architectural design combining old-world Georgian elegance with America's late nineteenth-century robber barons' penchant for a gargoyle perched over every window. Robert Stern's grandfather had been one of those robber barons who, following in Andrew Carnegie's bold footsteps, had moved so far uptown in Manhattan that high society scorned the uncharted territory, saying settling there would be as unfashionable as living in New Jersey. Today, our neighborhood, Carnegie Hill, is the most desirable one in the city. And—to think—if Mom's grand-aunt hadn't died and left us her co-op on 92nd Street, I'd still be living in Queens. I guess both the Sterns and the O'Haras can thank our ancestors for our current lifestyles.

I climbed the steps, caressing the wrought-iron railing interlaced with cupids, complete with bows and arrows. Then, without a script or even a sane reason for doing so, I raised the big Delft knocker and banged it on the front door. A butler, dressed in formal morning coat and school tie, stood in the foyer, averting any eye contact, as stony as a guard at Buckingham Palace. Silence, that lasted long enough to make me nervous. My smile fading along with my patience, I finally said, "So, hello. I'm Jake O'Hara. Will you please tell Mr. Stern that I'm here?"

Still not looking at me, the butler asked in an icy English accent, so upper class it made Queen Elizabeth sound like Eliza Doolittle, "Is Mr. Stern expecting you?"

I'd be damned if I'd let this Jeeves wannabe intimidate me. "Why don't you ask him?" I used my most imperious tone. And, by God, it worked. He ushered me into the foyer, and took off, "to see if I can locate Mister Robert."

The chandelier reminded me of *Phantom of the Opera*. I inched away from a direct hit if it should fall and looked around. The foyer had to be as large as our co-op and, even to my untrained eye, loaded with unique antiques which, if sold, would feed the Balkans for decades. Then the artwork could take care of Central America. So much beauty left me breathless and seriously pondering the benefits of socialism. When the revolution came, I'd like the Van Gogh hanging near the sweeping center staircase.

Judiciously mixed with the grand masters' originals, inlaid mahogany armoires, and Chinese curio cabinets was Delft. Dozens of blue and white vases, bowls, and plaques were promiscuously prominent wherever my eyes roamed. I wondered if the daggers had a place of honor all their own.

"Mr. Stern will see you in the morning room," the butler beckoned. The morning room. Shades of *Rebecca*. And didn't these people know it was three thirty in the afternoon?

Stern was stoking a lazy fire as I walked through the off-white enameled French doors. The room's decor ran a palette of neutrals from whole milk to eggshell to crème caramel. The perfect backdrop for all that Delft. The furniture was shabby chic. Grandma's front porch, liberally infused with Dutch Colonial. I loved it. "Jake, how nice to see you." Stern's smile managed to be warm while his eyes remained puzzled. "I trust you haven't reached an impasse on your first column." Did I hear an employer's rebuke behind the fatherly sounding concern?

"Oh no, Mr. Stern. Jennifer's copyediting that at home this weekend. You'll have it on your desk Monday morning."

"Well, that's fine. Good work. But then to what do I owe the...er, unexpected pleasure of your company?" Not for the first time, I wondered just how old this guy was. He always sounded so Victorian, and this afternoon, dressed in a narrow, wine velvet jacket, he looked like Edwin Drood or Nicholas Nickleby. I'd have to ask Gypsy Rose if Stern had been around during a previous incarnation in the England of Charles Dickens. Jeez. Had I become as weird as Mom and Gypsy Rose?

"Yes. Why I'm here. First, forgive me for intruding..."

Stern made a sweeping gesture with his right hand, almost landing on my left shoulder. "Please, that's just nonsense, Jake. You could never intrude. Now what can I do for you?"

"It seems I'm on the police's shortlist of suspects—well, I guess it's a long shortlist..."

"But why? You didn't even know Dick Peter before Tuesday. Did you?"

"No. However, I did wind up with his job at *Manhattan*, and the chance to complete...to edit, that is, his manuscript. Motives, you see. Listen, Mr. Stern, I'd like to find out who killed Dick and Allison and I think you might be able to help me."

"There's nothing I can tell you. I've shared what little information I have with the police. It may be small comfort, but I'm on their list too. Incidentally, did you find anything, any clues, that is, in Dick's notes for the book?"

Who was asking the questions here? And how did he know about the files? "No, I haven't had time to read through them all yet. Do you think there will be clues somewhere?"

Stern shrugged and started poking around the logs again. "Would you like a drink? Coffee or tea?"

"No thanks. Mr. Stern, I know you were working in your office—until nine or so—on the night of Dick's murder, but that you saw nothing. Heard nothing. Are you sure? If he had a visitor, would you have heard him or her? Did you go downstairs to use the copier, for example, or maybe you went to the fourth floor for coffee or..."

Robert Stern wagged his right index finger at me. "I was alone in my office that night, working. Late, as I often do. Then I went directly home. I never saw Dick Peter or his killer, and if one of my Delft daggers was the weapon, I wasn't the one who wielded it. For the record, Jake, I was also at work—as you were—on the morning of Allison's murder. I didn't see or hear anything then either."

That wagging finger convinced me that he was lying; he

knew something. But before I could form another question, the French doors opened and Barbara Ferris, out of uniform and into black satin, swept in.

Eighteen

After an abrupt, awkward farewell to Stern and Ferris, I collapsed on a bench in front of Central Park, watching the tourists and local photography buffs entering and exiting museums. Barbara Ferris and Robert Stern? Totally wild. Isaac Walton was next up on my afternoon's agenda. But I just sat, letting the fading sun warm my face and wishing my mind would go blank. A bold pigeon plopped down next to me and used his spot on the bench as a john. A sure sign it was time to move on.

Tonight would be the big finale for the Pledged-For-Lifers. Their last hurrah would be covered on the news and Madison Square Garden would be filled to the rafters. I'd need to catch Isaac Walton before show time, and I'd read that the old-time revival meeting—featuring religious rock music—was scheduled to start at seven thirty. Where was Isaac now? What hotel was he staying at? If I ever knew, I'd forgotten. Christian would know. The irony of one murder suspect calling another to check out a third was not lost on me as I pulled out my cellphone and looked him up. Holmes lived on the West Side and, thank God, he was listed. His voicemail picked up. His recording informed me that he could be reached at a very familiar phone number: Gypsy Rose Liebowitz's bookstore. I decided to just head over there, drop in, and browse. After all, I was in the neighborhood. The pigeon and I vacated our shared place in the sun.

My mother and Gypsy Rose had turned the New Age bookstore into an eerily attractive set design: *Children of the Corn* visit *The Wizard of Oz.* Hey, maybe Mr. Kim's seven pumpkin heads could be recast as disembodied Munchkins. Too perfect. I'd mention it to Mom. The store's two part-time sorceresses who doubled as salesclerks were draping cobwebs over a coffin in the corner, but there was no sign of either my mother or Gypsy Rose. Customers were getting into the spirit of things. The tearoom was packed. Cafe Diablo, Gypsy Rose's homemade devil's food cake, and a witch's brew, served with a cinnamon stick in the shape of a broom, were the hot items. And the lines, snaking around the tombstone where the book section's cash register was now precariously perched, were long. Aaron Rubin, of all people, was busy ringing up sales.

I called to him, trying to out-shout the chatty crowd. "Where're Mom and Gypsy Rose?"

He spotted me, and without the slightest pause in counting money, checking credit cards, and having the customers sign on the dotted line, yelled, "They're upstairs in the office, working with the witches. I'm in charge here." The former district attorney for the City of New York was obviously loving his new job.

Climbing the wonderful old wooden staircase to Gypsy Rose's third-floor office, I found myself chuckling. It was no wonder I was nuts. It was in my genes. In my Irish bones. However, a man as rational and normal as Aaron Rubin must have caught this craziness like you would the flu or—more likely—the love bug.

Before I reached the second-floor landing, I could hear the screaming. A strident woman's voice, filled with venom: "If we can't have a four-foot cauldron and the live snakes, the deal's off. Just what kind of a witch do you think I am?"

"A very unreasonable one. We have a contract here." The usually unflappable Gypsy Rose sounded angry.

"You can take that contract and shove it up your crystal ball. We're outta here. And our entire coven will boycott your Halloween Happening. Come on, Lucretia." A door opened, then slammed. I jumped to one side of the narrow step as two large ladies, looking more like Merlin than Samantha on the reruns of *Bewitched,* came flying down the stairs. Jeez. Mom and Gypsy Rose were having problems with the hired help. I really didn't want to get involved. All I wanted was an address from Christian.

I found him sitting next to my mother; Gypsy Rose, looking forlorn, was behind her desk. "Hi, guys," I said. "What's the problem?" Now why did I say that? I asked myself. I already knew the answer. I'm crazy.

Ten minutes later, we'd solved Gypsy Rose's labor strike. I volunteered Modesty, Jane, and me to be witches du soir on Monday. And since I figured Too-Tall Tom must have firsthand knowledge of what it was like to be a warlock—having dated one—I volunteered him too. Now all I had to do was sell this solution to the ghostwriters.

My mother beamed. "I'm so proud of you, Jake. What a great idea. Now listen, darling, why don't you come to dinner with us tonight? Gypsy Rose and Christian are joining me and Aaron when we finish here."

"Sorry, Mom, I'm meeting the ghostwriters. I left a note for you at home." Humph—and I was worried she'd be alone. No doubt about it, my mother had a far better social life than her darling daughter.

"You see, Maura," Gypsy Rose smiled, "Jake's not running around poking her nose into murder, she's planning a nice evening with her friends. So we don't have to worry." I felt grateful that Gypsy Rose's psychic powers seemed to have taken the afternoon off.

I turned to Christian. "Is Isaac Walton staying at the Marriott Marquis? One of my friends thought she saw him there."

"No. Sally Lou would have loved the glitz, but Walton knows the Marquis wouldn't be the right image for a country preacher. As a matter of fact, he's right across the street at the Wales. Says their bed-and-breakfast style makes him feel at home."

As I danced down the stairs, I heard Gypsy Rose say, "Christian, as we were discussing before those wicked witches interrupted us, I want you to know that you were very brave when you faced the guillotine."

Nineteen

The Wales stands on the east side of Madison Avenue, midway between Gypsy Rose's townhouse and our co-op. It's a small hotel that may be the best bed and breakfast in New York City. Europeans as well as Carnegie Hill's Museum Row tourists from across America fill its rooms. The century-old building had a face-lift some years ago and looked great. Its eclectic facade, featuring stone balconies, round, arched windows on the top floor, and decorated escutcheons above the middle stories' windows make for an intriguing architectural hodgepodge. In the tiny but elegantly refurbished lobby, there's a salute to Puss in Boots. And the decor in the grand salon on the second floor, filled with potted palms, geraniums on the sills of lace-curtained windows and Victorian settees, continues the theme; the walls are covered with paintings by some of the finest turn-of-the-century children's artists. Elegant old New York. Edith Wharton would have approved. An oak sideboard provides a great breakfast and every afternoon, tea and cookies are offered, together with harp music at five. That's where I found Isaac and Sally Lou, dressed in matching powder blue jogging suits—I hoped to God they'd be changing before the revival meeting—and sipping tea, just as the first selection began.

When the desk clerk had told me that the Waltons weren't in their room, I figured they might be catching a little culture at the afternoon concert. Now I'd have to wait 'til the performance was over to talk to them. I grabbed an empty chair in the back of the salon, closed my eyes, and let the beauty of "Clair de Lune" sweep over me.

The Waltons were coolly cordial when I interrupted their mad applause for the lady harpist. "Jake O'Hara, isn't it?" the reverend asked, mustering a wan smile. "What can we do for you? I'm afraid our time is very limited; we have the Pledged-For-Lifers closing tonight, you know."

Sally Lou seemed excited, but not over seeing me again. "I'm wearing a new chiffon gown covered in velvet angels. All white. Isaac says it's heavenly."

"I'm sure it is." I tried to sound sincere. "Look, I've come to take a few more shots for the *Manhattan* article." I pulled the just-purchased disposable camera from my bag with the panache of a professional photographer. "Maybe I could take a few of you in that heavenly outfit, Mrs. Walton. This Pied Piper Room would be the perfect backdrop."

"Oh, my, what do you think, Isaac? Could we squeeze that in?"

Isaac was nothing if not pragmatic. He knew we had him two to one. "If you really want to, Mother, I guess we could, but only if we move this along as fast as possible."

"I'll come up to the room with you guys. That way I can ask you a couple of questions, Reverend Walton, while Mrs. Walton's getting ready." Despite my calculated charm, Isaac looked suspicious. But by then, we'd arrived at the tiny elevator and I just stepped in behind them.

The suite, though small, was grand. Mahogany French doors separated the living room—still graced with its original fireplace—from the bedroom, the windows stretched from floor to ceiling, and those ceilings had to be twelve feet high. The wallpaper was William Morris, reminding me of the pattern on the walls of *Manhattan*, and all the desk, chairs, and settees were either Victorian pieces or damn good copies.

Sally Lou gave me an opening. As she applied neon green eyeshadow, she started out discussing the great breakfast at the Wales. "Fresh peach preserves from Sarabeth's Kitchen, Jake, and I couldn't have made them any better myself. All included in the price of our room. With plenty of food left over to have a free lunch too." She proudly pulled open a dresser drawer filled with bananas, muffins, pound cake, and soft boiled eggs, all neatly secured in sandwich bags—enough to feed a family of five. Then she segued to Dick Peter's final journey. "Well, for sure that wicked man was met and welcomed personally by Satan at the gates of Hell. Now all he's smelling is fire and brimstone. I believe that our punishment fits our sins, so Dick will be shoveling coal throughout eternity."

I wondered if—based on Sally Lou's theory—the opposite also applied. Then, when Isaac arrived in Heaven, he'd be assigned an Ivy League dorm room instead of a cloud.

While Isaac changed into his preacher suit, I offered to help Sally Lou tease the back of her sparse hair. "Oh, that's looking much better, Jake. Now, if you'd just fluff out the sides. Kinda like an angel's wings." She held her plump arms straight out, fluttering her hands in demonstration. "You know I once worked as a beauty consultant."

"Really?" Good thing I wasn't playing *What's My Line?*.

"Yes indeed. I sold cosmetics at Walgreens. That's how I met Isaac; he bought a large bottle of Old Spice." Sally Lou actually tittered. "I knew then that he wasn't married or keeping company, so I flirted a little."

"How did you know that?"

"Jake, married men, or even those steady dating, don't buy their own cologne. The ladies in their lives shop for them and select much more—hmm—sexy scents than Old Spice. Now I make sure that Isaac only uses Polo." She tittered again "Even for a man of God, it can't hurt to smell rich."

Isaac Walton emerged from the bathroom swathed in head-to-toe white silk. The collarless jacket was accessorized with a heavy chain holding a gold cross that could have topped a small church. His flared trousers draped over white suede loafers. And he smelled like a man about to rake in a pile of money when he passed around the collection basket. With some help from her new lady's maid, Sally Lou got into her chiffon and velvet creation, and we went back to the second-floor salon—at least the background would be attractive—to shoot the pictures. I prayed we wouldn't run into anyone.

I posed them at Mom's favorite table. We recommend the Wales to all our out-of-town friends and often join them in the salon for the concerts. The far corner table looks out on our building, and even in the fading twilight, the old white five-story stone house, with its bay windows and turrets, made me smile. As the Waltons said "cheese," I started asking questions.

"It's quite a coincidence that my editorial assistant, Jennifer Moran's, husband is so active in the Pledged-For-Lifers movement, isn't it, Reverend Walton?"

"Yes. Michael's been an active cell member for about three or four months, I'd say. He's done wonderful work for the ministry, recruiting several other bikers and distributing our pamphlets door to door. But I'd never met him and, of course, had no idea that Michael was in any way connected to the magazine where my cousin worked until after Dick had been murdered."

Of course.

"So how did you found out?"

"Let's see. Well, it seems to me that Michael may have stopped by to pay a condolence call right after the news broke on Friday morning...and he'd discovered Dick Peter was my cousin. Ah, yes. I believe that's when he mentioned that his wife worked for Dick."

It seemed to be such an unnecessary lie. Or was it Michael who'd lied? Could he really have been visiting his girlfriend? I probed further. "Well, Jennifer thinks Michael had spoken with you earlier—at the preconference social on Thursday, right before your opening service. You'll recall Christian Holmes and I met with you directly after the prayer meeting."

Sally Lou jumped in, "There were dozens of delegates at the social, cell leaders from across the country—the reverend can't possibly remember meeting all of them. Maybe Michael did speak to Isaac at that gathering."

I nodded and let it go, having other fish to fry with Isaac Walton.

The reverend, surprising me, lighted the fire. "Jake, I assume you've heard I visited Dick's office the night he was killed. Do you really think I'm capable of killing both my cousin and that gossip monger, Allison Carr? As you know, I was at *Manhattan* that morning too."

Admiring his directness, I answered honestly. "I don't know who the killer is, but I'm trying to find out. The police have no doubt grilled you on all this, so please indulge me. When you left Dick's office Tuesday night, did you see or hear anyone else?"

"No. I told Detective Rubin all I'd noticed was a light in an office—its door was ajar—as I passed by, heading for the elevator. I later learned it was Allison Carr's office. She'd worked late that night."

"And what timeframe are we looking at here?" I asked.

"About nine thirty. I can't be certain, I was too upset."

"Things hadn't gone well with Dick?"

"Sally Lou urged reconciliation. We were kin. As a man of God, I decided to try. But Dick behaved like the devil himself. Gloated over his Yale education, taunted me about my lack of same, mocking my correspondence-school theology degree, and made lewd remarks about Sally Lou's...er, large bosom. The deviant even suggested group sex. I wanted to kill...not literally, but you can imagine how I felt."

"So, you..."

"There was one more thing. I mentioned it to the police. While he was berating me, Dick kept checking his watch as if he were expecting someone. I finally just gave up and came back to the Wales and Mother." Isaac smiled at his wife.

"He arrived before ten," Sally Lou said. "And I'm sure about that, because I was reapplying my makeup, getting ready to go down to the dessert table, and that starts at ten."

I couldn't give it up. "So, Reverend Walton, you didn't see, hear, taste, touch, or smell any—"

"Hey, wait a second. You're on to something there, Jake."

"Where?" I couldn't even guess.

"An aroma. There was this...perfume or heavy cologne, first in the hall, as I passed the ladies' room, then lingering in the elevator as I rode down. A smell like—forgive my vulgarity, Mother and Jake, but I don't know how else to describe it—a smell like a bitch in heat."

Twenty

Time was running out. I had to meet the ghostwriters at eight, and it was now almost seven thirty; however, I stopped at home to check my messages, try to contact Mila Macovich, and put on fresh lipstick. Overseeing Sally Lou's toilette may have inspired me. More than a little late for their revival meeting under the big tent that usually houses the circus at Madison Square Garden, the Waltons had hailed a cab from in front of the Wales about fifteen minutes ago.

Mila's voicemail informed me that she was at her country house in New Jersey's horse country but would be home late Sunday morning. I appreciated, while being puzzled by, people who shared their daily itineraries on their recorded messages. Did they hate to miss a call, or were they showing off what busy, wonderful lives they were out about and enjoying, while the caller had nothing better to do than listen to their voicemail?

Still no word from Ben. Just how busy—and how angry—could he be? Well, I could be bigger than that. I dialed first his office, then his house, and left two identical messages: "Please call." Then I sent him an email.

There was a long report from Too-Tall Tom: "Jake, I've managed to set up a cocktail date with Barry DeWitt." Too-Tall Tom sounded proud of himself, as well he should. "Turns out an old buddy of mine is also an old friend of DeWitt's. He's the one who made the arrangements, but when we get to the Kit Kat Club, my pal will remember another engagement, leaving me alone to question DeWitt. So, being down in Chelsea and all, if I'm a tad late for our dinner at Grazie, I wanted you to know that I'm on the case. I also have news regarding Michael Moran, but I'll save that for des—" The recording cut off, as it almost always did when Too-Tall Tom left a message.

Jane and Modesty were sitting at a round table in the back room drinking Chardonnay and munching on Italian bread when I arrived at Grazie at 8:10. "Let's order before we get into the results of our investigations," Modesty said by way of greeting. "I'm starving and so is Jane."

"Oh, Jake, I've had quite a day. Being a detective certainly beats researching those boring self-help books." Jane glowed. The thrill of the hunt or the vigor of the vino?

"Okay," I said, picking up a menu. "Too-Tall Tom's interviewing Barry DeWitt and might be a while."

The next few minutes were devoted to a serious discussion of food. Jane and I chose the pollo caprese—grilled chicken breast with artichokes and marinated tomatoes. Modesty, a vacillating vegetarian, ordered gnocchi—potato dumplings with tomato sauce and fresh mozzarella. "I think they may use animal fat in the preparation of those dumplings," Jane said.

"No way," I said, as if I knew what I was talking about, before Modesty could verbally abuse Jane or interrogate the chef. "I eat here all the time with Mom and Gypsy Rose.

Gnocchi's a veggie dish, safe for purists." And Modesty bought it, either because she chose to believe me or she really wanted those dumplings.

Over salad, we agreed to let Jane go first. "But try to wind it up before the main course arrives," Modesty told her.

"I crashed an AA meeting," Jane began, and I knew her saga wouldn't be finished 'til dessert. But it was a great opening line, one that grabbed Modesty's attention. No wonder Jane was in such demand as a ghostwriter. "When we left Sarabeth's I realized I'd misplaced my sunglasses. You know, the Ralph Lauren wraparounds—three hundred and forty-six dollars, for heaven's sake. I backtracked. They weren't at the restaurant, and I knew I'd been wearing them when I left my apartment this morning for our Ghostwriters Anonymous meeting. I deduced that my glasses could only be at the Jan Hus church."

"Wow," Modesty said. "A regular Perry Mason."

Jane ignored her. "However, when I arrived, the three o'clock AA meeting was just starting, so I couldn't search the room. I figured recovery's recovery—I didn't know then that it was a closed meeting—and took a seat. My God, the alcoholics' qualifications are ever so much more exciting than our fellow ghostwriters' are."

"Just think what vicarious thrills you could have enjoyed if you'd crashed a Sex Addicts group," Modesty said. "Well, maybe next week."

"Modesty, let Jane finish," I said.

"The lead speaker was Steve, and the man chairing the meeting, who introduced Steve, was his sponsor, Hans F. By now, I knew this was a closed meeting, and only for recovering alcoholics, but I also knew this was no coincidence. God meant me to hear these two guys share, and no way was I leaving."

"Jesus," I said. "What did they have to say?"

"Hans introduced Steve, describing his suffering in terms one might associate with Mother Teresa—or maybe sainted martyred virgins. I'm telling you, some of these recovering drunks make Serial Sue seem serene." Jane took a sip of her wine. "Turns out Hans Foote had twelve-stepped Steve into the program. Your elevator operator's last drink had been at that *Manhattan* Christmas party Glory told you about, Jake. And Steve's sexual encounter with Peter and Flagg during their post-party sadomasochistic ménage à trois shocked him into sobriety. He cried when telling us how Dick had used the tree ornaments. Shaken and hungover, he'd approached Hans, who'd been a member of AA for years. After sharing his experience, strength, and hope with Steve, Hans brought him to his first meeting."

The main course arrived. Jane opted to keep her salad, which she'd hardly touched. We all had a taste or two of our meals and Jane continued, "When Steve spoke, I felt his pain."

Modesty groaned. "You would."

"No, Modesty, you just listen to this. The bottom line of Steve's current crisis centers on the need to protect both his own as well as other fellow recovering alcoholics' anonymity. Even a miserable ghostwriter like you can relate to that." I'd never heard Jane scold Modesty like that, and I rather enjoyed it. "Hans and Steve attended an AA marathon meeting on the night of Dick Peter's death. It went on to the wee hours of the morning; then they and several other AA members went to an all-night diner." Jane's voice had taken on a dramatic tone. "If they tell the police where they were that night, they'd each break not only their own anonymity, but that of the rest of the group, who'd have to confirm their alibis."

"Holy God," I said.

"Like the seal of the confessional," Modesty said, as she nervously twirled her rosary beads.

"And now," Jane sighed, "we're faced with a real problem. As good ghostwriters who respect anonymity and deal with it on a daily basis, dare we disregard another's? I shouldn't even be sharing this with you, but I didn't know what else to do. I do know this: Steve and Hans may still be considered suspects by the police, but they're off our list."

Stunned, we took a dinner break.

With no answers to Jane's questions regarding our two former suspects' anonymity, we decided to move on to Modesty's investigations before ordering dessert. And we were all wondering what had happened to Too-Tall Tom.

"I simply called Glory Flagg and invited myself over to discuss how to reinforce energy at the fifth chakra. Poor management of a chakra can cause an energy leakage. Glory was surprisingly receptive—grateful for the growth opportunity. She knows that by practicing self-control or empowering others, you can rebuild your fifth chakra's energy level. But that's easier said than done, you know." Jane and I stared at each blankly.

"Modesty, I don't have a clue what you're talking about," I said, "but, hey, if it got you in the door, congratulations."

"You two should study the energetics of healing before it's too late. Now I have several tapes by Caroline—"

"Please, Modesty, save that for another time. What did Glory tell you?"

"I'm trying to tell you. This is all tied in with moving Glory out of her existence in an energetically stuck place. In addition to exercising self-control and empowering others, one has to speak honestly to generate energy at the fifth chakra." Jane rolled her eyes but said nothing. Modesty gulped a large mouthful of her wine and rattled on, "So, if telling the truth can prevent illness, feeling inferior, and having your love life off center..."

I was losing patience here. "Damn it, Modesty, what did Glory say?"

"Well, after I advised her that the truth could set her free, she said she'd spent the night of her ex-husband's murder with Keith Morrison."

"What?" Jane and I shouted together, bringing the waiter over to inquire if anything was wrong.

Modesty smirked. "And that's not all. As I was leaving Glory's apartment—incidentally, she lives on First Avenue, right across the street from the United Nations. Great building. Bobby Kennedy kept an apartment there when he was the senator from New York. Lots of windows, facing all those flags and the river. Being Dick Peter's ex-wife and a part-time stripper must be a lucrative position to be..."

Jesus H. Christ. Do all writers tell a tale as if they're plotting their next chapter? Or was Modesty just trying to drive me crazy? "Get back to Morrison. What about him? Did you question him?"

"Philip Marlowe couldn't have done it better." Modesty poured the last of the wine into her glass. I guess Perry Mason wasn't a cool enough role model for Modesty.

Jane stopped our waiter and ordered another bottle. It looked like we were in for a long evening. Where was Too-Tall Tom?

"So, Modesty," Jane was saying, "did you just march up to Morrison and ask him 'where were you while Dick was being stabbed?'"

"Yes, as a matter of fact, I did. I told him I'd been hired—I didn't mention at no pay—to clear a colleague. He asked who. I said Jake O'Hara. And he said he'd do anything he could to help that pretty little lady. Barf. Barf."

Even though I'd told Stern that I was a suspect, I wrestled

with annoyance at Modesty's blabbermouth and admiration for her boldness. "And?"

"Count Morrison out. He confirmed that he and Glory Flagg spent the night of Dick's murder together...'til five in the morning. Get this: 'discussing a business project.' Morrison says he suffers from insomnia and often pulls an all-nighter. Jake, did you know that Keith Morrison had spent the night before you'd discovered Allison Carr's body with Dennis Kim? So it seems Morrison has an alibi for most of that murder's window of opportunity as well. And he wasn't among the crowd of possible killers who were on the scene that morning, was he?"

"No. But..." Feeling petulant and asking myself why, I said, "That doesn't mean he didn't do it. Morrison and Glory Flagg could be in this together. Alibiing each other. And just because I didn't see either of them at *Manhattan* on the morning of Allison's murder doesn't mean one of them couldn't have been there."

"What's wrong with you, Jake? I thought we were trying to eliminate suspects here." Modesty drained her glass and poured herself a fresh drink from the second bottle. I reached across the table and did the same.

Jane said, "Of course, Modesty, you've done a fine job. Jake may be a tad too close to all this."

I glared at her. "What the hell is that supposed to mean?"

"Good evening, ladies." Too-Tall Tom—as agile as Ray Bolger's Scarecrow—folded his frame into the empty chair next to Modesty. "I do believe I've found the killer."

Twenty-One

"Here's my theory on how these murders happened," Too-Tall Tom was explaining, as he waved away Modesty's offer of wine. "I've been nursing the mother of all martinis—two, in fact—for the past hour and a half while DeWitt was downing double Dewars. Fortunately, my legs are as long as Tommy Tune's and hollow to boot. But there's no doubt, Barry's our boy." He paused, stopped our waiter, then ordered a Pellegrino and the poached salmon, asking for a plate of penne pomodoro on the side. We ghostwriters were used to Too-Tall Tom's habit of eating two dinners at once. It wreaked havoc when it came time to divide the bill.

"Go on," Jane said, as soon as the waiter left.

"First, all the information in the 'D' file turns out to be true. He often was the second man in a Glory Flagg-Dick Peter trio, and DeWitt—the famed ladies' man—is bisexual. Jake was right to suspect him; Barry had motives galore. And the scene in the bookstore, where Modesty overheard that Barbara Ferris woman accusing DeWitt of killing Allison Carr, makes perfect sense. I'm sure he did stab her."

"What?" Modesty asked. "Did Barry just empty out his soul, upchuck his guilt, then vomit his motive, means, and opportunity into your face? I know you're charisma incarnate, dear boy, but..."

"Well," Too-Tall Tom said, brushing his long, sandy-colored bangs out of his eyes, "actually, Barry did seem to take an interest in me and chat away quite freely; however, most of my deduction comes from cerebral detective work. Very much in the order of Sherlock Holmes, don't you know?"

"Would that be why you suddenly sound like a castrated Ringo Starr?" Modesty demanded.

Before things really got ugly, I said, "Let's just order our desserts. That will give us all something to do while Too-Tall Tom eats his dinners, then we can kick back with a decaf cappuccino or espresso and listen to what he has to say." And—to my surprise—that's exactly what we did. Even Modesty.

Sipping his Pellegrino, having wolfed down his food in decathlon time, Too-Tall Tom had caught up to us, ordering hot apple pie with gelato and continuing his theory. "You ladies all know that people tend to tell me secrets. I don't ask; they just tell." This was true. There was an aura about Too-Tall Tom that encouraged confidences. "I think Barry DeWitt needed a friend. Or, in my case—a friend of a friend. After his second scotch, DeWitt told me that he found me attractive and asked what I was doing later tonight. After the third, he groused he was sick of being a society stud and whispered into my ear that I was really his type. Said he had to keep his gay affairs quiet, so he trusted I'd be discreet."

We all giggled. Despite that aura, Too-Tall Tom sometimes gossiped as much as Mom.

"After the fourth double, Barry literally cried. Toxic tears of hate. He said he was glad Dick Peter was dead. Unlike Glory

Flagg's autobiographical book, where she doesn't name DeWitt, Peter's novel would out the fictional—yet totally recognizable—DeWitt character's bisexuality and his frequent participation in those tawdry trios. After the fifth double, he was slurring that Allison Carr—Barry referred to her as Robert Stern's lapdog—believed that he'd killed Dick, but now she was dead too. Then he laughed like a demon. Remember I once dated a warlock; I know these things."

I became distracted for a moment, thinking about my rash promise to deliver the ghostwriters as witches for Gypsy Rose's Halloween Happening. Then Too-Tall Tom was winding down. "And, of course, he has no alibi for either murder. As you're all well aware, Barry was at *Manhattan* on the morning of Allison's death and he just shrugged, then chortled when, after he ordered his sixth drink, I'd asked where he was during the timeframe for Dick's. Elementary, my dear ladies."

The ghostwriters concluded that Barry DeWitt acted and sounded like a killer—albeit a crazy one—but that we couldn't take our case to court, or even to Homicide...yet. Too-Tall Tom agreed to stay on DeWitt's trail. "I'm worried about you, Jake. You're ghostwriting Dick Peter's book and DeWitt doesn't want that mystery published. You could be in danger."

As we split the bill—Modesty always did the math—we made plans for Sunday. And I still hadn't shared the results of my day's investigations. Jane wanted to check out Barbara Ferris. She'd stopped by her apartment building on 84th Street, off Lex—"Pretty snazzy for a receptionist"—but the doorman told Jane that Barbara had left Friday evening carrying an overnight bag. Telling the ghostwriters about running into Barbara at Robert Stern's, I wondered aloud if her bag had held a black satin dress.

"Maybe this woman had taken over Allison Carr's job as

Stern's chief comforter. Didn't you say Barbara Ferris seemed overprotective of him, Jake?" Too-Tall Tom asked.

"Yes," I said, scribbling down Stern's address for Jane. "Stern's lying about something, that's for sure. I guess he could be covering for Ferris. But...Jane, I have a suggestion. When you find Barbara, ask about her knowledge of the Allison Carr-Barry DeWitt connection. Why had DeWitt been warning Allison to lay off? What sordid secret did the gossip columnist know that would have threatened our nasty theater critic? And when did she know it?"

"Don't worry, Jake, I want to clear my third suspect too," Jane said. "I'll find Barbara first thing in the morning." Good God, were the ghostwriters assuming all the other suspects were innocent just because Too-Tall Tom had decided that Barry DeWitt was our killer?

Modesty must have read my mind. "I'm sure we've cleared Santa Steve, Hans Foote and, Jake's reservations notwithstanding, probably Keith Morrison and Glory Flagg. Jake may have a point though. They could be covering for each other. But remember, it ain't over 'til it's bound and in print. We don't even have the galley proofs yet. As for me, I'm going to have breakfast with Jennifer and Michael in the morning."

"How did you manage that coup?" I asked.

"Rang them up, Michael answered. He was dashing off to the Garden for that Pledged-For-Lifers bull session. I told him I was doing a freelance story on the movement. First time that biker's ever been civil to me; he usually just grunts and hands the phone to Jennifer. But tomorrow, I'm invited over for eggs Benedict. They're his specialty."

"Lying is yours, Modesty," Jane said.

"Thank you." Modesty almost smiled. "I am rather good at it, aren't I?"

"Michael Moran is mine," Too-Tall Tom complained. "That's not playing fair, Modesty. I couldn't see him today, what with that prayer thing at the Garden—he'd been down there setting up this afternoon—and my spending all that time lining up a date with DeWitt. I never even got to check out Christian Holmes. Now you'll talk to Michael before I do. Jennifer's your suspect, not Michael."

"They live together, for God's sake," Modesty said. "It just worked out."

"Then I'm going with you. I found out something very intriguing about Michael today. While you're 'interviewing' him, I'll have a word with Jennifer."

"Like hell." Modesty shook Too-Tall Tom's arm. "Tell him, Jake. I'm assigned to track Jennifer."

Jesus. I felt like King Solomon, about to suggest splitting that biblical baby in half. "Well, what did you hear regarding Michael?" I asked Too-Tall Tom, hoping his answer would inspire me.

"That he's having a hot affair—positively torrid—with some rich, older broad."

"Are you sure?"

"My darling girl, I heard it straight from a scorned biker babe's mouth. She rode with Michael, and she used to, er, pump the pedal with him. You can take this to the sperm bank. I'd bet my lifetime allotment of Viagra on it."

Before I could respond, Modesty said, "Okay, Too-Tall Tom, you're on as my breakfast date; we'll roleplay good cop/bad cop with both of them." I didn't have to ask which one would be cast as the bad cop.

When I finally gave my report, it sounded anticlimactic, even to me. I now felt fairly certain that Reverend Walton, weird as he was, hadn't murdered either his cousin Dick or Allison, but

I tried to present all the facts as Sally Lou and Isaac had related them to me—including the new information, a lingering scent of a mystery woman—without bias or editorial comment. Not easy for a ghostwriter.

"So, are you telling us that the good reverend didn't kill his cousin or Allison Carr?" Modesty asked.

"Could be," I said. "If he really left *Manhattan* at nine thirty and arrived back at the Wales Hotel by ten on the night Dick died, he didn't do it. Remember, the medical examiner says Dick was stabbed between ten p.m. and two a.m. I'm going to stop at the Wales before I go home tonight. Maybe someone, in addition to Sally Lou, can confirm Isaac's alibi."

"Jake," Too-Tall Tom said, "I'm sure the police have already investigated that."

"Yeah. And if Ben ever calls me again, I plan to ask him, but for now, we're on our own here."

Modesty collected our cash and stood. "I'm history." Her slang always seemed a decade off the mark. "Who's walking uptown?"

"Me," I said. "Just one more thing, actually two. First, Christian Holmes was over at Gypsy Rose's this afternoon, helping with the arrangements for the Halloween Happening. If you want his number, Too-Tall Tom, I have it. He's smitten with our Gypsy Rose, so if you don't reach him at home in the morning, try the bookstore."

"What else, Jake?" Jane yawned. "Excuse me, I'm bushed."

"Well...er...that is—" I began, as Modesty frowned. "Look, guys, Mom and Gypsy Rose have a big labor problem." I turned to Too-Tall Tom. "Those witches you helped hire quit cold, and Halloween's the day after tomorrow...and..."

"And what trick have you planned for us?" Modesty shouted, shoving the money in the startled waiter's palm.

"Since we'll all be there anyway, I told them we'd serve as their witches and warlock. You know, the double, double, toil, and trouble bit. Think about how good Mom and Gypsy Rose have been to us ghostwriters. And it's Halloween, for heaven's sake. Our holiday. If you'll do it, I'll treat for the costumes."

"Look, enough already," Too-Tall Tom said. "I'm coming to the séance on All Soul's Day; I want to go to the Halloween parade in the Village. It's tradition." He wiped his forehead, though it wasn't hot. "I have my outfit all ready. I've had six fittings and paid over two hundred dollars for it. Not to mention the wig. And the horse. Now you're asking me to toss my costume and my plans aside and dress up as some boring warlock at a Carnegie Hill party. Not only would that bring back unpleasant memories of the warlock I once loved, but you uptown people don't have any idea of how to celebrate Halloween."

"Who are you going as?" Jane asked.

"Lady Godiva. And I look great." Too-Tall Tom colored becomingly.

"There you go," I said, wondering how it could cost more than two hundred dollars to ride naked. The wig should cover everything. But Lord only knows how expensive that hair must been; there was a lot of Too-Tall Tom. I tried another tack. "Godiva's timeless. Pack the wig and whatever away for next year. Please, Too-Tall Tom. This year, Gypsy Rose, Mom, and I need you in our coven."

Twenty-Two

In the end, Too-Tall Tom agreed, citing his longstanding friendship with Gypsy Rose, Mom, and her devious daughter, then quoted Walt Whitman; "You call me inconsistent. You are correct. I am very large, I can contain all those contradictions." His acquiescence, however reluctant, shamed Jane and Modesty into helping too. Down deep, they were all great ghostwriters.

On our way home, with Modesty chattering on and on about her Gothic saga's neglected edits, we passed by a woman whose scent sent me reeling. I'd smelled it before, recently—sweaty, smutty, sexual but not sexy. And then, in a movie-image-of-the-mind moment, I saw a swirl of black satin and recalled its accompanying aroma. Oh my God—Barbara Ferris, wearing the perfume Isaac had described, doused with the odor of overripe passion, not her usual clean Ivory Soap, dressed-in-uniform smell.

I didn't answer Modesty's goodbye, as she hung a right on 86th Street. Desperate, I tried to hail a cab—but this was Saturday night—then stepped up my pace, almost jogging. The Wales would have to wait. I had to get to Robert Stern's. At the corner of 90th and Madison, while waiting for the light to change, I pulled out my cellphone and called Ben. No luck. Had I really expected him to be there? I left a message at the precinct and then another at his home, telling him to meet me at Stern's. I would have called 911, but what would I report? A suspicious smell?

We'd closed Grazie, and it was now almost eleven o'clock. Even from across Madison Avenue, I could see Mr. Kim's painted pumpkins were covered in heavy plastic, protecting them from the elements. A steady, chilling rain had begun to fall, but I didn't want to waste any time stopping at the apartment for an umbrella. I turned my blazer's collar up, grateful that I'd worn wool, tied my silk scarf babushka style, then jammed cold hands into my pockets, and ran faster. Ninety-third Street could have been Death Valley. Madison Avenue, as usual, had been full of life, and dead ahead, I could see the traffic drifting down Fifth, but Stern's block was so quiet, I could hear the rustle of the falling leaves. Did the very rich go to bed much earlier than most of us ordinary folks did on a Saturday night?

The house seemed to be in total darkness, so as I climbed the stoop's steps, I didn't notice that the front door was ajar. Odd. Should I just go in? Wouldn't Nancy Drew, no matter how foolish that might be? The answer to both questions was yes. I walked into that enormous foyer, calling, "Mr. Stern?" It came out in a raspy whisper. Then echoed vibrantly. Okay, now what? There were several doors exiting the foyer on either side of the center staircase. Would I remember which one led to the morning room? And, if I did, would Stern still be sitting in the dark in his morning room at this hour of the night? Well, he might be, if he were dead. I did know that the butler had led me to a door on the left. Where was Jeeves anyway? Working by Braille and the dim light of a street lamp shining weakly through the half-opened front door, I entered the first door on the left at the foot of the stairwell.

God, now that I was actually in a room, did I dare to put a light on? And if I dared to, would I be able to find the bloody switch? Fortunately, the room ran parallel to Fifth Avenue. The two floor-to-ceiling French windows had no blinds, and from the outside, light from the passing cars' headlights, as well as from a street lamp, filtered through the sheer curtains. However, there wasn't enough illumination to prevent me from stumbling over a body.

Trying to break my fall, I bent both knees and stuck my arms straight out in front of me, and my open palms landed on soft flesh. Someone's bare, flabby thigh? I figured if my mother had returned home, she could hear my screams on 92nd Street. But after three yelps, I stopped, becoming aware of another noise—footsteps clicking hard against the marble flooring in the foyer and sounding as if they were heading my way. I silently crawled forward.

Suddenly all the lights in the room were shining brightly. Had someone—the killer—pulled the circuit breaker back on? Jesus, Mary, and Joseph. Where could I hide? I was in the dining room, and while there were two magnificent mahogany breakfronts, there didn't seem to be any closets. Midway up the wall behind the long rectangular table there was what appeared to be a built-in cabinet. I opened it.

Inside, I found a large shelf with a pulley attached to it. An old-fashioned dumbwaiter. Big enough to hold dinner for twelve. Big enough to hold me. I stood on a Chippendale chair, hoisted myself up and onto the shelf, using the cabinet door as leverage. As I was folding my legs yoga style on the shelf, someone came into the room. I pulled the cabinet door shut with one hand, while working the pulley with the other, glimpsing only a flash of black material as my pursuer headed for the dumbwaiter.

It seemed a long way down. As I scrambled off my shelf, sliding onto the terracotta floor of a huge downstairs kitchen, all the lights went off again. The killer seemed hell-bent on playing hide-and-seek with me in the dark, and if it were Barbara Ferris searching for me, she probably would have a real game advantage, no doubt being very familiar with the house's nooks and crannies.

Counting on the killer's coming on down to the kitchen—most likely any moment now—I climbed back up on the shelf, tugging on the ropes with all my might, praying this baby went to the third floor. Or higher. Wouldn't the master of this mansion have ordered drinks in his room or a cozy breakfast for two via this rig? God, I hoped so. Sailing—far too slowly—past the dining room, I opened the dumbwaiter's door, ever so slightly, just for a fast peep. No one. My biceps were straining, and I'd about decided that if I lived I'd join a health club when, out of the corner of my left eye, I got a better look at the corpse. I stifled a scream. So much for sordid smells and senseless suspicions, I thought. There, on the Persian carpet, in an ever-widening pool of blood, hair matted, legs and arms akimbo, lay Barbara Ferris.

Crying for Barbara, whom I'd totally misjudged, and for my own frustration, I pulled the ropes with renewed vigor, born of fear and fury, wishing I could rummage in my bag for a tissue. The dumbwaiter did stop at the third floor, opening into a study. Robert Stern's. The walls were full of pictures of a beautiful, dark-haired woman. The late Catherine Stern, I presumed. I kept pulling. I wanted to get to the top floor, but I didn't know why, or what I'd do when I arrived there. Maybe I'd be like the Flying Dutchman, steering this dumbwaiter through eternity.

On the fourth floor, I sat on the shelf for a few seconds, jarred back to reality when the dumbwaiter started to descend. Someone was yanking my chain. Scurrying, I literally fell out of its door and onto the plush cream-colored carpet.

Even in my terror or, maybe, because of it—I couldn't help but notice the Delft. This had to be Mister Robert's suite. The room exuded masculinity and money. Heavy on wood and white, the Delft established the decor. Armoires full of it. An entire wall of plates, bowls, and cups. And a glassed-in cabinet, with a highly visible lock, displaying daggers. Dozens of daggers. In complete panic—would my killer arrive in the dumbwaiter or take the stairs?—I spun around, away from the daggers, as I sensed rather than heard someone behind me. It couldn't be the hunter who'd been stalking me. He or she wouldn't have had time to get up here. Who? I came full circle and stared into the glazed eyes of Robert Stern, looking a decade older than when I'd left him this afternoon and holding a bloody dagger. This time I didn't stifle the scream.

"Barbara's dead. Do you know that?" Stern spoke in a monotone, eyes downcast. "She came to tell me something. About Barry DeWitt and Dick. And Allison, I think. Now Barbara's been murdered too. You must help me, my dear. You always have, Catherine. And I've always counted on you, darling, but now..."

The dumbwaiter had stopped moving. If Stern had killed Barbara, who was chasing me? And wouldn't that person soon be joining us? I eyed the door. Stern blocked my way, but he seemed totally disoriented. I didn't even look like Catherine. How could I escape and what—or who—awaited me on the stairs? Wait—of course—back stairs. All these old mansions had servants' staircases. If I could just maneuver past Stern; maybe those stairs were located behind this room.

Once, with Modesty, on a tour of the turn-of-the-century Carnegie Hill homes, we'd learned that the rear staircases sometimes led to the master suites. But did I dare turn my back on a man wielding a dagger? Robert Stern made that decision for me. He lurched forward; it was hard to tell whether he'd felt faint and had fallen forward or if he'd taken aim at my abdomen. When he staggered, without thinking it through, I snatched the dagger from him and did an about-face. There were two doors. I ran toward them. The first entered into a basilica-sized bathroom; the second led to a stairwell. I bounded down those steps so fast that my heart now hurt almost as much as my upper arms.

After five flights, I wound up in the kitchen. Maybe I could sneak out the back way. As I mulled over that idea, I heard a loud rap on the kitchen door and a gruff voice demanded, "Let me in." I fled out into the hall as someone started to break down the door.

If I could just climb up the staircase to the foyer, maybe the front door will still be open...or at least Stern and my stalker might be upstairs and I could get out anyway...

I'd made it to the Van Gogh, certainly not pausing this time to admire the painting, when a large figure descended the grand staircase, then swung around in my direction. I lifted the dagger, still dripping blood, as Ben Rubin yelled, "Jake, what the hell are you doing?"

Twenty-Three

By one thirty Sunday morning, we still hadn't sorted it all out. But Ben no longer believed that I'd tried to kill him. He said he never had—not for a split second—however, the look of horror that had marred his handsome face and the extraordinary testy tone he'd used when he spotted the dagger, had told me otherwise. And Joe Cassidy, who'd battered down the kitchen door in time to see Ben's reaction, treated me like Jake the Ripper. Hey, I was an intended victim here. Talk about your tangled webs.

Robert Stern, totally incoherent, had been taken to Mount Sinai, where a police guard would be posted outside his room. While he wasn't officially under arrest yet for any of the three murders, he was being held as a material witness in Barbara's stabbing.

Around midnight, the butler—his name was Lawrence Mann—had returned home. Mann had every other Tuesday and Saturday evening off, and as he did every week, he'd been visiting his sister in the Bronx. When he'd left the house, Barbara Ferris and Robert Stern had been eating a light supper and playing gin rummy in the library. "Yes," the butler said, in response to Ben's question, "Miss Barbara was indeed a frequent guest since Miss Catherine had passed away."

"What was their relationship?" Ben asked.

Mann looked offended. "That information would not have been necessary for me to know in order to carry out my duties, sir."

"Well," Ben said, "it may be necessary for me to know in order to carry out mine. Just answer the question."

"A gentleman's gentleman doesn't indulge in gossip, Detective Rubin. Even if I knew the length, breadth, and depth of their friendship, which I don't, my lips would remain sealed." Lawrence sounded like the insufferable prig he was, and Ben's grim expression certainly intimidated me if not the butler.

"So, Lawrence," I said, "was Mister Robert a player? You know, rumor has it he slept around and sexually harassed his employees, first Allison Carr, then Barbara Ferris. I might remind you that both those ladies have been stabbed to death with a Delft dagger. Probably from your gentleman's collection. If you really want to help Robert Stern and not become an accessory after the fact"—this was the line Ben had used to scare me—"you'd better start talking, fast."

"How dare you imply such salacious untruths about Mister Robert?" Lawrence was sputtering, spittle flying. "You little guttersnipe."

I jumped out of the line of his sprinkle and then tried the line Modesty had tried on Glory Flagg. "The truth shall set you free." Every once in a while, it's good for a ghostwriter not to have to be creative.

Mann seemed to consider what I said. Then he sat, sinking into the cushions on the camelback sofa—we were in the library—and said, "Mister Robert deeply grieved for his wife.

Visited her crypt once a week, kept her bedroom exactly as it was when she had slept there, never cleared away her clothes. Her closets and armoires are filled with her dresses, hats, and furs, all arranged as they were on the day she left us to live at that dreadful institution. Even Miss Catherine's hairbrush is still on her vanity." God—this really reeked of *Rebecca*. "I'm certain that his relationships with Ms. Carr and Ms. Ferris were companionable, not sexual."

"And how would you know that?" I asked. Ben paused in his note taking, frowning, then giving me a glance that shouted "shut up."

"Miss O'Hara, a butler knows these things. And if Mister Robert were indulging in that sort of unseemly behavior, it was not happening here." Lawrence Mann squirmed for a second, then regained his composure.

"Unless, of course," I said, "he only had sex with those ladies on alternate Tuesday or Saturday evenings while you were in the Bronx. Or in their homes or a hotel?"

The butler looked at me with disgust. "There were never any mussed—or stained—sheets when I returned home. Nor had Mister Robert changed the linens. Nothing untoward." Mann lowered his eyes, then turned to Ben. "I suppose anything is possible, Detective Rubin. But I will never believe that of Mister Robert. And I assure you, there was never any evidence of a woman in this house."

When the butler went to bed, I explained to Ben what had made me return to Robert Stern's tonight.

"So it was the scent of a woman?" Ben shook his head. "That's no reason to blithely bounce back into a murder scene. And why were you checking out Stern this afternoon? I thought you'd promised your mother—not to mention me—no more Nancy Drew."

"Well..." I began, thinking now's the time to confess, to share with Ben all the stuff that the ghostwriters and I had found out, share our theories, and to share my fear that his partner, Cassidy, remained convinced I was a killer.

"Jake, if you believe you're helping, you're not. So would you please stay out of this? All you are doing is making the case and my life more complicated." His voice chilled my aching bones.

A ringing phone halted our conversation. Ben and I could hear it, loud and clear, but neither we nor the crime scene investigators could find where it was located. After the sixth or seventh ring, I heard someone shout from down the hall, "Miss O'Hara, it's your mother." When I walked into the dining room, the cop laughed. "The phone's in your bag on the shelf in the wall." I retrieved my tote from the dumbwaiter's shelf, assured my mother that I was alive and well, and though I lived almost around the corner, was driven home at Ben's command in a patrol car.

Gypsy Rose and my mother were waiting up for me, simultaneously relieved, upset, and angry with me. "Your mother's been frantic, Jake. What were you thinking?"

"A mother never wants to see her daughter in danger," mine said. "And you revel in it, even seek it out. But at least you usually call. I didn't start to worry 'til midnight. Then I tried to reach you on your cellphone, but..."

"The phone had taken a solo ride in the dumbwaiter. Finally one of the cops heard it ringing."

"God Almighty." My mother rolled her eyes at Gypsy Rose. "Are you going to tell us what happened?"

Putting as positive a spin as I could on the evening's events, I tried to reenact for my mother and Gypsy Rose what might have happened at Robert Stern's. But I wasn't sure myself.

There seemed to be several scenarios; I gave a synopsis of each.

My mother poured hot chocolate. "So Barbara Ferris had been at *Manhattan* on the night of Dick Peter's murder. And Isaac Walton had caught a whiff of her. Then you remembered a strong scent of..."

"Sex, Mom. Not romantic or passionate. Just basic, raw sex." I sounded like a perfume pusher, waltzing around Bloomingdale's cosmetic department spraying the helpless customers.

"Now Barbara's dead too," Gypsy Rose said.

"Right," I said. "But did she kill Dick Peter? Had Robert Stern had an awakening? He'd worked late that night. Maybe later than he'd said. It's possible that he saw or heard something and only connected it to Barbara today. Like Isaac recalling the scent. Stern could have remembered that Barbara sometimes wore that perfume. Or stumbled on some other clue or evidence. If he accused her and she attacked him—well, did he then grab the dagger and stab her?"

"Weren't the daggers locked up in that cabinet?" my mother asked. "Would Robert Stern have handed his killer a dagger?"

"I don't think so," I said. "And, while Ben seriously considers Stern as a suspect in all three murders and is convinced that he went totally crazy tonight, none of the above explains who was chasing me around the mansion."

"Obviously, the real killer," Gypsy Rose said. "I've known Stern for decades, Jake. And I'm telling you, Robert Stern is no killer."

"But..." I began.

"Now you just listen to me," Gypsy Rose said. "During dinner—all four of us were having your favorite, honey, the sauerbraten—Christian asked if I could contact my spirit guide. For God's sake, that old heathen wanted proof there is an afterlife, smack in the middle of my eating a divine potato pancake."

"Even Aaron thought that was poor timing," my mother said.

"Yes." Gypsy Rose sighed. "And you both know how flighty Zelda Fitzgerald can be. I couldn't contact her. My body must have craved the potato pancakes more than my spirit sought Zelda. Or maybe she was busy with the Murphys. So I failed Christian in his feeble search for faith. I know I can try again in future lifetimes, but I'd kind of hoped this lifetime would be it for Christian and me. Meeting so late into it and all. We're destined to flirt through eternity, I guess. It reminds me of Paris right after World War I, when Christian—his name was Armand then—fell in love with a much older writer. Colette. He died so young that time around—from his war wounds—I never had a chance. Later, I fell in love with Edgar Cayce. Lord, I do wish Zelda had shown up. But guess who did? Though just for a cameo appearance. I certainly hadn't channeled him. Not with Aaron Rubin at the table."

"Who?" Once again, I found myself hanging on every word of Gypsy Rose's conversations with the dead.

"Your father, Jake." Gypsy Rose smiled. "But I spoke to him by telepathy, without revealing who he was. No need to make Aaron jealous, right?"

"Right," I said, thinking Dad's long gone; why should Aaron be upset if he'd popped back for a visit? Then I shivered. Sometimes my thought processes proved to be every bit as weird as Gypsy Rose's.

"Jack's very worried about you, Jake," Gypsy Rose said. "He gave me a message for you. 'Tell Jake to *cherchez la femme*. And to never turn her back on anyone.' Now there's your proof. Robert Stern is an innocent—if crazy—man."

Who was left of the women suspects, now that Barbara was dead? Mila and Glory. The long shot—Jennifer Moran. I searched my mind. No one else, unless...unless Sally Lou hadn't been covering for Isaac, but for herself. Maybe the message from the world beyond only meant that a woman would tell me whodunit. Or maybe there wasn't any message except in the medium's mind.

I stared at Gypsy Rose. "Well, for sure someone other than Stern was after me tonight and managed to slip out the front door while Ben was checking out the second floor. And I'd bet that someone is our killer." The stricken look on my mother's face made me wish I could swallow those words.

"Jake, this has to stop. Now. Ben Rubin called me while you were being driven home. You are not a detective, and you could be the next victim. I want you to come to Mass with me in the morning. We'll talk to your father, light a few candles, pray for a resolution. Maybe Gypsy Rose can contact Dick Peter, but you are off this case."

Knowing when to quit, at least temporarily, I kissed my mother and Gypsy Rose good night and went to bed.

Twenty-Four

Returning from Mass at Saint Thomas More's, where we'd left a blaze of candles in our wake, I suggested breakfast at Three Guys. The diner, located at Carnegie Hill's northern border at 96th and Madison, was something of an area anomaly, reminding Mom and me of our Queens roots. And today, on the Sunday preceding All Soul's Day, my mother's nostalgia roared full throttle ahead.

First, there hadn't been enough space on the envelope provided to all the parishioners to list their dearly departed for special remembrance during the All Soul's Day masses. "Only twelve lines," my mother complained. "I have at least fifteen people in Purgatory needing prayers. Well, certainly some of them, like your sainted grandmother and your father are in Heaven, but I like to hedge my bets. And that number doesn't include your father's Aunt Bess. She was a tough old bird, drank like a longshoreman, but I believe she deserves to be remembered. Bess was a spinster, you know. And she has no one else left behind to fill in her name or to pray for her—and let that be a lesson to you, Jake—so I feel responsible." My mother stuffed twenty dollars in the envelope, licked it sealed, and started another. "There'll be some blank spaces left on this second one. Do you have any dead souls' names you'd like to add, dear?" I gave her three.

Then the candles were in short supply. My mother, who dropped a bundle on blazes on an ordinary Sunday, wasn't to be thwarted so close to All Soul's Day. The dead were counting on her. Mom tapped an angelic-looking altar boy on the shoulder, while the kid was still part of the recessional, for God's sake, and sent him trotting back to the sacristy to dig up some candles. The pastor himself hand-delivered them to Mom. He knew better than to rebuff a regular at his vigil lights' slots. Leaving more candles glowing in the dim vestibule than in any soap opera's hottest sex scene, we finally walked out of church and into the clear, bright sunshine.

The pre-Halloween weather had us wrapped in layers. There's an unwritten law in our house—you can't don a winter coat before Veterans Day. A raincoat over a blazer over a cotton turtleneck, swathed with a scarf, worn with gloves and boots is acceptable, but a winter coat must remain closeted 'til November 11th. So I suffered, both from the cumbersome clothes and the chill wind. Poached eggs, pancakes, and lots of hot coffee would be the perfect breakfast. And Three Guys was the perfect place to get it. I began to cheer up.

After we ordered, Mom said, "Let's watch *Terms of Endearment* tonight, Jake. I do so identify with Amanda." It didn't take Freud to figure out that Mom was worried about losing her only daughter and, none too subtly, letting her know it. I counteroffered, suggesting *All of Me*—one of my favorite movies—and a far more positive approach to death. We were still debating when our poached eggs arrived. I changed the subject back to our dear departed relatives, and Mom launched into six consecutive cancer-deathbed horror stories as we ate.

Later, in the spirit of compromise, kind of a happy medium, we decided on *Ghost*. When I told my mother I would be spending the afternoon with Dennis—I'd abridged my plans to meet Mila Macovich and to check out Isaac Walton's alibi—she started humming some old song. Mom steadfastly refused to listen to any music, except for show tunes, that had been written after the mid-sixties. Foolishly, I broke one of my cardinal rules and asked what its title was.

"'Isn't it Romantic?'" she said. "Don't you remember it from *Sabrina*? You know, the movie where Audrey Hepburn married the multimillionaire." Then she suggested we watch that too.

During a series of phone calls earlier this morning, I'd set up my game plan for this afternoon. Jane's call had awakened me at 8:10. She'd heard on the radio that Barbara Ferris had been murdered and lamented the fact that her three suspects were now either cleared or killed. "It's not fair, Jake. Modesty has three really hot prospects. I don't believe Jennifer's a triple murderer; she's afraid of dead people, you know. She refuses to attend wakes or funerals and would rather visit Hell than view an open casket. But maybe being married to Michael Moran all these years has finally driven her over the edge. Glory Flagg's my first choice. Probably aided and abetted by Keith Morrison."

"Really? Last night I thought you'd agreed with Modesty's assessment—that their mutual alibis proved their innocence."

"I've changed my mind. I've spent half the night analyzing this." Jane did sound tired. "Keith Morrison has to have been the other man in the Glory-Dick ménage à trois. I don't buy that his relationship with Glory is business. And if he lied about that, what else is he hiding?"

"You're right," I said. "And his last name begins with an 'M,' doesn't it? I can't get that file out of my mind. One of the "M's" has something major to hide. Morrison's married, isn't he? He surely wouldn't want his wife to know he'd played sadomasochistic sex games with Glory and Dick. Now there's a motive."

"You don't think that we could be dealing with a screwy serial killer here...you know, one who hates *Manhattan* magazine and wants all its staff dead, do you, Jake?"

"Well, yes and no. I think the killer may be crazy and may hate the magazine's staff, but I'll bet our murderer knew all the victims intimately, and had a much more personal motive. Maybe that's what we should be concentrating on."

"How can I help, Jake?"

"Make a few calls to your agent and publishers. See what you can dig up about Morrison's personal life."

Jane laughed. "Oh, they'll love that on a Sunday morning. But I can call in a few favors. I'll get back to you. Will Modesty murder me for infringing on her suspect?"

"Only metaphorically, Jane. Don't worry, I'll take the verbal onslaught. Modesty's given Morrison a pass; we have to do something."

Then I'd called Dennis. I didn't have any favors to call in, but I'd think of something. We agreed to meet at one o'clock. I'd ride along as Dennis delivered his father's pumpkins to Gypsy Rose's bookstore. And having Dennis on my agenda would make it easy to ditch Mom. She really liked Dennis, had no objection to his enormous wealth, and would welcome him as her son-in-law. But at this point I decided she'd welcome almost anyone.

Dennis seemed pleased, if puzzled, by my inviting myself along on his errand. But it was a good thing I had. The pumpkin heads weighed a ton and their felt hats kept slipping off as we gingerly loaded them into the trunk of his Rolls Royce. I couldn't wait to get a look at Gypsy Rose's face when we presented her with these Halloween treats.

"Sometimes modern art eludes me. I didn't want to upset Dad, but are these pumpkins as ghastly as I think they are?" Dennis asked.

"Ghastly would be a good review of this guy's talent. But not to fret. 'Tis the season to be scared. Hey, Dennis, before we leave, do you mind if I run into the Wales for a minute?"

"Renting a room for later, Jake? Love in the afternoon? What kind of a guy do you think I am? Well, hurry up. I haven't got all day."

The day manager told me the waiter who'd worked the Pied Piper Room's ten-to-eleven o'clock dessert table last Wednesday night would be in at four. I said I'd be back.

Gypsy Rose, dressed in what I thought was a costume—with her fashion flair, ranging from Chanel suits to Granny's Attic, sometimes, it's hard to tell—and looking like a reincarnation of Zelda Fitzgerald's flapper era, was hosting a pre-Halloween book signing. The New Age author, a heart transplant recipient who'd fallen in love with the donor's widow, reminded me of a wannabe Tom Wolfe, or maybe the white suit he sported was his costume. The place was packed. But Christian Holmes rushed over and offered to help Dennis and me carry the pumpkins. Jeez. Had he moved in? When we reached the Rolls, double-parked outside the 93rd Street entrance to the bookstore, a burly cop was writing a ticket. All of Dennis Kim's considerable talent for lawyerly persuasion only resulted in a long lecture and a fat fine for blocking traffic. I buried my face in a pumpkin head so Dennis couldn't see me laughing.

While Dennis, Christian, and I debated about where to place the pumpkins for least visibility, and the New Age author rattled on about our eternal hearts, Gypsy Rose joined us. "Oh, too divine. I love them. These jack-o'-lanterns just ooze the essence of Halloween; don't you think so, Jake? Let's add one or two of them to the window display."

As we dutifully followed her lead, I decided there's absolutely no accounting for taste. Once the pumpkin heads were ensconced in their new home, Gypsy Rose insisted we all take a coffee break. Over cappuccinos, totally ignoring my fierce frown, she proceeded to fill Christian and Dennis in on my dumbwaiter flight through Robert Stern's townhouse.

Dennis said, "I thought you'd given up."

"Listen, the last thing I need is another scolding." I aimed my frown toward him.

"But he's right, Jake," Christian said. "There's a serial killer on the loose here. And what's really frightening is that it has to be someone we all know." He patted my hand. "We don't want you to be hurt."

Emboldened and warmed by his concern—and convinced, in my gut, that this good man couldn't be the killer—I trampled on Too-Tall Tom's territory and asked about Christian's alibi.

"All night at the New York Public Library." Christian chuckled. "Sounds as fishy as Isaac Walton, doesn't it? However, Girlie, that's where I spent the night of Dick Peter's demise. The Society to Debunk the Dead Sea Scrolls held an all-night marathon hunt for evidence to prove that the paper they'd been written on was manufactured centuries after the scrolls were supposedly crafted."

I asked, "But how...?"

"One of my ex-wives still has a yen for me," Christian said, grinning at me and Gypsy Rose. "And she's a devout atheist. Like me, she's much happier now that she's given up hope. Anyway, my ex arranged for our society to use the main reading room, even provided coffee and sandwiches for our heathen research, and there were twenty of us to feed. So I couldn't have stabbed Dick, but I think you knew that already, didn't you, Jake?"

As I watched Gypsy Rose's face flush with relief and Dennis nod approvingly, it was my turn to pat Christian's hand.

Dennis had moved his car at the officer's request. It was now parked on 87th Street, off Lexington; he said he'd walk me home on his way there. Then, to both his and my surprise, I accepted his invitation to dinner. A date with Dennis. Mom would be watching *Sabrina* alone, but happy.

Twenty-Five

I didn't dare go upstairs. Mom would be filling little orange and black Halloween bags with candy corn and miniature Milky Ways, getting ready for tomorrow's onslaught of neighborhood ghosts and goblins. She'd always taken trick or treating seriously. Edith Head couldn't have provided me with better costume design than Maura O'Hara. But, given Mom's heightened state of perpetual worry, if I'd ventured into the kitchen, I'd either be pressed into stuffing the sacks or suffer an inquisition about why—and where—I was going out again. As Dennis made a right on Park Avenue, I doubled back, crossed Madison, headed west to Fifth, and boarded a downtown bus. Mila Macovich lived in a townhouse on 68th Street, right around the corner from *Manhattan* magazine. I would have walked, but I was just too weary.

At 68th Street, I plopped on a park bench, and with one eye on the lookout for low-flying pigeons in my vicinity, I pulled the cellphone from my tote and dialed Modesty's number.

"How did it go at the Morans?"

"Jake, it was weird. Wild. I've left two messages for you.

And Too-Tall Tom and I were worried after we heard about Barbara Ferris. I wish you'd stop acting so stupid and putting yourself in dangerous situations. You don't want to get yourself killed, Jake." For sure, this had to be the absolutely kindest remark I'd ever heard Modesty make. Touched, I wanted to respond, but she moved on, "Then I spoke to your mother. She told me you were okay and out for the day with Dennis. Any romantic news you'd care to share with a fellow ghostwriter?"

"That was only a cover story. But Dennis and I did deliver Halloween pumpkins to Gypsy Rose's. All carved out to be the ugliest version of the seven dwarfs you ever laid eyes on, and the big item is I'm engaged to Dopey."

"It's not nice to call your future husband names."

"Modesty, now I know why you never joke. Just tell me what happened at Jen's."

"Well, I have to say Too-Tall Tom proved helpful. The Moran marriage would make even your mother glad you're single. Michael sucks up to Jennifer, sweet as a Hershey Kiss, but anyone can see it's all an act. If Jen had a brain cell left, she'd spit him out. Did you know she's become a morning drinker? Polished off three Bloody Marys for breakfast but ate nothing. When I told them you were a suspect, Jake, and we need information, Michael only smirked; but Jen offered to help. That's when Too-Tall Tom threw down the gauntlet."

"Maybe the drinking explains why Jennifer's stomach's always so bad. It certainly explains why she's been behaving so peculiarly. And she admitted the marriage had crossed some rocky roads but said things were getting smoother. Sex was still a problem, though." I thought about that for a second, then asked, "What did Too-Tall Tom say to them?"

"That you were innocent and the rest of the suspects—and he reminded Jennifer and Michael they were included in that motley crew—had better start answering his questions. He's so big, Jake, I think he scared the truth out of Michael."

"Where did they say they were on the night of Dick Peter's murder? Together?"

"No. Jennifer claims she had a tad too much wine with dinner and fell asleep. Alone. And she'd eaten alone too. Michael had gone out for the evening. Biker Boy woke her up when he came home—at one a.m."

"Where had he been?"

"At a Pledged-For-Lifers' cell meeting. He refused to give the names of his fellow cell mates. This anonymity stuff is really getting boring. Of course, I don't believe him for a minute. And I wonder if Ben Rubin's talked to him yet. He couldn't pull that confidentiality garbage with the cops."

"I think Jennifer told the police they were home together that night."

"Well, well," Modesty said. "The best is yet to come, Jake."

"What?"

"Yesterday, Michael spent most of the afternoon turning that circus tent at MSG into a chapel. When Reverend Walton arrived, very late, he insisted on going to his dressing room before mounting the flower-bedecked pulpit. And the Pledged-For-Lifers were getting really restless."

"That's true. Isaac and Sally Lou were running way behind. Remember, they'd been with me at the Wales."

"Yeah. Well, Sally Lou took her place on the dais, but when another five or ten minutes passed by, Michael went to get Isaac. Guess who the good reverend was engaged in a screaming match with down in the dressing room?"

"I'm totally clueless. Who?"

"Keith Morrison," Modesty snarled in my ear. "Seems my presumption of his innocence may have been premature."

"Good God. What were they fighting about? Did Michael say?"

"Oh, yes. Michael said Morrison accused Walton of reneging on a promise, saying that, after all, that was the reverend's stock in trade. There was something else about Pax Publishing House's honor being challenged. But mostly, they were fighting over Glory Flagg. Walton anti. Morrison pro. To Michael, it sounded like a major battle over sex and money. But Michael says he missed the details. He was more concerned about getting Walton to the pulpit."

"Wow. Good work, Modesty. Do me a favor, call Too-Tall Tom and say thanks. I'm on my way to Mila's. Isn't it amazing how all these suspects keep intertwining? I'll catch up with you guys later." I didn't mention my dinner date with Dennis.

When I hung up the phone, I sat and thought. This case had more crosscurrents than *Murder on the Orient Express,* where it turned out all the suspects were guilty—each having stabbed the victim in turn. If I could gather the remaining suspects together in one room, then, maybe, like Hercule Poirot, I could trick one of them into confessing. If, at that time, I'd have any idea who that might be. With the ghostwriters on the case, I'd bank on that happening. And wouldn't Halloween be the perfect night to host that party? At the witching hour the murderer would be unmasked.

I picked up the phone again and called Gypsy Rose. Where better to hold the denouement than her New Age bookstore? My favorite psychic didn't disappoint me. Said it was in the tarot cards. I compiled the guest list, then called Jane.

"I'll issue the invitations in person, Jake. No one has gotten back to me yet with any dirt on Morrison and this will give me an excuse to see him in person. Too-Tall Tom can come with me on my rounds."

I filled her in on what Modesty had reported. "Why don't you ask her to help too? You can divide the list, if necessary. But don't bother asking Mila or the Waltons; I'll be seeing them this afternoon. Thanks and good luck, Jane." Then I stood, shooing away an aggressive pigeon who seemed to be aiming for my spot, and walked to the curb. Motives, means, and opportunities boiled in my brain, and the plot thickened as I crossed Fifth Avenue.

The house was a four-story Georgian limestone, complete with turrets and stained-glass windows. Graceful and gorgeous. It reminded me of a Gothic cathedral, and it must have cost Mila millions. All those quivering loins and heaving bosoms had paid off. Big time. The suspects in this case were offering me a peek into the lifestyles of the very rich. And Fitzgerald was right on. They are different from you and me.

Mila answered the chimes, which played a medieval chant, wearing jodhpurs, high boots, and carrying a crop.

"Going riding?" I sputtered, somewhat overwhelmed by the smell of incense, the foyer's wall-to-wall gargoyles, and the chandelier of lighted candles.

"No, my dear, this is my writing attire." Mila pouted, then perched on a recycled pew, zipping up a boot. "Sorry to sound brusque, Jake; I am glad to see you, but I have an appointment to go horseback riding in a half hour." She looked up, giving me a smile so dazzling it rivaled the candlelight. "Can we cover whatever it is that you want to talk about in a gallop?"

I cut to the chase. "I have a question and an invitation for you, Mila. I'm sure you've spoken to the police, but it's really important that I know where you were on the night that Dick was murdered."

She stood and stared down at me. This was one tall lady. "Why? Do you think I might have been at *Manhattan* stabbing my husband?" Then she gave a raspy chuckle. "The truth is I was here, writing in my study 'til two in the morning, and I have the chapter to prove it. I date all the pages in my manuscripts. To keep a record of how many hours of blood, sweat, and typing go into all my books. Romance is such a difficult genre, Jake. Even the vanilla characters have to be covered in hot fudge." Mila sighed. "Of course you're correct, the police—that charming Detective Rubin and his gauche associate, Joe what's-his-name indeed have asked that same question. And received the same answer. Actually, Dick couldn't have been killed at a more inconvenient time. I'm on deadline."

The brass of this broad. As if I didn't know computers can be programmed—I'd bet even Joe Cassidy knew that.

I stared right back up at her. "Well, it's great when a writer's creativity can also provide an alibi, isn't it?"

Mila never stopped smiling. "Yes, Jake. Isn't it?" Then she looked at her watch. A Rolex. "Now, I do have to trot. What sort of an invitation do you have for me?"

"I know you're coming to the Halloween Happening at Gypsy Rose's tomorrow night. Plan on staying late. The name of the killer in the three Delft dagger murders will be revealed at midnight."

"Really? I wouldn't miss that for the world. But do we still get to come in costume? I have this magnificent mask..."

"By all means, wear it, Mila."

From somewhere in the deep recesses of the house, church bells tolled. Three o'clock. I looked for the holy water fountain on the way out.

*   *   *

I decided to take a stroll through Central Park to clear my head, plan my party, and then cab it back to the Wales. Near the entrance, I passed a food truck with its vendor standing in front of his truck, hawking the hot dogs. I resisted temptation. They smelled divine and looked so delicious, smothered in sauerkraut, relish, and mustard, but I was my mother's daughter and not about to allow "dirty water dogs" to run amok through my digestive track.

At three thirty, I treated myself to a bag of roasted chestnuts and a diet soda, then sat on a bench, watching the riders go round and round on the carousel. Rodgers and Hammerstein's music filled the air. Parents stood next to their kids on horseback, holding them tightly, and the children squealed with delight as the merry-go-round picked up speed. I spilled the Coke all over my good Burberry raincoat when I spotted Mila Macovich astride a painted pony, hand in hand with Michael Moran. *Carousel*'s Billy Bigelow and Julie could not have looked more in love than Dick's widow and Jennifer's husband.

Twenty-Six

I trekked through Central Park and the echo of the organ music's haunting refrain traveled with me. Good God Almighty. Mila Macovich and Michael Moran. Way beyond belief. Their romance not only confirmed Too-Tall Tom's information that Michael was having an affair with a rich, older woman and Jennifer's hunch that her husband was sexually otherwise engaged, it provided two more motives for Dick Peter's murder.

Horses of many hues raced around in my mind, their hammering hooves taking me on a wild ride more like a tilt-a-whirl than a merry-go-round. And I didn't ride alone. A befuddled Robert Stern straddled a Delft blue colt. Next to him, Glory Flagg sat sidesaddle on a tricolor striped stallion. Barry DeWitt's mount was a white gelding and he wore a cowboy hat to match. In front of them, Isaac Walton rode bareback on a palomino. Sally Lou had squeezed on behind him, her chubby arms wrapped around his waist. Jennifer Moran, looking forlorn and eating a cotton-candy cone, rode a pink pony. Keith Morrison, singing along to the music, sat on an ass. Michael Moran and Mila Macovich, eyes locked and fingers intertwined, ignored their fellow riders. The carousel's benches, painted with colorful carved enameled flowers and usually reserved for grandparents and timid toddlers, were filled with bloody daggers. And, on this murder-go-round, Dick Peter, Allison Carr, and Barbara Ferris were the pale riders seated on pale horses. I rode with them.

A scream brought the carousel to an abrupt stop. From the curious stares of passersby, I realized I'd been the one who screamed. Of course, this being New York, none of them were curious enough to inquire what might be wrong with me. All that hammering had left me with an Excedrin headache; I left the park and hailed a taxi.

In the cab, I swallowed two tablets neat, then closed my eyes, relieved that the whirling images had vanished. But no way could I relax. Questions nagged; answers were in short supply. The Mila Macovich-Michael Moran equation changed everything. Mila got around. Dick Peter's "D" file indicated that she'd also slept with Barry DeWitt. Had Dick been killed so that Mila would inherit his money and Michael could marry the merry widow once he'd dumped Jennifer? Did Jen know Mila was the other woman? Had she really been protecting her philandering husband? Good Lord. Could Jennifer have killed Dick, knowing the police would find out about Mila and Michael? A double-barrel frame?

Robert Stern's need to revenge Catherine's suicide may have driven him to murder Dick and then Allison. Because she knew too much? Why would Stern have waited so long to exact his revenge? Maybe he'd feared the whole sordid story reappearing in Dick's book. On the morning I'd copied the manuscript files, he'd been in the mailroom, holding on to a folder as if his life depended on reading it. If he wasn't the murderer, what had driven him over the edge yesterday? If

Stern hadn't stabbed Barbara himself, had he witnessed her murder?

He wound up holding the bloody dagger, seemingly convinced that I was his dead wife, Catherine. If the daggers used as the murder weapons were from his collection, who, other than Stern, had access to them? What had transpired in that mansion right before my trip in the dumbwaiter? Could his confusion be an act? Had Ben been able to get a statement from him? Was there any way I could visit Stern at Mount Sinai? Murderer or not, he certainly played a pivotal role in all three of these deaths, and I wanted to invite him to be part of our Halloween Happening.

If Barbara Ferris and Allison Carr were killed because they knew too much—and I believed they were—what had the women discovered? Had they shared the same information? Or did they each have different evidence pointing to the killer? Allison Carr had worked late on the night of Dick's death. Probably later than she'd admitted. I'd no doubt she'd seen something. Barbara Ferris had been there too. Isaac Walton and probably Stern—or whoever had murdered Dick—had smelled her heady perfume. Who or what had these women witnessed that night? I was convinced if I had an answer to that question, it would lead me to the killer.

Isaac and Sally Lou weren't out of the woods either. Family feuds, especially those involving jealousy and money, frequently ended in murder. The reverend's motive remained one of the strongest and God knows he was such a snake. Wouldn't I have loved to find out why Keith Morrison had been calling on Walton last night at MSG? My earlier hunch about *Our Gal Sunday* and Dick and Isaac's West Virginia roots resurfaced. Were their lives crossed somehow? What might the preacher and the publisher have been plotting? Yet, as much as I disliked

Isaac, a confirmation of his alibi would help prune this list.

Even more intriguing was the relationship between Glory Flagg and Morrison. A business arrangement, he'd told Modesty. I didn't buy that. Morrison owned Pax. Glory's publisher was Harvest House. Since Keith Morrison had had Dick Peter under contract, how could he have been dealing with Glory? An affair? Were they only another odd couple—or two-thirds of an odder ménage? Or were they partners in murder? While Glory had a twenty-million-dollar motive, Morrison's motive could have been to cover up an extramarital fling. Morrison, not DeWitt, might be the other man.

But then what would be the real reason that Barry DeWitt had threatened Allison Carr at the Algonquin? And could it be mere coincidence that Barbara Ferris had overheard his threat? I didn't think so. Our Ghostwriters Anonymous twelve-step program teaches us there are no coincidences. Barbara must have been tracking Barry or, more likely, Allison. Maybe Barbara knew Allison was in danger. Too-Tall Tom's conviction that Barry was our murderer seemed too simplistic for such a complex case. Yet when it walks like a duck...

"Miss, we're at the Wales. Do you ever plan on exiting my vehicle?" The cabbie sounded really irritated.

The Waltons were in the lobby admiring the Puss and Boots display. Damn. I didn't need them hanging around while I checked out Isaac's alibi.

"Jake, how nice to see you." Sally Lou beamed. "We're going up to the Pied Piper Room for a spot of tea. Won't you join us?" A week at the Wales had turned Sally Lou into English landed gentry. Now if she could just lose that West Virginny twang.

"Thanks, I've had a busy afternoon. Tea would be terrific." Hell, the waiter would be on duty 'til midnight. I'd catch up with him later. This would be a great opportunity to gather a few more facts and to invite the Waltons to the Halloween Happening and the confession that I hoped would follow.

Sally Lou sipped her tea with her pinkie practically extending out to Madison Avenue. "It's all so sad. Will you be attending Dick's funeral tomorrow morning, Jake?" Hypocrisy hugged her words like a shroud.

"Yes. Though I have to stop at *Manhattan* first."

"Won't they be closing up shop for my cousin's service?" Isaac asked. "I'd have thought Dick mattered more to the magazine's management. Wouldn't you say that Dick deserved the respect of a full day of mourning, Jake?"

Having no idea how to answer that, I ate a cookie. Not to worry, Sally Lou jumped in.

"*Manhattan*'s a dangerous place to work. With that hotshot Robert Stern in custody, is there anyone in charge over there? Who could have thought that puny ole Mr. Stern stabbed Dick? And those two innocent women. They must have had something on him. What a pity. I have read Allison Carr's 'Bites From the Big Apple,' of course."

"As I understand it," I said, "Robert Stern is being held as a material witness. He hasn't been arrested for the murders."

Sally Lou put three cookies into her mouth at once, but managed to continue talking. "Don't be silly, Jake; he's guilty as sin."

"With what judgment we judge, we shall be judged," the reverend said. "However, in this case, I agree with you, Mother. Robert Stern had more than sufficient reason to want Dick dead." Isaac slammed sugar into his cup, stirred it with vigor, and turned to me. "Isn't that right, Jake?"

"Reverend Walton, I assure you, Stern wouldn't be my top candidate among this large slate of suspects. That's one of the things I wanted to discuss with you."

"Who is?" Sally Lou asked, grabbing another fistful of Social Teas. "Your top choice, I mean."

"Actually, I'll be revealing that tomorrow night at Gypsy Rose Liebowitz's Halloween Happening. Her New Age bookstore's right around the corner on 93rd Street, just off Madison. Please join us. All the suspects will be there. I know you both want this mystery solved as much as I do."

"Jake, I don't think we can do that," Sally Lou said. "Don't you understand that New Agers consort with Satan?"

Isaac Walton coughed and his big nose turned even redder than the rest of his face. "God forbid that I would ever enter into such a den of evil."

"Well," I said, "you'll risk looking guilty if all the other candidates show up and you don't. And, Sally Lou, this would be the perfect opportunity for you to wear that heavenly white dress again. You can come as an angel."

"Jake could be right, Mother." Isaac seemed to be reconsidering. "Maybe God will forgive us, if our presence would end all these ugly accusations and help find the real killer. A march into Hell for a heavenly cause."

I stood.

"Oh, by the way, I heard that Keith Morrison caused a bit of a scene at the Garden last night. What happened?"

Isaac stood too.

"Mr. Morrison's brief visit concerned a private business arrangement, and as far as I can recall, was most cordial." He turned to Sally Lou. "Come along, Mother, we have an appointment."

Sally Lou sighed. "We'll attend your Happening. But I think

you're drawing to an inside straight, Jake. If I were a betting kind of woman, I'd give you ten to one odds on Stern."

"Think of it as bingo, not poker, Sally Lou. See you in church." I left them in the Pied Piper Room to go and search out Isaac's alibi, praying I wouldn't find one.

Twenty-Seven

"That little fat lady?" the handsome young Albanian—whose name plate read Fredric—asked. "Yes, Madame. She has not missed a dessert hour since arriving at the Wales. However, her husband, the one who is leading the men's prayer group at Madison Square Garden, did not make it every night. Sometimes, the lady ate her cake alone. I do not recall if he joined her last Wednesday night. It is possible—I am sorry, but I cannot be certain."

"It's okay. Is there any way I can get a list of the guests who were staying here last Wednesday night? Maybe someone who went to the late dessert will remember seeing Reverend Walton."

"We will inquire at the front desk. But I believe an investigator—a Detective Rubin—already has made such a request. Is Madame associated with the New York City Police Department as well?" This man sounded like a cultured Middle European who'd studied English at Oxford.

Though tempted, I didn't want to add impersonating a police officer to Ben's litany of my transgressions. "No, just checking out alibis, trying to clear a friend from a possible murder charge." No need to mention I too was a suspect.

"I regret having to inform you of this, Madame, but I am certain the manager will not share the hotel's register with a...how you say...random citizen. Not even in America is there such liberty."

By the time I'd left the hotel and arrived home to be greeted by Mom and Gypsy Rose—both in a twitter about my dinner date with Dennis—two strange things happened. Fredric had willingly replied to my puzzled questioning. He'd been a doctor in Albania. Now, while awaiting certification in the United States, he was working three nights a week at the Wales. Then, as Fredric held the lobby door open for me, I glimpsed Keith Morrison stepping out of a limo across the avenue. Why would the multimillionaire publisher be dropping by the Hotel Wales, if not to visit Isaac Walton? What was going on between them? I ducked out, hanging a left before Morrison could spot me, but not before I'd accepted a date for next Saturday night with Fredric.

My mother said my phone had been ringing all afternoon. I checked the answering machine. Two hang-ups. A message from Dennis. He'd be here at seven. Jane and Modesty had called. Not a word from Ben.

Jane's message was surprisingly short, though hers usually rivaled Too-Tall Tom's tomes. "I met with the Morans. Michael and Jennifer will—though not happily—attend the Halloween Happening. Jennifer said, 'If we don't come, people will assume one of us is the killer.' Michael looked as if he could kill her about then. Anyway, they'll be late. He has to stop somewhere first." After all the squabbling Too-Tall Tom and Modesty had done about just whose suspects Jennifer and Michael were, I found it amusing that it now appeared Jane had taken them over.

Modesty's message was long. "Glory Flagg's canceling her own polyamorous Halloween plans to attend both the Happening and our Name the Killer follow-up. Says we should have a pool. Her winning pick would be Barry DeWitt. With Isaac Walton to place. When I asked her if Keith Morrison had been going to that polyamorous affair with her, and now might also be available to join us, she jumped all over me. Keith Morrison, says Glory, is an overstarched Puritan. And did I realize that he was almost seventy? And she's never seen such a case of total second chakra shutdown. Even if he had the passion to pursue polyamorous pleasure, he wouldn't have the passion to perform. Anyway, the Puritan's not answering his phone. I'll keep dialing."

I called Modesty back and told her to page Keith Morrison at the Wales. That should shake up his chakra.

Gypsy Rose had brought her entire makeup case. "Trunk" would be a more correct term. Rows and rows of pull-out drawers, filled with creams, lotions, lipsticks, shadows, and multiple baggies that contained blush, highlighter, and contouring brushes. Some of the boxes were so arcane that I didn't even question their mysterious, albeit colorful, contents. Knowing I couldn't fight the two of them, I sat at Mom's vanity table, allowing her to fasten a plastic cape around my neck. Gypsy Rose went to work redoing my cheekbones and brows, while Mom plugged in her hot rollers. It had been a long time since I'd seen the two old friends looking so happy.

Women who came of age in the late fifties and early sixties

still spend a lot of their time planning what to wear and getting ready. Mom and Gypsy Rose were no exceptions. "You haven't even decided which dress," my mother said. "I could be pressing it for you." She jabbed a stick into the big roller under my bangs with more force than I felt was necessary.

"Why does it have to be a dress? I only own three: one for funerals, one for weddings, and that green velvet, Scarlett O'Hara's drapes number that you bought me last Christmas. How about my camel silk pantsuit?"

"And I'd hope you wouldn't be wearing that with a white cotton shirt from the Gap," my mother said.

She had me there. I did own four silk blouses, and one even matched the pantsuit in question; however, all of them were at the cleaners. In the mirror as Gypsy Rose arched my eyebrows, I watched a frown furrow my forehead.

"Jake, don't worry," Gypsy Rose said. "I've brought along three of my prettiest camisoles. One black, one taupe, and one ivory. I know they're a little fancy for your plain...sense of style, but, darling, a bit of lace never killed anyone. And they all come with built-in bras. So uplifting. And no one would ever guess it wasn't all yours."

Agreeing to consider the camisoles, as Mom scurried off to get the pantsuit so that I could try it with all three of my options, I switched subjects with Gypsy Rose, going from this evening's fashions to tomorrow night's suspects.

"I don't know what I'd do without you, Gypsy Rose. You always come through." I jumped as she tweezed a wild curly black hair from my eyebrow. Jeez, where had that come from? Maybe I'd better invest in a magnifying mirror.

"My pleasure, darling. Am I hurting you? Sometimes we have to suffer to be beautiful, you know." Gypsy Rose applied a bit of witch hazel—what else?—to the blood her last pluck had drawn. "Too-Tall Tom stopped by late this afternoon, just as I was closing up shop. He brought one warlock's and three witches' outfits over. Said he knew you wouldn't have the time to rent them—even if you could find anything left in the stores at this late date. And they're the right stuff. His former boyfriend, the warlock, conjured them up for him."

"I'm a lucky woman to have friends like you guys."

Gypsy Rose beamed. 'Tell that to Too-Tall Tom. He also had a report he asked me to pass along to you. Don't dare call him tonight; he has a date. But he finished his assignment. Barry DeWitt will be at the Halloween Happening and will stay for our private party. Too-Tall Tom wants you to know he went way beyond the call of duty. You and the other ghostwriters must be aware he believes that pompous theater critic is the killer. Well, DeWitt would only attend our Happening if Too-Tall Tom came with him. As his date."

"Oh, God. Does Too-Tall Tom think he'll be stabbed in the back on his way to the bookstore? He could be right. Maybe we can have Modesty ride shotgun for him."

"I've already arranged for a limo to pick up Too-Tall Tom and his date, the potentially deadly DeWitt."

Gypsy Rose smiled as she brushed my brows, filling in their bald spots with a soft pencil. Why do women pluck out the hairs from our brows, then crayon them back in? Why had I been crazy enough to let Gypsy Rose do it to me? This is one of the few areas where—though I hate to admit it—men might be smarter than we are.

"Seems like you and Christian are getting pretty cozy," I said as Gypsy Rose rolled on the mascara.

"Charcoal gray, Jake. That's the right shade for you. And it curls as it lengthens, isn't that wonderful? You can buy it in any drugstore. Never pay department store prices. All that money's for the packaging. Remember, you can't beat Maybelline." She stood back, like a true artist, to admire her work. "I'm thinking of bringing Christian with me to the cemetery next Sunday to visit Louie. Unless, of course, he turns out to be the killer."

I laughed. "You know he has an airtight alibi—his ex-wife. Can't get one any better than that."

"Well, it's time Louie Liebowitz and Christian Holmes met, Jake. Did I tell you Louie knew Christian—as Armand—in Paris in 1918?"

"No..."

"Why, Louie was Colette's publisher. He really couldn't stand Christian that time around. I'm hoping they can work things out in this incarnation."

"But Louie's been dead for years. How can they...er...be on the same plane?" I knew I'd regret asking this question.

"Don't you see, Jake? I'm the go-between. It's my destiny to smooth out their relationship before Christian dies or Louie makes a comeback. He's on a holding pattern—between planes—for now. Sit still while I line your lower lip. A pout is always sexy."

The color was coral. I actually liked the way my face was shaping up. "So what's the game plan for tomorrow night, Gypsy Rose?"

"We'll have booths, like a fairway. Two fortune-tellers. You witches, not being the real thing, can act as hostesses. I thought Too-Tall Tom could man the cauldron. It will be filled with cider and emitting mysterious vapors. Dry ice, not witchcraft, you understand. We'll have a hypnotist doing regressions. And a fire walker from the downtown Unity Church will give a demonstration. Our guests can enjoy a hands-on experience. I guess I should say a putting-their-feet-in-the-fire experience. Have you ever watched anyone walk on burning coals, Jake?"

I shuddered, then shook my head from side to side, admiring my heightened cheekbones.

Gypsy Rose continued. "And lots of great food. Then the grand finale will be your unmasking the murderer."

"We hope."

"I didn't mention anything about that to Maura. Your mother's frantic enough without having to worry about the killer now knowing that you plan to expose him. Or her. This really is a dangerous game you're playing, Jake. I only agreed to help because I knew you'd go ahead without me. There may be safety in numbers in an environment I can control."

"I'm not sure the ghostwriters can pull this off. We'll need your help. Do you think we can move the séance to tomorrow night? The spirits could help with the solution. Since we won't be getting started 'til after midnight, technically it will be All Soul's Day anyway."

"If you hold the séance at the Halloween Happening, Mila Macovich won't come." My mother had returned, holding a carefully pressed pantsuit over her arm.

"Oh, I don't think you have to worry about that, Mom. I can assure you Mila wouldn't miss it for the world. And that's straight from the horse's less-than-original mouth."

When Dennis Kim arrived an hour later, I realized that despite the curls, color, camisole, and my complete cooperation with Mom and Gypsy Rose, he looked far better than I did.

Twenty-Eight

Somehow the French country decor at the restaurant reminded me of the carousel in Central Park. Or, maybe, as it had before, sitting this close to Dennis and sipping champagne cocktails made me feel dizzy. The soft lighting should have soothed; instead, the tilt-a-whirl inside my head spun round and round.

Popping an exotic canape into my mouth, I watched in wonder as Dennis placed our order in French, chatting up the maître d' as if he were an old friend. As soon as we were alone—the staff had hovered over us since we walked in the door—I told Dennis about the Halloween Happening's anticipated surprise ending and how all the suspects would be there, stressing that if the ghostwriters couldn't come up with the killer, surely Gypsy Rose would. "You know how effective her channeling can be. Why, Dick Peter could return from hell and tell us whodunit."

"Comme ci comme ça, Jake." Dennis was on a French roll tonight. "Haven't you yourself said her séances have a fifty percent no-show rate?"

"I never said fifty percent." I hated it when my words came back to haunt me. "Maybe thirty-five."

"Whatever. I'm more concerned that you won't be around

to see which—if any—spooks do show up. Have you and the ghostwriters gone totally crazy, girl? You've issued an invitation to a serial killer. His or her response certainly will include an attempt to stab you. And need I remind you, this murderer's had a damn high success rate so far. Does Ben Rubin know what insanity you've been planning?"

"Well, no, but I'll invite him too." This was a spur-of-the-moment decision, made more to quell Dennis's objections than to keep Ben informed.

"All we can do is damage control." Dennis's gold-flecked eyes held mine. "You can't be alone between now and that Halloween Happening tomorrow night. Not even to go to the john. Give me your itinerary. I want someone with you at all times." His tone scared me into complying.

Dennis would pick me up and drive me to Dick's funeral at St. Thomas's in the morning. We'd get one of the ghostwriters, either Modesty or Jane, to meet me in front of the church after the service and accompany me to *Manhattan* to deliver my column. I'd wanted to turn it in early in the morning, before the funeral, but Dennis vetoed that idea.

"And, Jake, we have to cover the late afternoon too. Since your mother has no idea of your Agatha Christie copycat final chapter, we can't count on her staying home all day."

"No. She'll be at the bookstore, setting up for the party. Christian Holmes and Aaron Rubin will be helping too."

"Okay, when will you finish at *Manhattan*?"

This babysitting tactic would cut into my agenda to continue the investigation tomorrow. Maybe I could take Modesty or Jane with me; however, I didn't consider it prudent to mention that idea to Dennis. He didn't seem to understand that desperate people used desperate measures. "I should be home about five."

"All right. I have a meeting with Robert Stern, but I can be there by six. Keep Modesty or Jane with you 'til I get there. Do you read me?" Dennis pulled out his phone, so tiny it hadn't even made a wrinkle in his Brooks Brothers jacket pocket. "I'm calling Modesty now. She's really a weirdo, but far sharper than that How-to-Doody Jane. What's her number?"

I gave him Modesty's number, then said, "Oh, I read you, Dennis. Loud and clear."

The waiter arrived with our first course. Escargot. Didn't Dennis know he was dining with an Irish peasant? I dipped French bread in the sauce, trying to avoid contact with a snail, while Dennis laughed. "Would you prefer something else?"

"Actually, if there's melon or a small fruit cup, I'd like that." Dennis just kept laughing, but he waved the waiter over. We chatted about his father, my mother, and how the old neighborhood had changed, not mentioning murder or anything personal until the main course arrived.

Our rack of lamb was served with as much flair as a Broadway production number. The roast more than lived up to the expectations of its presentation. Absolutely delicious, if a tad too rare. And the potatoes were the best I'd ever eaten.

"Dennis, this is really a wonderful meal." I sipped my white wine. All his House of Rothschild snobbery had failed to convert me to red.

"Don't you know there's nothing too good for you, Jake? Your wish..."

Boy, would Dennis live to regret those words. "Well, I do have a wish you might be able to fulfill."

"Yes?" I could hear the slightest hint of terror. "And what would that be?"

"Who's Robert Stern's lawyer? I mean, I know you represent him, but has he hired a criminal attorney yet?"

"Why?" His voice was becoming shriller by the second.

"I want Stern at the séance. Some of the suspects think his being found holding a bloody dagger has let them off the hook. I want to cause a stir. You know, shake things up. Besides, I don't think he did it. Someone else chased me around that house. I'd bet my poached pear that someone is our serial killer."

"The police seem to share your theory. Or at least they're considering it. Evidence indicates there was another person on the premises. Stern's still suffering from shock. He can't tell them anything. However, I've convinced them to send him home in the morning. I'm meeting with him tomorrow afternoon. And yes, I'm bringing a defense attorney with me. How come you didn't know about Stern's status? What's the matter, Jake? Aren't you talking to your boyfriend, Detective Rubin?"

"Don't change the subject, Dennis. So can you bring Stern to the unmasking tomorrow night?"

"I don't think he's well enough. He's completely disoriented. I understand he thought you were Catherine."

"Look, he doesn't have to come to the party, but I need him at the séance. Come on, Dennis." I'd show him what shrill really sounded like. "You said my wish..."

"Okay, okay. I know you've been through hell these last few days, kid. Let me see what I can do."

I leaned over to kiss him on the cheek. But my lips landed on his. He tasted like red wine. Not bad. Not bad at all.

"Well, well, if it ain't the mouthpiece and the ghostwriter." The unmistakable Brooklyn vowels of Glory Flagg jarred me. I bit Dennis's lip. As he wiped the blood away with his napkin, Glory said, "Why don't you guys join me and Keith for a nightcap?"

As it turned out, they joined us. Glory had a double Remy Martin. Keith Morrison had a Canadian Club and ginger ale.

Dennis had an espresso and I savored the poached pear, a cappuccino, and a cornucopia of information from Glory.

"How about that Ferris broad getting herself stabbed at Robert Stern's?" Glory Flagg asked, fussing with the red feather boa that appeared to be tickling her chin. "If she'd killed Dick and Allison, Stern woulda had mixed emotions. Been thrilled that Barbara had bumped off Peter, but been really upset if she'd stabbed my former schoolmate, Allison Carr. The old boy dug Allison. She'd stuck by him after Catherine's suicide. Ya know, when *Manhattan's* board voted to keep Dick and Stern really needed a friend. The hitch here is this fact: while Stern woulda wanted Barbara dead, he wouldn't've had the guts to kill her. Besides, not for anything, I don't think Barbara killed anybody."

"Was Stern having an affair with Allison?" I asked. Dennis's and Christian's comments, as well as my own powers of deduction, made me sure Glory's answer would be affirmative.

"The only affair Robert Stern ever had was with that prissy butler of his. It's lasted for decades." Glory grinned. "That's why Catherine was so receptive to Dick's devilish charms."

"What?" I shouted. The only surprise Dennis evidenced was an inhale of breath, bordering on a gasp. He swallowed an oversized swig of espresso to mask it.

"Yeah, ain't that amazing?" Glory asked, clapping her hands. "Them keeping it a secret, I mean. But I promise you Stern and his valet were in the closet together. Ya can read all about it in my book."

Keith Morrison remained silent, smiling at Glory with what appeared to be fatherly affection. But, then again, what did I know? I wondered why Morrison wanted Pax to publish Dick's posthumous manuscript when it was obvious that Glory's book would have all the gore.

While digesting the information about Stern's sex life, I

managed to eat a mouthful of the poached pear, as Dennis asked Glory, "Why don't you think Barbara's the killer?"

"I've known Barbara for years." Glory said. "She's...er, she was a very religious woman. A Bible belt in karate, ya might say. Didja know she fought and won a sexual harassment lawsuit against Dick? Him and *Manhattan* had to cough up a pile of dough. But the board still wouldn't fire him. Dick's sass sold millions of copies. Ya probably haven't heard anything about that lawsuit. The magazine's settlement included a confidentiality clause, but I do know Barbara told that hunk Detective Rubin all about it." Dennis shot me a smirk.

"But, Glory," I said, "it seemed to me that Barbara was very interested in Robert Stern. Romantically, I mean."

"You got that right, Jake. I told ya, Stern was so deep in the closet, poor Barbara didn't realize he was gay. Most people didn't. Barbara had mistaken his kindness for desire. That might be tragic, but it ain't a motive for murder. Not in my book." Glory adjusted her tiara. "Enough already. Now let's get on to the important stuff. What are ya wearing to Dick's funeral? And to the Halloween Happening? Me and Keith are really looking forward to learning who killed Dick. Ain't that so, Keith?"

"Indeed," Morrison said. "I was delighted when Miss Modesty called to invite me to join you for the denouement. You're one fine detective, Jake, tracking me to the Wales this afternoon." He sounded as sincere as when he'd discussed his high regard for *Our Gal Sunday*.

Dennis put his arm around me in the Rolls. It felt great. Then, though I had several of Dick Peter's files to read tonight and his funeral to attend in the morning, I consented to go dancing with Dennis at a South America nightclub down in Tribeca. "If you haven't danced the tango, you've never really danced. This orchestra takes traditional Argentine music to poetic dimensions—not to mention dips. Come, tango with me."

"But I don't know how."

"Just let me lead, Jake. I can tell you'll be a natural." And after two practice spins and another white wine, I believed I danced better than Al Pacino.

Twenty-Nine

When the alarm went off at seven thirty on Monday morning, I had a hangover. I crawled out of bed, brushed my teeth with baking soda, swallowed two Tylenol, put the water on for tea, dialed Ben at the Nineteenth Precinct's Homicide Department, and left a message inviting him to tonight's séance. Then, as guilt galloped through my soul, I added, "I'd really like to talk to you."

With such an aching head and queasy tummy, I wouldn't think my heart could still jump every time I thought of Dennis Kim's good-night kisses, but it did. Why? Would I never get over my childhood crush? Did I really want that overconfident, mega-rich, far too sexy, womanizing, know-it-all pain in the ass in my life? I knew the answer was yes when I started worrying if—and at what time—he'd call before he came to pick me up this morning. But I wanted Ben too. And what about that handsome Albanian I'd flirted with at the Wales? If I lived through the week, I had a date with him on Saturday night. I took another Tylenol.

The phone rang and I jumped, sloshing tea all over my

bagel. Not that it mattered, I couldn't eat it anyway, even devoid of cream cheese or strawberry jam.

Modesty yelled in my ear, "Jake, Jennifer's leaving Michael! Your line was busy, so she called me. She's meeting with an attorney this morning—remember, Jen doesn't do funerals—then going into the office this afternoon, but she wants to talk to you."

"Good God. I'd say a divorce would be in her best interest; but I'm still surprised. I'll catch up with Jennifer at *Manhattan* later." I then told Modesty about Glory's revelations last night, observing, "She's like a sink in an airport. You know, the no-hands-on kind, where the faucet spurts out automatically, splatters you for a few seconds, then stops—just shuts off—whether you're ready or not. Glory, seeming spontaneous, will shower you with startling, apparently accurate information, then just as suddenly, her stream turns into a sprinkle and she dries up. Changes the subject. She drives me crazy. And I can't figure out what's going on with her and Morrison. Any ideas?"

"Call me gullible, Jake. But for what it's worth, I still believe Morrison is crackers, but not a con. And that their relationship could be all business. Maybe Morrison's going to appoint Glory as Pax's editor-in-chief. Just consider all the recent publishing takeovers. The book business gets stranger by the merger. What did Dennis Kim have to say? He represents Morrison, doesn't he?"

"Yes. But we didn't get into the odd couple's relationship." I felt no need to tell her that my tango lessons had taken precedence over any discussion of murder suspects. "Dennis is paranoid about client confidentiality."

"And I'm sick to death of hearing about that, not to mention Dennis Kim's convenient code of legal ethics. Now there's an oxymoron. Anyway, as I promised the counselor to the stars, I'll be waiting right outside St. Thomas's when you leave the funeral. And I'll tag along with you all afternoon. So you won't be alone."

I reached for the Kleenex. Either my sore head or her show of heart made me teary. "Thanks, Modesty."

"What the hell? I'll work it into a future plotline," she said, and hung up.

Dennis hadn't called; he just showed up, handing me a single, perfect white rose. No kiss this morning. Not even a hug. My mother took the rose, looking at it with such rapture you'd think she was holding the Holy Grail, and went off to put it in water. She returned with a tray of coffee and Sarabeth muffins. No question about it. Mom had turned Carnegie Hill into Camelot and Dennis Kim into Sir Galahad. I felt a little better— my appetite had made a major comeback—and since I seemed to have been suddenly struck speechless in Dennis's presence, I was happy to eat and let Mom do the talking.

"Jake tells me you're coming to our Halloween party, Dennis. What kind of costume will you be wearing?"

"Now, if everyone answered that question, Maura, there'd be no element of surprise, would there?" Dennis's sugarcoated charm was curdling my delicate stomach juices. "I'll give you a hint though. Expect the unexpected." Whatever the hell that meant.

"I think that's a terrific theme for our Halloween Happening—that spirit of our sharing unexpected and scary adventures should hold true for the entire evening," my mother said. Sometimes, she spooked me. Mom, never in your life have you been more right on.

Dennis spent the twenty-minute drive downtown lecturing me on today's safety precautions. Fifth Avenue was jammed from Fifty-ninth to Fiftieth. Limousines lined the curbs and basic black filled the avenue as mourners gathered on the steps of St. Thomas, grumbling that their taxi drivers had been forced to drop them off blocks away from the church. Dennis managed to secure a spot directly behind the hearse.

As we entered the church, he wrapped his arm around mine like a boa constrictor. And he wouldn't let go, not even when we collided into Ben Rubin in the vestibule. I'd been watching the less-than-teary-eyed crowd and not where I was going.

"Jake. Hi. I returned your call, but your mother said you'd already left for the funeral." Ben stared at Dennis's hammerlock hold on my triceps. "What's up?"

"There's some stuff I really need to tell you, Ben," I said. The organist opened the service with a resounding rendition of "Nearer My God To Thee," almost drowning me out.

"Sounds like we're going down with the Titanic." Ben smiled at my upper arm.

"The most important thing of all is that you show up at Gypsy Rose's Halloween Happening tonight," I said. "We may unmask the murderer." Ben stopped smiling.

But before he could reply, one of the assistant funeral directors came up to us. "Would you three mourners kindly take your seats? We're about to bring in Mr. Peter's remains."

As Dennis and I, stuck together like Siamese twins, obeyed the pallbearer and headed for our reserved seats in the fifth pew on the left side, I twisted my neck around and stage-whispered back at Ben, "I'll be at *Manhattan* most of the afternoon."

We were among the last to be seated. The organ music ceased. Then what sounded like a small jazz band in the rear of the church began to play as a cabaret-style singer's throaty voice wailed, "I'll take Manhattan, the Bronx, and Staten Island too..."

Dick Peter's remains were carried down the aisle by his grieving widow. In a cut-glass Tiffany vase. One of the few items that store sells for under one hundred dollars. I know. I've often sent that very same vase as a wedding present...but only when I'm not a close friend of the bride. I'd always thought its round shape had been designed to show off short-stemmed flowers. Holding Peter's ashes proved the vase's versatility. Mila wore all black—a fitted jacket, long skirt, leather riding boots, and an enormous Edwardian hat almost spanning the center aisle.

Glory Flagg, escorted by Barry DeWitt, trailed in Mila's wake. As always, Glory showed her colors. Today's catsuit was solid blue, but her gloves, scarf, and shoes were tricolor. And a crown of thirteen stars topped her thick hair. DeWitt looked handsome in an expensive, custom-tailored morning jacket and striped pants. He'd placed a white rose, not unlike the one Dennis had given me, in his lapel.

Isaac and Sally Lou Walton, wearing matching black polyester, marched in step behind them. He fingered the huge gold cross hanging around his neck while weeping copiously; she sang along with the sexy soloist. Sally Lou caught my eye and waved. I'll bet this macabre parade was a funeral first for St. Thomas's. I glanced up at the altar. The priest's, if not sad, at least resigned, expression had been replaced with one of total disapproval.

The players in this drama were all acting out some bizarre script that I couldn't follow. I thought both Dick Peter's widow and his ex-wife had as little use for Barry DeWitt as they'd had for dead Dick. Yet there Barry strode, center stage, holding on to Glory's waist with one hand, while patting Mila on the shoulder with his other. And how about those Waltons? They had miraculously turned into the dearly departed's long-lost kissing kin.

Keith Morrison sat in the pew in front of us. All dressed up in his Sunday best, he'd traded his signature t-shirt and vest for an Armani suit, worn with a black shirt and silver tie. With his full head of steel-gray hair, Romanesque nose, and jaded, jowly face, he reminded me of an aging don. In lieu of a missal, he was thumbing through an old issue of *Manhattan*. Dennis, who'd finally released my arm, whispered in my ear, "Morrison's giving one of the eulogies." I figured the magazine had to be part of his research. Kind of like a kid cramming ten minutes before the exam. But it couldn't be easy to find nice things to say about this dead man. Maybe Morrison would have to resort to quoting Dick Peter's own words.

"Hey, can I squeeze in next to you, Girlie?" Christian Holmes poked my shoulder.

Hating to relinquish my aisle seat, with its excellent view, I said to Dennis, "Slide over."

"If I do, I'll be sitting in Harry Brett's lap."

"Don't exaggerate, just move it, Dennis." I craned my neck around Dennis's back to get a look at the famous author whose book I'd just reviewed. Wow. I'd been a Brett buff since college. I couldn't wait to chat with him. I wondered if he'd like my critique. Mostly raves, but a few rants regarding the plot. There was none. Just a bunch of midlife-crisis guys on a hunting trip in West Virginia, sitting around a fire, spewing venom. Well-written venom, of course. Brett lived up to my long-standing ideal image of him. All British tweed and wide-wale corduroy. Wearing a black turtleneck sweater as his only sign of mourning. When he noticed me staring at him, from behind Dennis's back, he flashed a megawatt smile that electrified my toes.

The funeral began. Boy, this High Episcopalian service at St. Thomas's had turned out to be more Roman Catholic than Sunday Mass at our parish church, St. Thomas More. The Latin liturgy, old favorite hymns, and pomp and pageantry would have delighted my mother. Maura O'Hara still missed the traditions her beloved Catholic church had shed after Vatican II. However, the jazz band alternating with the organ and Cole Porter's "Anything Goes" following "Ave Maria" proved disconcerting. I wondered if Steve, *Manhattan's* elevator operator, had selected the music.

The priest didn't even attempt to eulogize Dick Peter. I'd bet that he'd never met the critic and probably rued being assigned as chief celebrant at the funeral of the man most Americans loved to hate. So, right after the gospel, Isaac Walton, accompanied by the band playing "I Get A Kick Out of You," stepped up to the pulpit. Who had choreographed this show?

The mourners had old-time country religion preached right in their sophisticated, big-city faces. Walton made Elmer Gantry sound a shy schoolboy. We heard every dirty little detail of growing up in a poor mining town in West Virginia. What would Keith Morrison have left to say? The reverend was stealing his *Our Gal Sunday* material. Walton's tabloid-style true-confession-as-a-eulogy held the congregation's complete attention. He closed, saying, "Though Dick and I never resolved our differences in this world, I'm confident that we will be seated next to each other, as kinfolk should be, at the Lord's big table in the sky. And, with God as my witness, I'll never leave Manhattan until my cousin's killer is caught." Many of the mourners gave him a standing ovation.

I turned to Christian Holmes. "Who produced this extravaganza?"

"Rumor has it that Mila Macovich had total control of the script and staging. I heard the widow gave Glory Flagg permission to handle all the arrangements. Musical, that is. And the flowers." So that explained the elaborate red, white, and blue floral pieces cluttering the magnificent altar and draping the entrance to every pew like a horseshoe.

"But, Christian, this entire funeral is a monument to bad taste."

"Consider the corpse, Girlie."

I laughed.

"Shush," Dennis demanded. But the giggles got the better of me, and I had to bury my head in my hands, covering my mouth, while hoping the row behind me might think I'd been overcome with weeping.

By the time I came up for air, Morrison had replaced Walton in the pulpit.

True to my prediction, he stood there and read Dick Peter's book reviews. Bitter, mean-spirited, cruel—even evil—and often, wildly sardonic and funny as hell. Gasps of shock and nervous titters filled the church. These savvy New Yorkers knew how wicked it was to respond to Dick Peter's lurid literary legacy with laughter. But, like me, they couldn't seem to control it.

The priest rushed through the rest of the service and when, mercifully, it finally ended, Mila took the microphone and invited everyone to a luncheon at Tavern on the Green. We all filed out of the church behind the official mourners, just in time to watch his widow dump Dick's ashes out of the Tiffany vase and into the middle of the Fifth Avenue traffic, causing a downtown bus to knock a mounted policeman off his horse. The officer picked himself up, adjusted his jodhpurs, and issued Mila a ticket.

Thirty

Very few of the mourners elected to join Mila at Tavern on the Green. Some offered work as an excuse. Some said they were sorry but they had plans that couldn't be changed. Some, like me, just walked away in silence.

As promised, Modesty waited for me on the steps of St. Thomas. And she was all riled up. "That cop ought to arrest Mila for polluting Fifth Avenue with Dick Peter's ashes. Don't we have enough dirt on the streets of New York?"

"Beyond bizarre," I said.

"Stay with Jake, Modesty," Dennis said, releasing his hold on my arm. "Don't let her out of your sight."

"Aye, aye, Captain." Modesty sounded snide but apparently took Dennis at his word. Her fingers latched onto my forearm. "Go play with your beads, Queeg. Jake's under my command now."

"Okay. But, ladies, don't venture out of *Manhattan* this afternoon. And when you finish work, go straight home. Don't let anyone into the apartment. Not Jennifer. Not anyone except Ben Rubin or me. Modesty, you stick with her. And get Jane over to stay with Jake if you have to go somewhere. Even for a few minutes. I'll pick you both up around eight thirty and drive you to Gypsy Rose's."

"Dennis," I said, "for God's sake, the bookstore's only a block away."

"Right. Maybe we'll walk. It's just that I hate to parade up Madison Avenue in costume. Even for one block."

"Who are you coming as?" Modesty asked Dennis.

"Be ready to roll at eight thirty and you'll be surprised, ladies. Ciao."

As Modesty and I descended the church steps, Glory Flagg navigated among the stopped cars on Fifth Avenue, attempting to scoop up Dick's ashes into her cosmetic case with a blush brush.

Manhattan seemed dead. Hans Foote stood sentinel in an almost-empty building. He issued Modesty's visitor's pass with an attitude of formality more somber than the funeral we'd just left. However, as we walked by him, headed for the elevator, Hans smiled. An absolute first. Then spoke, *"Manhattan* will never be the same now that Dick Peter's gone." His new expression could only be described as a happy face.

Steve's music selection for our elevator ride was a catchy number from the land of Oz that Mom used to sing while sweeping the kitchen floor: "Ding Dong, the Witch Is Dead." Today Modesty sang along all the way to the fourth floor. Her performance dazzled Santa Steve. "Welcome to *Manhattan,* miss. And may I say how much I like your outfit. It's every bit as smart and stylish as your voice. I'll bet you were the best-dressed woman at the funeral."

Modesty, wearing one of her basic black shrouds, seemed

delighted. It's so hard to tell with her. She dropped the refrain, fingered her rosary beads—she really shouldn't talk about Captain Queeg—and favored Steve with a shy smile.

"I wasn't in the church. I didn't have a ticket; I caught up with Jake outside on the steps. But you're right. Based on the weirdo mourning attire I observed waltzing out of that service, I probably would have been one of the most tastefully dressed women there."

"What did that tramp Glory Flagg wear?" Steve asked, no doubt recalling the ménage à trois that had led him to AA.

Modesty launched into a vivid fashion critique and I rudely interrupted. "Come on, this is our floor, let's go. I have work to do."

As we started down the hall, I said, "We have no time to waste on Steve. Remember, he has an alibi."

Fortunately, you can't insult Modesty. She admired the William Morris wallpaper, the dentil moldings, and the Persian carpets, then asked if she could have a quick look at the murder scenes. I did value her insight; we began a mini tour of *Manhattan*.

Allison's office, its entrance still covered by yellow tape, had no policeman on duty. Maybe he'd gone to the john. For all I knew, Ben could have solved the murders and pulled out the troops. We stepped over the tape and went in.

"Nice." Modesty's fingers traced the tops of Allison's highback chairs. "The lady had interesting taste."

Images of my first meeting with Allison raced through my mind. She'd been so alive. So vibrant. Then flashes of that morning when I'd found her with the dagger in her back flooded through me.

"Modesty, let's go. I don't feel well." We stopped for a drink of water. The halls remained eerily quiet. Were we the only ones on this floor? I forced myself to show Modesty Dick's office. Again, no guardian stood at the door. Maybe the investigation was over.

"What a mess," Modesty said. "Did the cops trash this place, or was Dick Peter as big a pig with his housekeeping as he was with his sex life?"

"A total pig."

She started to poke around the piles on his desk. "Hey, I don't think you should be touching anything, Modesty. The police may not be finished here." I knew I was. Suddenly I felt sick again. God, had I become as fragile a flower as Jennifer? And where was she? "Come on, Modesty, put that damn appointment book down. Let's see if Jen's arrived yet. She may be working away in my office."

We were en route there, when Barry DeWitt, who seemed to spend an inordinate amount of time in the men's room, once again rushed out of its door and this time slammed into Modesty.

"Oh good lord, ladies, you scared me. I didn't know there was anyone else here," he said, rubbing his shoulder. "Didn't you go to the luncheon at Tavern on the Green, Jake?"

"Well, obviously not," I snapped, then helped Modesty regain her footing.

"You're Modesty, aren't you?" Barry appeared flustered. "I think we have a friend in common. That is, besides Jake." Barry's voice brightened and he blushed. "Please don't tell Tom that I almost knocked you on your fanny."

"Just what are you doing here?" Modesty asked him. Torquemada's inquisition would have been gentler.

"Well, I do work here." Barry caught himself. I had to laugh. As furious as he must have been with Modesty, he couldn't compromise his chances with Too-Tall Tom. He forced a smile.

"I'm on deadline. Late with the old column. Gotta run. You know how that goes, don't you, Jake?"

"I'd suggest you look where you're going in the future, Mr. DeWitt." Modesty's icy tone stopped Barry cold. 'Too-Tall Tom hates a klutz."

Modesty approved of the view from my window. "Sixty-ninth Street has damn fine architecture, Jake."

"Where's Jennifer? How long could that appointment with her attorney have taken?" I walked over to my desk. Then I screamed. A Delft dagger, covered in blood, had been stuck in my calendar, the tip of its blade firmly centered on today's date. Happy Halloween.

Thirty-One

The blood turned out to be tomato sauce. Ben had arrived within fifteen minutes in response to my frantic phone call. He'd actually stuck his index finger in the red gook clinging to the dagger and covering most of my calendar and then tasted it. Yuck.

After I'd discovered the dagger, Modesty locked my office door and we stood side by side at the window, watching and waiting for the police to arrive. And discussing whodunit. When I'd stopped shaking and started thinking, I dialed Hans Foote and asked, "Which staff members came into the office this morning? Before the funeral?"

"Barry DeWitt showed up here about nine. Just for about a half hour. He came back again right after the funeral."

"Right. Did he have any visitors? I mean when he was here earlier."

"Yes. Glory Flagg and Keith Morrison arrived about five minutes after DeWitt. I passed them through. Then Mila Macovich showed up. They all left for the funeral together."

"Anyone else?"

"That Preacher Walton and his wife are here now. They came about twenty minutes ago, right after you and your friend got here."

"To see DeWitt?"

"No. Jennifer Moran stopped by early this morning. I don't think she went to the funeral, but she left around the same time as DeWitt, Flagg, and Morrison. Anyway, she left instructions to pass the Waltons through if they arrived here before she returned."

Curious and curiouser. Why were all these people running around *Manhattan* today? What were they up to? Had one of them thrust that dagger into my desk calendar as a Halloween trick that could only be taken as a threat?

"Has Jennifer come back?"

"I haven't seen her. She seemed very nervous, you know, and she looked sick, pale and wobbly, like she was frightened or something."

I was surprised, not only by the information Hans was sharing, but the change in his attitude. Maybe he'd been to an early AA meeting. Some of them started at six in the morning. I asked the next question gingerly. "Now don't take this as any sort of a criticism, but I really do need to know, did you leave your post at any time this morning?"

"Well, yes. I went to the men's room around eight thirty or so, and I just brought a cup of coffee down to the lobby a few minutes ago."

"From the coffee room on the fourth floor?"

"Yes."

"Did you take the elevator?"

"No. I always use the stairs. I need the exercise."

"So there's the chance that while you were away from your post—of course, for good reasons—someone else could have entered the building. An employee with a pass card or a visitor who could have been escorted up by an employee."

"I'd have to say that's correct. There's a third possibility. That someone else could have used an employee's card with or without the staff member's permission. However, I'm sure you've thought of that. Why are you asking so many questions, Miss O'Hara? Has there been another murder?"

"No. But..."

"Never mind. You can tell it to the police. Detective Rubin has just arrived. I'll send him up."

Before Ben reached my office, I made two decisions. I would tell Ben all I knew and all I didn't know but suspected. To do that I needed to be alone with him. So I suggested that Modesty go out, find a deli, and bring back three corned beef sandwiches and cream sodas for lunch. She had to be starving too.

"But, as you may recall, I promised Dennis I wouldn't let you out of my sight."

"For God's sake, Modesty, I'll be with a New York City Homicide detective. How much safer can anyone be?"

"Well, I don't like this; however, I would like to eat sometime today and you'd like to be alone with your other boyfriend. Right? You'd better plan on doing some fast talking. I'll be back in less than thirty minutes."

"Thanks. Now one more thing, Modesty. On your way, will you get on the phone and try to track down Jennifer? See if you can find out the name of her attorney. Did she ever get to see him? Maybe Michael knows where she is. I wonder what she wanted to tell me. Why did she come here this morning? And why did she arrange to meet the Waltons? They're somewhere in the building as we speak. This merry-go-round of suspects gets murkier by the minute." I rummaged in my tote bag and handed her my cellphone. "I'll ask Ben to check out all the offices on this floor, plus the ladies' room, the copy room, and the coffee room. Maybe Jennifer is here. But where? Why would she be avoiding us? God, maybe the killer's still here. Actually, the cops will need to search the entire building. Who knows who's lurking where?"

"I guess Mila Macovich had mighty few guests attend that post-funeral luncheon in the Tavern on the Green." Modesty wrapped her shawl around her shroud as Ben walked in the door.

A half hour later, the cops had scoured the building. No sign of Jennifer. Joe Cassidy was interviewing Isaac and Sally Lou Walton, separately, and Ben was keeping Barry DeWitt waiting in the wings for his interrogation. Then the partners would switch suspects. After several false starts—hampered by Ben's blank expression—I'd made my confession regarding the withholding of evidence and said mea culpa. I ended up in tears, had to borrow Ben's handkerchief for only about the twentieth time in our relationship. Then as a grand finale, certain that my playing detective would make him totally ticked, I shared the results of the ghostwriters' and my own investigations. To my amazement, something I said along the way prompted a confession from Ben.

"So Dennis Kim spent the night before Allison's murder holding Keith Morrison's hand. Then he picked you up at dawn in front of his father's fruit stand and drove you to work? Is that right?" A lock of Ben's thick black hair tumbled appealingly over his left brow.

"Yes. Why? Is that important?"

"Well, yeah. It gives Morrison an alibi for most of the window of opportunity. Cassidy interviewed him at length. Morrison never mentioned that all-nighter. Strange. But...the truth is..." Ben brushed the unruly curl out of his eye.

"What?" I asked.

He stared at the floor. Then he shrugged, turned, and walked over to the window.

"For God's sake, Ben, tell me."

Still looking out the window, he said, "When you drove up so early that morning, I watched you step out of the Rolls. I thought you'd spent the night with Dennis."

The door opened. Modesty strode in, out of breath, carrying a bag that filled the room with the divine Jewish deli aroma of corned beef on rye and sour pickles.

We plotted strategy while wolfing down our food. Each of us juggled a yellow pad, a sharp pencil, and a thick sandwich. Though Ben's dramatic last line prior to Modesty's entrance had shaken as well as stirred me, it also had explained much of Ben's strange behavior. I realized that any real discussion of our relationship would have to wait 'til after the Halloween Happening and Gypsy Rose's séance; however, I felt better knowing we were working together again.

Ben was duly distressed that I'd invited all the suspects to the séance with a promise of unmasking of the killer, but he certainly wanted to be in on the action. Modesty's marvelous memory provided him an accurate reportage of the ghostwriters' conversations with their assigned suspects and the conclusions they'd reached.

"I'm impressed," Ben said. "You ghostwriters have uncovered some great stuff. But, Jake, you keep dancing with death. And, despite some fine—if unorthodox—detective work, we still can't be sure whodunit."

The dancing brought back memories of Dennis. I'd left the tango out of the tangled tale I'd told Ben. But now all the information Glory Flagg and Dennis had revealed regarding Robert Stern—and that I had shared, in brief, with Ben—jumped back into my mind. I'd bared my soul as well as the ghostwriters' heartfelt theories to Ben. It was time for him to reciprocate. "What about Robert Stern? Is he off your suspect list? Have you released him from the hospital?"

"He's home free, Jake," Ben said.

"Why? For what reason?" Modesty demanded.

"Actually, there are two reasons. Stern rallied this morning. Regained his memory and became totally lucid. Absolutely amazing. And, facing a possible indictment in Barbara Ferris's death, he asked to make a statement."

"Wow," I said. "He was totally crackers yesterday."

"First, Stern admitted he'd lied about a dagger missing from his collection. However, he'd given a set of six Delft daggers to Dick Peter. Years ago, before Dick's affair with Stern's wife. He didn't want to tell us before, because he'd been protecting Allison Carr. Stern had seen her at *Manhattan* after ten the night of Dick's death. They both lied about what time they'd gone home. Furthermore, she was one of the few people who knew where Dick had stashed the daggers, and Stern believed she'd killed Dick. His butler confirms the dagger gift-giving, citing records and receipts to prove it." Ben took a swig of his cream soda. "When Allison Carr was murdered, Stern realized someone else had not only used one of Dick's daggers to stab him, but had stolen the other five and subsequently used one of them to stab Allison. Stern then was convinced Allison must have witnessed something incriminating. The night of the murder, Stern had smelled a heavy perfume, which he later connected to Barbara Ferris. He liked Barbara and couldn't accept that she'd killed Dick and Allison. He'd invited Barbara over so he could ask her some questions."

"Did she sleep there Friday night?" I asked, expecting a no.

"I see one of you ghostwriters spoke to her doorman too,"

Ben said. "No. Barbara and a girlfriend went to a singles dance in Yorkville. Then she stayed overnight at her friend's."

"Go on," I said.

"The butler had Saturday evening off, leaving Stern and Ferris alone," Ben said, "but before Stern could query Barbara, he had to use the john. She waited in the dining room. When he came back, she was dead. Stern lost it."

"But, Ben, how do you know Stern didn't kill Barbara?" Modesty asked. "How can you be so sure?"

"Because of the second reason that he's no longer a suspect," Ben said. "All three victims were stabbed by a right-handed killer. The doctors at Mount Sinai say Stern couldn't have closed his right hand over the dagger. Couldn't get a grip. He suffers from advanced carpal tunnel syndrome. Stern's hidden evidence, but he's no killer."

Jeez. I'd just bet... "Ben, did Stern swipe the 'M' file?"

"There you go. Good work, Nancy Drew." But Ben was teasing, not scolding.

"Why would he do that?" Modesty asked.

"Because his butler's last name starts with an 'M,'" I said. 'To cover up their affair. Stern suspected Dick Peter's notes would drag them out of the closet and through the mud."

My cellphone rang. Modesty retrieved it from somewhere within the cavernous folds of her black bundling. "This could be Jennifer. I've left messages for her all over town." However, Michael was on the line. After a few terse yeas and nays, Modesty hung up. "Well, he claims he knows nothing and, get this, is worried about his wife. Right. Anyway, Michael checked the Morans' answering machine and just wanted to tell me that he hasn't any idea where Jen might be. When she left the house this morning, Jen told him she'd be working most of the day with Jake O'Hara here at *Manhattan*."

Michael wasn't the only one worrying. My lunch lurched in my upper digestive track. "You didn't find out her attorney's name?"

"No," Modesty said. "But I talked to Too-Tall Tom; he's calling all her friends and going over to her building. Someone must know something."

"Let me ask the Waltons." Ben stood up and started for the door. "Since Jennifer had an appointment with them immediately following her visit to her attorney, there may be a connection. I need to talk to them and Barry DeWitt anyway. In the meantime, keep writing. Fill those yellow pads. The solution to this case lies somewhere in all these cross currents."

I stared at my pad. I'd doodled a merry-go-round. Every one of its riders had a dagger in his back.

Thirty-Two

Ben assured me that I'd never been considered a suspect. Well, not really. He did admit that my unwelcome detective work had convinced Cassidy that I was not only a danger to myself, but to their investigation. How I wish I could have been a butterfly on the wall during that exchange. I knew Ben and I had reached a temporary truce. If the murderer wasn't unmasked tonight, even if I remained alive, my detective days were numbered. That's why we had to arrive at the solution during the séance. When Ben left my office to interview the Waltons and Barry DeWitt, carrying on the business of the NYPD Homicide Department, I went back on the job too.

Modesty grumbled, but I could see she'd been bitten by the detective bug. And she had promised Dennis Kim she'd stand by me. No matter where I roamed. We took the stairs, and while Hans Foote was answering one of the detective's questions, ducked out the back door of *Manhattan* and into a cab.

Morrison, who—I believed—held the string that could unravel this mystery, lived way up north on Fifth Avenue near the Museum of the City of New York, another of my favorite

Saturday morning haunts. Modesty and I were about to torment him with a Halloween trick-or-treat visit.

I'd called Pax Publishing to make sure Morrison hadn't gone into his office after the funeral, and after learning he was at home, I'd decided to surprise him. The Brisbane, a nineteenth-century landmark located at 1215 Fifth Avenue, had the distinct possibility of being the only building in Manhattan with its own monument. A bust, prominently displayed across the avenue in front of Central Park, salutes Mr. Brisbane and his publishing achievements. Now if we New Yorkers could only find out: Who the hell was Major Deegan? And why had we named an expressway after him?

The sun had vanished behind a pile of gray clouds, and though it was not yet three o'clock, the day was dark. A cold rain and high wind whipped across our faces as Modesty and I left the cab and ran for the lobby. The Brisbane's doorman was ushering in a small group of children all decked out in expensive, trendy costumes, toting designer trick-or-treat bags and accompanied by their nannies. Modesty and I attached ourselves to their merry little band. I adjusted an angel's damp halo as we trooped through the ornate entrance, hoping the doorman would think I was one of the nannies. I figured Modesty could pass for a big kid all dressed up as death.

When the doorman smiled down at my little angel, I said, "We promised her grandfather, Mr. Morrison, that we'd be sure to stop by and say happy Halloween to him. What's his apartment number again?"

Fortunately, he'd given me the number—Morrison's apartment took up an entire floor—and had turned away to admire a purple dinosaur when my annoyed angel announced, "My Pop-Pops lives in Palm Beach. And, lady, will you get your hand off my halo?"

Modesty and I rode the elevator to the fourteenth floor and walked directly into a twenty-foot foyer, featuring marble floors, crushed velvet wall coverings, and gaslight sconces. A red door, not unlike Elizabeth Arden's, was straight ahead.

"How come there's never a thirteenth floor in any of these fancy old buildings?" Modesty asked. "I can understand the Marriott Marquis not having one, but wouldn't you think an architect of this caliber would have had better sense? I think thirteen has been given a bad rap. My numerologist says it's my best number and it works well in any combination..."

"Modesty, please."

The red door opened and Marilyn Monroe stood in front of us. "Happy Halloween, kiddos," Marilyn said in a whispery voice. "Well, don't be shy, Sugars, you two just come on in here. Have I got a treat for you."

It wasn't until after we were seated in the dimly lighted drawing room—about the size of the Waldorf-Astoria lobby and filled with candlelight and flowers—that I realized this Marilyn Monroe was Keith Morrison in drag.

"Gotcha, Jake O'Hara. You too, Miss Modesty. I do love a good trick on Halloween. Glory did my makeup. What a hoot. You ladies awarding prizes tonight for best costume? I figure unless that fruitcake DeWitt comes as a naked Madonna, I'm your winner."

"Everyone will be a winner," I said. "The prize will be learning the name of the killer."

"Hell, Jake, I know that already." Morrison stood, removed his wig and carefully draped it over a lampshade. "Now how about some caviar and champagne? Come on, ladies, it's my favorite holiday. Let's start celebrating."

Modesty dropped her shawl on top of Keith's wig, settled into the downy couch, then turned to our host. "So, start spreading the news along with the caviar, Mr. Morrison. Who's your choice for killer? And, more importantly, why? While you're telling us, you might just go ahead and pour some of that champagne."

"Barry DeWitt. *Manhattan*'s fabulous switch hitter," Morrison, wearing a white chiffon halter dress, three-inch spikes, and double-thick false eyelashes, said with a straight face. "Who else could it be? Motive. Means. Opportunity. Barry had them all. It's a classic crime case. And the solution's self-evident. I'd be truly disappointed, Jake, if you of all people haven't come to the same conclusion."

"It's certainly a good possibility," I said. "But, Mr. Morrison, how can you be so sure Barry's our killer?"

"Glory's shared her galleys with me." Morrison slipped out of his white satin sandals and kicked them under the bar cart. Where had he ever found a pair big enough? I stared at his scarlet painted toenails. His feet had to be at least a size twelve. "I've been in the book business a long time, Jake. I can read a serial killer with one eye closed. Every paragraph devoted to DeWitt proves he's a psychopath. The evidence leaps off the pages."

"Well, I have three questions for you," I said. "And your honest answers would help convince me of Barry's guilt." The champagne cork popped.

"I only know how to give honest answers, little lady." Morrison poured three drinks. "As a child, listening to *Our Gal Sunday*, my ethics were set in stone. Shoot."

I stood and held my fluted glass high. "Happy Halloween! Here's to the unmasking of a murderer."

Modesty, who'd been downing the beluga at record speed, now jumped up. "I'll drink to that, but then, with Dom Pérignon, I'd drink to anything. Cheers." Had Modesty actually made a little joke? The three of us smiled and clicked our glasses. The moment of toasty warmth passed.

We all sat down again and I began my cross-examination. "Okay. Mr. Morrison, there are several things about your involvement in this case that bother me. First, a reasonable person might assume, based on your recent behavior and despite your denials, that you're having an affair with Glory Flagg. Where's your wife? Just what is going on between you and Glory? Then there's your relationship with Isaac Walton. Why have you been hanging around the reverend and his Pledged-For-Lifers? But what I'm really dying to know is why you and Glory were visiting Barry DeWitt—your very own candidate for serial killer—at *Manhattan* this morning?"

Morrison crossed one leg over the other, resting his left ankle on his right knee—somewhat incongruous amid all that flowing chiffon—and finished his champagne. "Well, Jake, that's four questions, not three; however, I'll be happy to answer all of them. My wife of almost forty years is in Salem. Sabrina spends every Halloween there. Most years I join her, but sometimes, as happened this season, I'm just too busy. Her family came over on the *Mayflower*, you see, and settled in Massachusetts. Sabrina never misses her annual pilgrimage to her hometown."

"Pilgrimage?" Modesty asked.

"Yes." Morrison sounded sad. "Sabrina's great, great, great-grandmother, Elspeth Bloodsworthy, practiced witchcraft and the good people of Salem burned her at the stake. My wife returns every Halloween to lay a wreath at Elspeth's grave. She'll be home tomorrow. We always celebrate All Soul's Day together with a special dinner. I can't tell you how much I miss my Sabrina."

I nodded. Modesty, for once, remained speechless too. Keith Morrison stood, walked to the bar cart, poured himself and us more champagne and continued. "Glory's a great gal. If Sunday had grown up in Brooklyn, I think she'd have been a lot like Glory. There's never been a romance or sex of any sort between me and Glory. That smart little lady has become my protégé as well as a potential business partner. But I really can't discuss the details—the deal's still under very confidential negotiations."

Maybe Modesty was right about the Flagg-Morrison arrangement. She smirked at me.

But Morrison just smiled. "Indeed, I've never cheated on my wife. If you knew my Sabrina, you'd understand. Which brings us to your third question, Jake."

I smiled back, nodding encouragingly.

Keith Morrison now glowed. Right through his pancake makeup. "I'm now a card-carrying member of the Pledged-For-Lifers." His eyes were bright, his voice full of passion. "God wants husbands to remain faithful to their wives. That's why I've become committed to the movement, to my Sabrina, and to help other men live up to their marriage vows. Isaac is a fine man. And if we can iron out a few things, there could be a book deal. His childhood memoirs about growing up with that son of Satan, Dick Peter, might make for an even more teary read than Frank McCourt's. But I may have a more tragic plot for Isaac."

I smiled. "Well, well. A little profit making for you and Isaac mixed in there with your old-time religion?"

"Now, Jake, you know the Bible tells us that what you reap is what you sow."

"I guess I never read your interpretation into those words." I sipped my drink. "Okay, three down. Barry DeWitt to go."

"Simple answer there, Jake. Did you know that Barry and I were both scheduled to present eulogies this morning? Never an easy performance to prepare for, under any circumstances, but especially difficult when the deceased was so hated by all the mourners. Killer or not, I didn't want Barry stealing my theme or my thunder. Glory, who has such marvelous stage presence, suggested that we'd better have a chat with Barry. She'd been having her own troubles with that manic Mila Macovich trying to hog the processional. Dick Peter's widow has always demanded center stage. Anyway, our visit to *Manhattan* was in the nature of a run through...who'd say what. A dress rehearsal, if you would. But while Barry and I were agreeing who'd say what, Mila arrived. She canceled Barry's eulogy. Cousin Isaac would deliver instead."

Unfortunately, all of Keith Morrison's answers made some perverse kind of sense. My Halloween trick had proved to be no treat. Modesty and I headed home.

Thirty - Three

We grabbed a taxi. Ordinarily, this would have been impossible on a rainy holiday afternoon, but another small group of fairy princesses and wicked witches were hopping out of a Gypsy cab—where except on Fifth Avenue do kids go trick-or-treating in taxis?—and we got lucky.

I checked my messages. Ben had left one. The Waltons said Jennifer had called before the funeral, saying she had to talk to Isaac about Michael. She sounded crazed, so they'd agreed to meet her later. Feeling antsy, I said to Modesty, "Let's make a quick visit to the bookstore. I want to see how Mom and Gypsy Rose are holding up."

"Your promises are as empty as my agent's," Modesty sneered. "You told Dennis Kim you'd go straight home. And now you've made me a part of your bald-faced lies."

As bizarrely as Modesty behaved, her standards have always been far higher than mine. "Come on, Modesty. Mom and Gypsy Rose may need help. A Halloween Happening doesn't just happen, you know. Maybe Too-Tall Tom or Jane will be there with some new information; they may have heard something from Jennifer. Where the devil could she be?" My words worked as I'd expected and I directed the driver to stop at the bookstore.

Dennis Kim's Rolls Royce was double-parked on the northeast corner of Madison and 93rd Street. Damn. Could he be at his father's fruit stand? Of course that would indicate that he'd actually walked an entire block. I thought he had an appointment this afternoon with Robert Stern, who was now officially removed from the homicide department's suspects list. Maybe Dennis had popped into the bookstore to celebrate his client's clean slate with a cup of cappuccino and a tea leaves reading. If so, would Stern be with him?

The store bustled with busy people spending money as if they were afraid that all New Age literature might be re-maindered this very day. As if that would ever be the way the fortune cookie crumbled. Once again Aaron Rubin manned the cash register. And Christian Holmes kept the lines, which stretched in two snaky circles round and round the store, calm so that Aaron could collect.

Every table in the tearoom was packed with those who were not grabbing Caroline Myss and Deepak Chopra off the shelves. These folks were devouring volumes of orange cupcakes topped with candy witches, goblins, and ghosts. Then washing all that gook down with apple cider. The two part-time sorceresses had been added to the wait staff.

Modesty and I did a quick walkabout. We almost tripped over Gypsy Rose, who sat in the lotus position in front of the floor-to-ceiling window that faced 93rd Street. Dressed as a Viking, complete with a wig of blonde braids and a homed headdress, she appeared to be in a trance. I was afraid she'd be trampled.

"For God's sake, Gypsy Rose, this is neither the time nor the place to meditate." I bent down and shook her shoulder.

She opened her eyes. "Jake? You're here. I just received a message for you."

"Long-distance from the grave?" Modesty asked.

"Now you know better than that, Modesty," Gypsy Rose said. "Spirits don't live in their shrouds. Life after death goes on in the world beyond the grave." She stood, then stared at me. "This message came directly from Zelda. I'd been rearranging the pumpkin heads. Jake, I've been having second thoughts about them. Anyway, unexpectedly and unbidden, Zelda arrived. She'd run into Glory Flagg's spirit guide and invited her to the séance. There's been a lot of peer pressure for Dick Peter's guide to show up too. But what really knocked me out was Zelda's message for you."

"What?" I asked.

Gypsy Rose took my hand. "Zelda said, 'Tell Jake to take another ride on the merry-go-round.' Then she vanished and you appeared."

"What the hell does that mean?" Modesty asked.

I shivered. "I don't know," I said. But I was afraid that I did.

Modesty stayed to help Gypsy Rose grapple with the pumpkin heads while I went to find my mother.

Too-Tall Tom stood on a small stepladder, attaching a sign atop an orange velvet-curtained booth. It read: 'Take A Fire Walk With Mrs. O'Leary. $35. Cash Only. No Refunds." He waved his hammer. "Hi, Jake."

"Have you seen or heard anything from Jennifer?" I asked.

"No." Too-Tall Tom inserted a nail into the garish fabric. "But Jane's still out searching down leads. I called everyone I could think of but didn't come up with a single clue."

"Well, thanks. I'll talk to you when you come down to earth. Do you know where my mother is?"

"When I last saw her, she was over there in aisle three."

Too-Tall Tom used his hammer to gesture to the right. "Between Joan Mazza's *Dreaming Your Real Self* and *Chicken Soup for the Teenage Soul*."

I pushed my way through the throngs of shoppers and discovered my mother mediating a battle over the strategic placement of two competing booths. Neither the East Indian alternative healer nor the Sioux shaman wanted to take the higher ground, which was located in an alcove above the fray. Not when this maddening crowd was so freely spending money on the floor.

The healer's heated position reflected his desire to present his video, "Alternative Angles for the Sexually Challenged," in the best possible light. The shaman felt just as strongly about his own medicine show.

The dispute had disintegrated into an impending disaster, with the shaman—a big attraction—threatening to return to his reservation if he couldn't have the television screen moved. Mom wasn't able to out-shout them and offer a compromise. As I was about to come to my mother's aid, Gypsy Rose and Modesty, charging like the cavalry, arrived to rescue her.

While Gypsy Rose, who could shout loud enough to be heard in Chicago, reminded the combatants just whose territory they were fighting over, I had one of the sorceresses bring Mom and me cafe au lait and croissants. Then we retreated to Gypsy Rose's third-floor den.

My mother looked tired. She ran her fingers through her short ash-blonde hair and sighed. "Jake, as a girl, I always preferred the Beverly Gray series to the Nancy Drew drivel. If you'd only agreed with my literary assessment, maybe you'd be a reporter now, instead of always being in the middle of murder."

"Mom, it seems to me that Beverly got into as much, if not more, hot water than Nancy." I sipped my cafe au lait. "So drink your coffee, eat your croissant, and quit worrying. This murder case is almost closed."

"I hope so. I want my daughter back. And where's Ben these days? I know he's working hard, but is there something wrong? Have you two had a fight?"

"More of a disagreement. It's over now. He'll be here tonight."

"Does Ben know whodunit?" my mother asked.

"By tonight we'll all know, Mom." I sounded far more confident then I felt.

Modesty banged on the door and came in. "Jake, Dennis Kim just stormed in here and yelled at me. He says I broke a solemn promise. You go right downstairs and tell him you're totally responsible for your own bad behavior."

"What's wrong, Modesty?" my mother asked. "Why is Dennis all upset? Oh, God, is Jake in danger?"

If I had a Delft dagger handy, I might have killed Modesty. "It's about those damned pumpkins, Mom. You know, the really ugly ones that Mr. Kim sent Gypsy Rose. I'd better go down and see what I can do to save their faces."

When Dennis calmed down, I asked, "Have you heard anything about Jennifer?"

"No. Is she missing? I've been at Robert Stern's all afternoon. I've just walked back over from Fifth. There were no spots, so I had to park outside Gypsy Rose's."

"That's really tough, Dennis," I said. "Imagine having to trek less than two blocks. Why, you must be weary." Modesty had delivered me to Dennis and disappeared. I watched her chatting with Christian Holmes. Any atheist in a storm. The crowd had thinned out. Gypsy Rose would be closing the bookstore from five 'til eight in order to complete the arrangements for tonight.

"Don't be such a nasty toad. You owe me one, Jake. Stern's coming to your séance."

"Really? That's great," I said, still looking across the room. Jane had joined Modesty and Christian, waving her hands and talking a mile a millisecond. Then the three of them descended on me.

"Jake, I spoke to Jennifer's Aunt Mabel," Jane said. "She gave me Jen's attorney's name. Of course, he told me nothing. But Mabel dished the dirt. Jennifer filed for divorce this morning. The grounds are adultery. And she named Mila Macovich as correspondent!"

Thirty-Four

I poured Modesty and myself two Devil Mountain Ales, kicked off my only pair of high heels, stripped off my mourning clothes, changed into rag bags, and crashed into the Eames chair. My mood matched the miserable weather. The short walk from the bookstore to our co-op had left me chilled and damp. Worse, the light drizzle had spotted the bottom of my basic black, lightweight wool Donna Karan dress and frizzed my hair. And, all too soon, I'd have to change again into Too-Tall Tom's recycled witch's wear.

During our walk from Gypsy Rose's, Modesty pointed out that the tiny tots who'd been trick-or-treating earlier in the day had disappeared. Ghosts, fairy princesses, and angels had been replaced by the Spice Girls and Elvis. Carnegie Hill had become a Halloween playground for shivering pre-teens traveling in packs. I'd hardly noticed. Zelda's message from the world beyond haunted me. Ugly thoughts that had come uninvited into my mind had settled in like horrific houseguests who didn't know when to leave. My body may have been moving along down Madison Avenue, but my mind had remained riveted on that *Manhattan* merry-go-round. A conundrum of clues continued to whirl with the horses, but Jennifer Moran's pink pony currently carried no rider.

"So what's with Jennifer?" Modesty spoke my thought. "Do you think...er, well, that the ditz is in real danger, Jake?"

"That's the first item in a messy lineup that keeps racing through my head. And the one that worries me the most." I took a long swig of my beer.

"Want to talk about them? The troublesome items, I mean."

I did. Suddenly, I felt grateful that the bizarre but totally loyal Modesty was sitting here with me, sharing a beer and ready to listen. "Okay, how about a long shot? Did Jennifer pull this vanishing act to run away from her marriage, or from the murderer, or to avoid Ben Rubin's questions? Could she possibly be our serial killer?" I asked, realizing my vague notion that Jen had murdered three people in order to frame her cheating husband seemed pretty lame.

Modesty shook her head. "Never. She once told me that before she married Michael, if she saw a cockroach in her apartment, she'd call down to the concierge and have him send up the porter to kill it. Then Jennifer would tip the guy two bucks. I told her at two dollars a roach in New York City, she'd soon be broke." Modesty twisted her beads. "After they were married, Michael became her exterminator. Jen's no killer."

"So why do you think she's running?"

"Fear? She could know whodunit. And, maybe—dumb as Jen can be—the killer knows that she knows. Which, of course, would make her a loser in the most dangerous game in Manhattan—Jennifer might be facing her own Final Jeopardy."

"Jesus. I just wish we'd hear from her."

"Meanwhile, let's look at the odds," Modesty said. "Who's your favorite contender for killer?"

"It looks like a dead heat. Isaac Walton and, thanks to all you ghostwriters and most of his fellow suspects touting him, the so-easy-to-hate Barry DeWitt. I'd say it's Isaac by a nose. Then there's a clue I can't quite grasp; it keeps nagging me. Somehow, I believe our dark horse could be Michael Moran."

"I like the ladies," Modesty said. "And one about-to-be-put-out-to-pasture stallion. I'd been convinced that Morrison couldn't have done it, but now my gut tells me that he and Glory could be co-killers. No matter what bologna he spreads, something's going on between Keith Morrison and Glory Flagg. And power is a great aphrodisiac. Their private business dealings may include a motive for murder. I never thought stabbing someone in the back would be Glory's style. I always thought of her as a shooter. But after our visit to Morrison's, I'm not so sure. Glory and Keith are neck and neck. And Mila Macovich's another front-runner. All that money—not to mention freedom—just waiting for her in the widow's circle."

"Well, the séance is at midnight." I looked at my watch. "Less than seven hours away. Let's hope the dead can come up with an answer. I'm still full of questions."

"Like what?"

"Like why did Keith Morrison paint such a placid picture of his relationship with Isaac Walton when Michael Moran said they'd had a major screaming match at Madison Square Garden over Glory Flagg's honor and some filthy lucre? Like why Morrison didn't tell Joe Cassidy that he had Dennis Kim as an alibi through the night and early morning that Allison Carr had been stabbed? Like why has Barry DeWitt—the man with the most blatant motive and Dick's heir apparent as the man most Americans love to hate—become so entwined with both Mila and Keith Morrison? Like why Glory wanted me to hand Peter's files over to her? She claimed they held the key to the killer, but could that really be why she wanted them? I don't think so. Like why did Jennifer refuse to talk to the police right after Dick's murder? Like did Dick Peter know about Michael and Mila's affair? Like what time did Isaac Walton leave Dick's office? Sally Lou could be lying. And, most importantly, like who else was present at *Manhattan* on the night of Dick Peter's death? If Allison Carr and Barbara Ferris were murdered because they knew too much, what had they witnessed?"

"Jesus, Jake." There was an edge of sadness in Modesty's anger. "The killer could be any of the above."

"Like you're so right."

My private line rang. I dashed into my bedroom to answer it. "Jake O'Hara."

"I'm leaving for Europe." Jennifer. And she was difficult to understand between the phone's static and her tears. "Don't ask where and don't tell anyone."

"Are you okay? God, where have you been?"

"I need to give you something before I go."

"Jennifer, Modesty and I will come and bring you back to my apartment. Where are you now?"

"Jake, listen to me," she sobbed. "Stop asking questions. I'm telling you this is a matter of your life or death. Go to that little Italian bakery on Christopher Street. You know, the one near Too-Tall Tom's place. The owner, Signora Giatto, is holding a package for you. Tell her that Jennifer sent you."

"But where..."

"There's no time for buts. Go. Leave now!" She hung up. Modesty stood in the doorway, arms crossed, one hand clutching her beads, as I pulled a sweater over my sweats and searched under the bed for my sneakers. She reminded me of Sister Mary Thomas, my eighth-grade teacher. Only more formidable.

"Just where do you think you're going?"

"Out. But I'll be right back. You stay here and wait for Dennis. And Too-Tall Tom said he'd drop by with the costumes."

"Yeah, right. As Ruth said to Naomi, 'Whither thy goest, I go,'" Modesty snarled.

"I think Ruth said that to her husband, not her mother-in-law."

"The mother-in-law came along as part of the package." Despite how frustrated I felt, I smiled.

"The package? Modesty, I swear sometimes your ESP is as good as Gypsy Rose's. Okay, let's go. I'll fill you in on our way."

Thirty-Five

Christopher Street appeared far more festive—and far more crowded—than Bourbon Street in New Orleans during Mardi Gras. We'd taken the standing-room-only subway to Astor Place, headed down to Broadway and West Fourth, then walked west. My mood may not have improved, but the weather had. The skies were clear and the air felt warmer. Greenwich Village seemed to be overrun with thousands of New Yorkers plus tons of tourists; the annual Halloween Parade always drew enormous crowds and tonight's was no exception. Organizers were attempting to bring a little order out of the cheery chaos, but the plumes, tiaras, baubles, beads, and boas, as well as the men wearing them, proved to be irrepressible.

Some of the marchers had spilled over on the sidewalk and were chatting with the onlookers. The colorful costumes ranged from a spectacular Marlene Dietrich, wearing a gown of transparent netting and several strategically placed sequins, to a Madonna, painted to look much prettier than the real thing. Everyone, except Modesty and me, who were struggling to wend our way through the packed streets to the bakery, seemed to thrive on the infectious gaiety. But even as distraught as I was, I could understand why Too-Tall Tom had wanted to be part of this huge, glorious parade and the gala parties that would follow.

We found the entrance to Giatto's blocked by a fantastic Auntie Mame float, featuring a replica of Mame's 1920s Manhattan townhouse living room, complete with a scaled-down staircase. In the jostling for parade positions, the float had been shoved out of the street and onto the sidewalk. Five extraordinarily realistic and fabulously garbed Patrick Dennis characters had jumped down from their assigned places and were struggling gallantly—though somewhat hampered by their high heels—in an attempt to tug the float away from the bakery's front door. Modesty and I aided and abetted their efforts.

"Your costume is like so Catholic," the eight-months-pregnant Agnes Gooch character said to Modesty, as the pillow under his maternity top slipped during his labor.

"Are you on a float or just a marching monk?" a second character asked Modesty. He was dressed in the outré but magnificent flapper outfit that Auntie Mame had worn at her wild party on the night that her young nephew, Patrick, arrived to live with her.

I'll never know with what degree of testiness Modesty might have responded to those comments because of a speedy confluence of events. The perennially hungover Vera character, a Bea Arthur lookalike, complete with an ice pack atop his Clara Bow bob-style wig, shoved, as another man, dressed in Mame's formal riding-to-the-foxhunt attire, pulled, and the float sailed back into the street. The bakery door whipped open, and as Modesty and I dashed through it, the third Auntie Mame, dripping in paste diamonds and dressed in a sex, black peignoir and matching sleep mask—announcing he wanted a biscotti and espresso to go—and a tall, masked, horned red devil, who appeared from out of nowhere, followed us inside.

The plump Signora Giatto, wearing a Holly Golightly cat mask and chef's whites, manned the counter. My visits to Too-Tall Tom's exquisite gem of an apartment on Christopher Street were often preceded by a purchase of Giatto's famous cannoli, so I knew her well.

"Ciao, Signora, do you have a package for me? My friend, Jennifer, told me to pick it up here."

"Bella Jake, whatsa matter? You wearing that brute face for Halloween?"

I guess I really looked like hell. "It's been a tough day, Signora Giatto."

"Say, could I order a biscotti and espresso to go?" the Auntie Mame in the peignoir costume asked. "And pronto. I have a float to catch."

"Wait your turn, Mame," Modesty snarled.

The Signora rummaged under the counter and handed me a small package—about the size of a trade book—wrapped in plain brown paper. As I reached for it, the devil swooped down from behind me and swiped the package, sticking it under his left arm. While I whirled in an attempt to grab it back, I saw the Delft dagger under his cloak.

As the Signora and I screamed in sync, the door opened, and the Agnes Gooch character stood—half of him still on Christopher Street, but with his belly in the bakery—blocking the red devil's exit.

"The float is leaving," he addressed the peignoir Auntie Mame. "Right this very minute, whether you're aboard or not." Then Agnes Gooch spotted the dagger, once again dropped his pillow, and slumped after it to the floor.

The devil darted for the door, stepping down hard with one

cloven foot on the heap that was Agnes, as Modesty grabbed his tail. Jesus, would he stop to swing around and stab her?

I dialed 911 on my cellphone and yelled, "Drop that tail, Modesty!"

Signora Giatto prayed noisily. I thought, based on my limited knowledge of Italian, that she was making an Act of Contrition. Auntie Mame shoved his sleep mask atop his chic chestnut curls, reached for Modesty's rosary bead belt and yanked her back into the bakery but failed to get her to release her hold on the devil's tail. Then, as I feared, the devil did turn and thrust his dagger at Modesty. I threw my phone at him, grazing his right arm and forcing him to take aim again. Agnes Gooch stirred, looked up, and shouted, "Begone, Satan!"

Distracted, the devil didn't notice the foxhunt Auntie Mame character charge the entrance and whip out his riding crop. A slap was heard through the bakery as the crop landed on the devil's left shoulder. Ignoring what had to be a painful blow, the devil now held the dagger dangerously close to the nape of Modesty's neck. She flung herself toward the counter, losing contact with his tail, but avoiding contact with his dagger. Its blade landed in a loaf of Italian bread. With a burst of fury, no doubt fueled by both the sting from the slap and having missed Modesty, the devil wrenched the riding crop out of the incoming Auntie Mame's grip and ran like hell down Christopher Street— still clutching my package—with Agnes Gooch, Vera, and two Auntie Mames in hot pursuit. The remaining Auntie Mame adjusted his boa, gracefully descended the staircase, swung off the float, forged through the panicked crowd and brought back a policeman.

The devil's long legs had outrun the drag queens' high heels. They'd lost him as the "A" train doors slammed shut in Agnes Gooch's face.

In an attempt to comfort us, Senora Giatto served Cafe Diablo and anisette cookies as we tried to explain this trick-or-treat tale to the police. Though totally depressed at the loss of what must have been important evidence, Modesty and I thanked our Halloween heroes, inviting all of them—including the cop—to lunch next week at Gypsy Rose's tearoom.

When the Auntie Mame float had rejoined the parade and the officer had gone to the station house to file his report, Signora Giatto insisted that Modesty and I follow her into the kitchen. "Jennifer said that if anything went wrong during the delivery of her package," Signora Giatto said, as she opened a warming oven, "or if I heard that something bad happened to her, I should give this copy to the police."

Speechless, I stared into the oven. There, nestled among the fresh baked breads, lay a videotape in an unmarked cardboard jacket. Signora Giatto continued, "You know Patsy doesn't deal with the police." I remembered that Too-Tall Tom had told me the Signora's husband ran numbers. "So you take this, Jake, and you decide if the police should see it." Wow. The devil didn't know I had this warm-as-toast video in my hands. I grabbed my cellphone and left messages at all three of Ben's numbers.

Thirty-Six

"Dead!" my mother screamed. She and Too-Tall Tom had been vacillating between rage and relief since Modesty and I walked through the front door. "That's what I thought. That you'd both been murdered on the mean streets of Manhattan. I started planning a double funeral while the two of you were out, God only knows where, embracing all sorts of evil."

Modesty gulped and took a tentative step forward from the foyer into the living room. "Actually, Maura, only I grabbed hold of the devil's tail. Jake never touched him."

"Jesus, Mary and Joseph." My mother shouted her prayer, then turned to Too-Tall Tom. "Please, dear, mix us a pitcher of martinis. I do believe we're about to hear a chilling tale, and we'll be needing some fortification."

Modesty's abridged account of our brief encounter with the killer held Mom and Too-Tall Tom spellbound. I, however, squirmed in my seat, itching to watch the tape, but not wanting Mom to know I had it. As Modesty's story reached a climax and my mother drained her cocktail glass, I jumped up. "Listen guys,

I'm sorry to cut this short, but we have to change into our costumes. Where did you put them, Mom?"

My mother looked aggrieved. 'They're hanging in your closet, Jake."

Too-Tall Tom chuckled. "Don't worry, Jake. Your mother instructed me to have all of the outfits dry-cleaned. Who knows what witches wore them last?"

"Are you two up to going to the Happening?" my mother asked.

"Absolutely," I answered with far more assurance than I felt. Then I turned to Too-Tall Tom. "Don't you have a date with Barry?"

"DeWitt's stood up our Too-Tall Tom." Mom started to clear the glasses. "Now hurry, Jake. Dennis will be here at eight thirty. You only have about a half hour to get ready."

"Come on, Modesty," I said, "let's turn ourselves into witches."

We carried our drinks into my bedroom. I shoved the tape into my old VCR and pushed the play button. Steamy sex crowded my small screen.

"Lord love a duck," Modesty squealed. "Did you know you could do it in that position?"

"Well, not in handcuffs!"

Modesty and I sat rapt and silent through the rest of the show. Dick Peter may have been rotting in his grave, but in this production, he appeared eerily agile. His office was the set. Costume design by Victoria's Secret. The critic had costarred with two very animated performers...currently rated as red-hot suspects. One of the players must have placed a camera on a tabletop in order to immortalize what would turn out to be Dick's last stand. The date and time on the video confirmed it had been shot the night of his murder. At the end of our six minutes of voyeurism, we'd been shocked by the video's twists and turns, but had been left with no doubts about who'd killed Dick. Or why.

"Bingo!" Modesty yelled.

I felt as if I'd finally grabbed that elusive brass ring off the *Manhattan* merry-go-round. Only a few hours ago, I'd been in total despair, convinced my Hercule Poirot dog and pony show would be a bust. Now, with Ben's help, Dennis's cooperation, and an opportunity to discuss direction and casting with Gypsy Rose and Jane, I should be a smashing success in the role of detective at tonight's séance.

However, I'd need a quick conference call dress rehearsal for my all-important supporting cast. I reached for the phone. Then, when the dialogue, props, and staging were in place, I made a dramatic return to the living room to go over Mom's and Too-Tall Tom's lines.

After some fast talking, I'd convinced Dennis, dressed as a sexy Zorro—an odd choice of costume since Ben looked so much like Antonio Banderas—to go on ahead and play the part of a gracious host while Gypsy Rose hastily rearranged sections of the bookstore to accommodate our spur-of-the-moment production, having assigned Christian and Aaron to oversee the Happening. Then our Carnegie Hill apartment turned into a miniature rehearsal hall and Ben, without whom a cast of thousands couldn't pull off this caper, gave Mom, me, and the ghostwriters sound direction while choreographing the denouement.

I'd reached him at headquarters on my first try. He'd been about to call me, having retrieved all three of my frantic messages. Several of his staff and the missing persons department were searching for Jennifer. Ben said he'd put a tail on each of our murder suspects and would be right over.

When, truly surprised that he'd agreed to participate, I asked Ben why he'd be going along with my theatrics, he'd said, "Confession is good for the soul, and in this case, might spare the City of New York and its taxpayers the expense of a long, tawdry trial."

At eleven o'clock, when Modesty and I—requiring no acting ability to look like two truly bedraggled witches—arrived, Gypsy Rose's bookstore seemed to have entered a postmodern New Age. Some of the otherworldly outfits—I never knew they were so many ways to look like an angel—were so far out there that they made Christopher Street's drag queen costumes seem like Halloween ho-hum.

Working with such a sketchy script, we'd have to ad lib our way through the rest of the Halloween Happening scene as well as the séance. Thanks to our years as ghostwriters, Modesty, Jane, Too-Tall Tom, and I were well versed in the art of creating dialogue as we went along. And the party was winding down.

The fire walk instructor had attracted a large crowd, resulting in some slightly singed soles. So naturally, the magnet therapy booth, directly to the left of Mrs. O'Leary's fire area, was doing a brisk, barefoot business.

The East Indian healer had been a bigger draw than the Native American shaman, but at this late hour, even his attendance had dwindled. Most of the other exhibitors had folded up their tents. However, many of our séance guests had not yet appeared. And that made me nervous.

"Jake, Modesty. Happy Halloween." Glory Flagg's curvy Catwoman costume—the comic book, not the movie version— and feline mask did nothing to disguise either her Brooklyn accent or her sensational figure. "Why ain't you goils wearing your witch hats and masks? You'll never fool anyone this way."

"Isn't that the naked truth?" I said, putting on my face mask and plopping the peaked cone on my head. Modesty grimaced but did the same.

Keith Morrison, now suited up as a paunchy Batman, clung to Glory's arm with one hand while he adjusted his ears with the other. "Where are all the suspects?" he asked, scanning the rapidly emptying room.

As one of the fire-walking wounded limped out of the bookstore, he held the door open, and Mila Macovich, dressed in an elegant royal blue Empire gown and tiara, waltzed in, accompanied by Barry DeWitt, wearing a huge white Russian fur hat and hospital scrubs.

"Josephine?" I said to Mila, venturing an educated guess.

Mila extended her hand as if expecting it to be kissed. "Nyet, darling. Natasha from *War and Peace.*"

As I shook her hand, I couldn't help but notice what appeared to be an engagement ring. The diamond covered her knuckle. "Beautiful stone," I said.

"What are you supposed to be?" Glory asked DeWitt. "An *ER* reject?"

"In keeping with Mila's Russian literary theme, I have come as Dr. Zhivago," Barry said.

"And no doubt in several other costumes," Modesty mumbled.

Mila smiled down at her diamond, winked at Barry, but spoke to me. "There'll be an announcement soon."

"We may have an announcement ourselves tonight." Morrison tightened his grip on Glory's arm.

"I told you so." This time, Modesty didn't bother to lower her voice.

"Show time in fifteen minutes," Gypsy Rose called out, right on cue, crossing the length of the bookstore as Christian Holmes ushered out the last of the Happening's stragglers. "Michael

Moran and the Waltons are in the tearoom with Robert Stern. Dennis Kim's serving decaf cappuccinos and apple tarts. Come on, everyone, let's join them."

Gypsy Rose had selected a pink Chanel as her channeling costume. Or, maybe, despite her serene, appealing appearance and calm, gracious attitude, it had been the far more simple choice. I knew she'd been working behind the scenes on my production for the last couple of hours. And the Marie Antoinette getup that she'd planned to wear included three crinolines, a weighty wig, and a hefty dusting of powder.

Robert Stern, smiling like a man with a new lease on life, sported a gray jogging suit and windbreaker; he had distanced himself from the Waltons and Michael Moran. Aaron Rubin—also sans costume—whose serious face and kind eyes reminded me so much of Ben, sat next to Stern. The reluctant-to-attend Waltons had gone all the way. Isaac's satanic attire caught my attention and elicited a gasp from Modesty. This was no red devil, though. Lucifer, cast out of Heaven, would be more like it. Ghastly and garish. Sally Lou had reprised her wing-like hairdo and the white angel-style outfit. She'd added a halo. Michael lurked in a corner, looking sullen, dressed like the biker that he was. When I said, "Hello," he grunted.

Jane and Too-Tall Tom, who'd been setting up the seats for the séance, came in. "Have you heard anything from Jennifer?" Too-Tall Tom asked Michael.

"No," Michael growled and stared at the floor.

Then Glory, Morrison, DeWitt, and Mila joined us, and the little group of suspects shared coffee, Halloween tarts, and painfully strained conversation. All as scripted. I wanted these unwitting players to be totally fed up with each other's company.

Just before midnight, Gypsy Rose led them back into the bookstore, which my mother had lighted only with candles. We arranged our séance participants in a semicircle, facing both Gypsy Rose and the television screen hidden above her in the alcove. From skeptic to believer, this audience was alive with anticipation.

Glory sat to Keith's left, with Barry DeWitt next to her, and Mila next to Barry. Too-Tall Tom and Jane rounded out the left side of the semicircle. Dennis, in an impromptu move, grabbed a seat between Keith Morrison and Isaac Walton. Why did I smell a book deal? Seated on Isaac's right was Sally Lou, then Michael Moran, Robert Stern, Christian Holmes, my mother, clutching Aaron's arm, Modesty, and me. Gypsy Rose slipped into her burgundy leather armchair, facing us, her posture perfect, a slight smile lighting up her face, so beautifully framed in the candlelight. And, awaiting his cue, Ben sat behind the alcove's curtain...which covered the large-screen television.

"Now, I want you all to relax," Gypsy Rose was saying. "I'll be, for lack of a better word, going into a trance—but don't let that intimidate you. I'll still look like myself, but my spirit guide will be in residence in my body. She'll be your channel to the world beyond. And while I'm gone, there's no reason to keep quiet; the spirits enjoy lively audience participation. So ask questions. We're all here to get some answers from the dead and solve this mystery, aren't we?"

"Who's your spirit guide?" Glory asked.

"Zelda Fitzgerald," Gypsy Rose said with pride. "And I've been told that when she's taking my place, I assume her accent and demeanor. Zelda will ask Dick's spirit guide to put in an appearance; then his guide will address our questions to Dick. However, Dick himself may choose to speak to us. Either directly or through another medium."

"Does Zelda always show up?" Barry DeWitt asked, sounding like less than a true believer.

"Well, a séance isn't always scientific," Gypsy Rose explained. "I currently have three guides. One of them, Gray Feather, is an old master who only appears on special occasions. Who knows? You may meet him tonight."

"Who's the third?" Sally Lou sat on the edge of her chair.

"Mother, please, stop trafficking with Satan," Isaac Walton said.

"The third's a newcomer." Gypsy Rose smiled. "Showed up for the first time last summer. But she values her privacy in the world beyond as much as she did here on earth. I've promised never to reveal her identity. However, I can assure you that she won't be putting in an appearance tonight. The lady abhorred the press and considered Dick Peter's column to be the most repugnant of all."

Good Lord. Had Jackie O become Gypsy Rose's latest spirit guide?

"For God's sake, Gypsy Rose, let's get started," Robert Stern said. Isaac Walton shuddered.

But Gypsy Rose was gone.

"You all better make this snappy," a flirty voice with a slight Southern accent said. Gypsy Rose's lips were moving; however, I knew we were listening to Zelda. "I left a marvelous All Hallows Eve affair to come here. Bram Stoker is the guest of honor. Gerald Murphy and Scott have been plying him with liquor. So you all can understand why I'm in a hurry to return."

"Zelda?" My mother spoke. Mom, of course, was well acquainted with the blithe spirit, who'd been a frequent conduit to my father.

"Hello, Maura. Jack sends his love." Zelda was both charming and disarming. "Now, who's Glory Flagg? There's a master guide present who wishes to speak to her."

"Me." Glory's voice faltered and she fidgeted with her fur.

I glanced around the semicircle. The crowd seemed mesmerized.

Then a gruff cough caught our attention. "This is Gray Feather speaking." All traces of Zelda had vanished. Gypsy Rose's posture and attitude had undergone a dramatic change and her voice now sounded stern and humorless. "The wretched soul of Richard Peter is residing on a plane in the far reaches of the world beyond where contact is almost impossible."

"So the show's over?" Mila asked, starting to stand up.

"Please be seated, Madame. Almost impossible, I said. Let me explain. Souls travel through eternity in packs. Therefore, some of your own current spirit guides may be acquainted with Mr. Peter's guide. Miss Flagg, I have had telepathic communication with your guide, who may be able to assist us in this endeavor. I ask your permission to channel her."

"Yeah. Like I could stop ya. Go ahead." Glory winked at Gray Feather.

"Miss Flagg?" A cold female voice inquired. "You have summoned me?"

"Are ya my spirit guide?" Glory asked. "What's yer name?"

"Betsy Ross." She sounded proper and pragmatic. I wondered—aside from the obvious patriotic name connection, and Flagg was really Fuchs—why Ross had been assigned as Glory's guide.

Dennis said, "I'm sure I dated Ms. Ross in high school during another lifetime. I recall sitting next to her during home economics. That girl revolutionized sewing."

Modesty said, "Shut up, Dennis."

Glory laughed. "So do we get to talk to Dick?"

Betsy Ross sighed. "I would suggest, Miss Flagg, that you reveal whatever it is that you're covering up. And why. Deception clouds any clear communication with the world beyond. Especially on the remote plane where Mr. Peter has descended."

Glory grabbed Keith Morrison's hand. "I guess now's as good a time as any."

He removed his Batman mask and beamed at her.

"Now, Jake, don't be mad at me," Glory began. "Ya gotta understand, business is business. Right?" Where the hell was she going with this? "Anyhoo, when Keith's Pax Publishing officially bought out Harvest House today, we came to our final decision that a mystery by Dick Peter, ya know, the one you're ghostwriting..." My gasp at her callous breach of confidentiality interrupted her, but not for long. "Well, it's just one Dick book too many. Keith thinks my manuscript about my life with Dick—which he will now be publishing—is destined to be a bestseller. Yours would only hurt my sales. Ya see, it's a question of literary supply and demand. Nothing personal, Jake."

"Are you crazy? I'd like to remind you and Keith Morrison that I have a contract."

"I'm afraid you don't, Jake," Dennis said. "Keith never got around to signing it."

"And you're just telling me this now." I could hear the quiver in my voice.

"Look, Jake, I knew about the pending merger." Dennis's voice wavered too. "That's the main reason why I've been sitting up nights with Morrison, but I only found out about the book today."

"Mr. Kim has also been kept busy working on my deal with Keith's new publishing empire," Isaac said, apparently in an effort to defend Dennis.

"I thought one book connected to Dick was all the market could bear," I said.

"Jake, dear," Sally Lou said, "Isaac's book has nothing to do with Dick. He's writing about some dirt-poor gal called Sunday, who comes from a small mining town but grows up to marry an English lord."

"And there's something else I want to confess," Glory said. This woman sounded like Bill Clinton. "I'm getting married."

"What are you planning to do with the current Mrs. Morrison?" Modesty asked.

Glory giggled. "Not to Keith, silly. All these years, I've never revealed who the other man had been in Dick's and my longtime ménage à trois. I only wanted Dick's files to see if he'd used my mystery man's real name—so I could expunge it. But with the book coming out and all, that man—the one true love of my life—said, 'Go for it, Glory.' Harry Brett and I will be married in Kenya next week."

Barry DeWitt led the scattered applause. However, I think I was more upset about Glory marrying my favorite adventure author than I was about giving up the ghostwriting deal.

Gypsy Rose, once again her own person, called the séance back to order. "Gray Feather's troubled. Before he left, he told me that Betsy Ross has reached Dick's spirit guide, the Marquis de Sade, and that Dick's ready to confront his killers."

Ben didn't miss his cue to push the VCR play button and pull open the curtain.

Three frolicking naked bodies—who appeared sad rather than sexy—filled the large television screen in the alcove. Though still more than a tad upset, I felt the pride that Poirot always displayed at his denouements when Mila screamed, "Michael, I told you to trash that tape! How could I, a Macovich, ever have slept with the idiot of the century?"

Epilogue

"So this case began with one devil and ended with another. I do like symmetry," my mother said, as she poured Too-Tall Tom a cup of tea. The ghostwriters had gathered at Gypsy Rose's tearoom for a recap. Mom and Gypsy Rose were fussing over us. It was Tuesday afternoon, one week, almost to the hour, since I'd signed on as Dick Peter's ghostwriter. And the only dangerous liaison remaining on my calendar was this Saturday night's dinner date with the doctor/waiter, Fredric. I found myself looking forward to the challenge.

Modesty said, "Jake, you do realize that Mila murdered Allison and Barbara because she *thought* they might know too much?" I shivered, nodded, then gulped my tea. I'd worried all along that I might be killed for knowing too little.

"Isn't Michael just saying that to save his own tail?" Jane asked.

"Well, he is going to testify against her," I said. "Mila's not talking, but Robert Stern told Ben that Barbara Ferris hadn't noticed anything unusual on the night that Dick was stabbed. And it appears our red devil, Mila, actually committed all the murders. I'd bet Mila must have regretted killing Allison. Remember, she'd stolen Dick Peter's six Delft daggers, using one to stab him, perhaps planning to frame Allison. According to Michael, neither Allison nor Barbara had witnessed Mila and Michael going into Dick's office or, for that matter, anywhere at *Manhattan* that night. Michael claims Mila spotted Allison, then smelled Barbara's perfume, and later panicked and decided they both had to die. Isaac Walton was more fortunate. He'd left before show time."

"But you didn't see Mila the morning of Allison's murder," Too-Tall Tom said.

"Michael was there. He says he let her in the back door. Remember, Mila lived right around the corner from *Manhattan*."

Gypsy Rose passed around the bagels. "Mila might have murdered Robert Stern too, except for Jake's dumbwaiter distraction."

Too-Tall Tom wrapped his arm around me, "Good work, Jake. Now, do tell, did you suspect Michael before you watched him cavorting on the video?"

"Only had a nagging itch," I said. "He remained a long shot. Michael had reported Walton and Morrison had a huge row at MSG; but neither Walton nor Morrison confirmed that. Now I realize Michael had been planting a red herring."

"Speaking of that skunk, Morrison," Modesty said, "why didn't he tell Joe Cassidy that he had Dennis Kim, a fellow skunk, as an alibi for the night and early morning of Allison's murder?"

"Dennis called this morning, full of apologies and promises," I said. "I asked him that very question. He said Morrison had been worried that the police might want to know what he and Dennis had been talking about. Keith would rather have been considered a suspect than reveal any discussion of his upcoming publishing empire."

Modesty slapped cream cheese on a cinnamon raisin bagel. "And of course Dennis Kim would have been bound by that confidentiality crap he thrives on, wouldn't he?"

"What about my favorite choice, Barry DeWitt?" Too-Tall Tom asked. "How come Mila Macovich and Keith Morrison seemed to have become his new best friends? Did Mila really plan to marry him?"

"No way," I said. "As the video shows so graphically, Mila stabbed Dick so she could be with Michael. All that money she would inherit was a bonus. This wasn't just another ménage à trois. The lady was in love, but Dick Peter wouldn't release her. And Jen suspected them from the beginning. That's why she didn't want to talk to the police." I sighed and took another sip of tea. "Mila was using DeWitt as a beard, a diversion to protect Michael until they could be together."

"And Morrison's reason?" Jane asked.

"I think he told Modesty and me the truth yesterday. He only went to see DeWitt because he thought Barry would be delivering a eulogy and Morrison didn't want him to steal the show."

"So where in the world is Jennifer?" Too-Tall Tom asked. Relishing the drama, I reached into my tote, pulled out a printed-out email, and read, "Arrived Venice this morning. Signora Giatto arranged for me to stay with her cousin. Chatted with a man on waterbus who looks just like that Italian guy in *Summertime*. Meeting him tonight in St. Mark's Square. Going on to Harry's Bar. Hope Michael rots in jail. Will return to testify, but first I'll dine at Cipriani's, walk across the Bridge of Sighs, and drift in a gondola. Love to the ghostwriters. Ciao, Jennifer."

Noreen Wald

Noreen Wald lives in downtown Sarasota, Florida with her husband, Steve. Their sons visit often. Hey, surf and sun are great lures. She has served terms as a local chapter president for Mystery Writers of America, as well as Executive VP and Secretary for their National Board of Directors. A winning contestant on seven television game shows—including Jeopardy!—Noreen later worked for Goodson-Todman and Merv Griffin Productions. She's lectured at the Smithsonian, the CIA , the National Press Club and aboard the QE II. Her Ghostwriter Series was a Mystery Guild selection and praised in *The New York Daily News, The Sun-Sentinel*, and hit #1 on *The Dallas Morning News* bestseller list.

**The Jake O'Hara Mystery Series
By Noreen Wald**

GHOSTWRITER ANONYMOUS (#1)
THE LUCK OF THE GHOSTWRITER (#2)
GHOSTWRITER TO DIE FOR (#3)
REMEMBRANCE OF GHOSTWRITERS PAST (#4)
GHOSTWRITER FOR HIRE (#5)

Available at booksellers nationwide and online

Visit www.henerypress.com for details

Henery Press Mystery Books

And finally, before you go...
Here are a few other mysteries
you might enjoy:

DEATH WITH AN OCEAN VIEW

Noreen Wald

A Kate Kennedy Mystery (#1)

Nestled between fast track Ft. Lauderdale and nouveau riche Boca Raton, the once sleepy beach town of Palmetto is plagued by progress. The latest news has Ocean Vista condo board president Stella Sajak and other residents in an uproar. Developers plan to raze the property and put up a glitzy resort. But when Stella says she'll go to City Hall and fight this to the death, no one thinks to take her statement literally.

And when Kate begins to investigate the murder, she discovers that this little corner of the Sunshine State is cursed with corruption, unsavory characters, and a very dark cloud overhead.

Available at booksellers nationwide and online

Visit www.henerypress.com for details

PRACTICAL SINS
FOR COLD CLIMATES
Shelley Costa

A Mystery

When Val Cameron, a Senior Editor with a New York publishing company, is sent to the Canadian Northwoods to sign a reclusive bestselling author to a contract, she soon discovers she is definitely out of her element. Val is convinced she can persuade the author of that blockbuster, The Nebula Covenant, to sign with her, but first she has to find him.

Aided by a float plane pilot whose wife was murdered two years ago in a case gone cold, Val's hunt for the recluse takes on new meaning: can she clear him of suspicion in that murder before she links her own professional fortunes to the publication of his new book?

When she finds herself thrown into a wilderness lake community where livelihoods collide, Val wonders whether the prospect of running into a bear might be the least of her problems.

Available at booksellers nationwide and online

Visit www.henerypress.com for details

FIXIN' TO DIE

Tonya Kappes

A Kenni Lowry Mystery (#1)

Kenni Lowry likes to think the zero crime rate in Cottonwood, Kentucky is due to her being sheriff, but she quickly discovers the ghost of her grandfather, the town's previous sheriff, has been scaring off any would-be criminals since she was elected. When the town's most beloved doctor is found murdered on the very same day as a jewelry store robbery, and a mysterious symbol ties the crime scenes together, Kenni must satisfy her hankerin' for justice by nabbing the culprits.

With the help of her Poppa, a lone deputy, and an annoyingly cute, too-big-for-his-britches State Reserve officer, Kenni must solve both cases and prove to the whole town, and herself, that she's worth her salt before time runs out.

Available at booksellers nationwide and online

Visit www.henerypress.com for details

NUN TOO SOON

Alice Loweecey

A Giulia Driscoll Mystery (#1)

Giulia Driscoll has just taken on her first impossible client: The Silk
Tie Killer. He's hired Driscoll Investigations to prove his innocence
and they have only thirteen days to accomplish it. Talk about being
tried in the media. Everyone in town is sure Roger Fitch strangled
his girlfriend with one of his silk neckties. And then there's the local
TMZ wannabes stalking Giulia and her client for sleazy sound bites.

On top of all that, her assistant's first baby is due any second, her
scary smart admin still doesn't relate well to humans, and her
police detective husband insists her client is guilty. About this
marriage thing—it's unknown territory, but it sure beats ten years
of living with 150 nuns.

Giulia's ownership of Driscoll Investigations hasn't changed her
passion for justice from her convent years. But the more dirt she
digs up, the more she's worried her efforts will help a murderer
escape. As the client accuses DI of dragging its heels on purpose,
Giulia thinks The Silk Tie Killer might be choosing one of his ties
for her own neck.

Available at booksellers nationwide and online

Visit www.henerypress.com for details

MURDER ON A SILVER PLATTER

Shawn Reilly Simmons

A Red Carpet Catering Mystery (#1)

Penelope Sutherland and her Red Carpet Catering company just got their big break as the on-set caterer for an upcoming blockbuster. But when she discovers a dead body outside her house, Penelope finds herself in hot water. Things start to boil over when serious accidents threaten the lives of the cast and crew. And when the film's star, who happens to be Penelope's best friend, is poisoned, the entire production is nearly shut down.

Threats and accusations send Penelope out of the frying pan and into the fire as she struggles to keep her company afloat. Before Penelope can dish up dessert, she must find the killer or she'll be the one served up on a silver platter.

Available at booksellers nationwide and online

Visit www.henerypress.com for details

www.ingramcontent.com/pod-product-compliance
Lightning Source LLC
Chambersburg PA
CBHW060536260626
47161CB00003B/922